I0756550

PERFECT FLAW

PERFECT FLAW

EDITED BY

ROBIN BLANKENSHIP

Published by Seventh Star Press, LLC.

ISBN Number: 978-1-937929-11-4

Library of Congress Control Number: 2013934970

Seventh Star Press
www.seventhstarpress.com
info@seventhstarpress.com

Publisher's Note:
Perfect Flaw is a work of fiction. All names, characters, and places are the product of the author's imagination, used in fictitious manner. Any resemblances to actual persons, places, locales, events, etc. are purely coincidental.

Printed in the United States of America

First Edition

Copyright Acknowledgements

DEDICATION:

For Andrew, through ups and downs and twists and turns, who always ends up on the other side still holding my hand.

ACKNOWLEDGEMENTS

If you had asked me two years ago if I would be editing an anthology I would have thought you were crazy, but one thing I have learned in the last two years is life is a wild ride, and you can always make your way with a little help, a strong will and a lot of luck.

Thank you Christian and Beatrix Grace for putting up with a scatter brained, occasionally loony mom.

To the rest of my family, by blood, by chance and by choice. My very own support team. Mom, Dad, James, Mary, David, Elinor, John, Glenna, Lela, Kate, Justin, Mike, Trahnel, Noah, Calla, Dorothy, Debbie, Angel, Beth, Pat, Kim, Stephen, Melissa, Aimee, Alicia, Dan and all the amazing people in my life.

I want to thank my friend, Stephen Zimmer, who has been a constant support personally and professionally. He is one of those rare people who is a natural encourager and I know I would not be where I am today without him. I am thankful every day for his friendship.

TABLE OF CONTENTS

COST BENEFIT ANALYSIS

BY CATHY BRYANT

There was only about a fifty per cent chance that I'd die. I'd followed all the suit protocols, found the safest place possible under the circumstances and done everything that the survival lessons teach you to do.

Well, OK, I shouldn't have been out there in the first place, but you'll understand why when I tell you that I'd just found eight k-weights of solaz stones just beyond the Rim. What was I supposed to do, leave them to the night winds because it was nearly time for city lockup? Yes, Mum and Dad would worry. I hadn't been an adult (scavenger class, two years early) very long, being just thirteen, but this was an opportunity I just couldn't let slip.

Eight k-weights! One k would pay three months' rent on our unit. Eight could do so many things...I ran the stones through my hands, marvelling at their muddy unimpressiveness. When polished they'd look like liquid sunshine and be harder than diamonds. They were rare this close to the city, and I'd never heard of a haul this size in this third at all, never mind just beyond the Rim. Mum earned about this much in two years; Dad, slightly less since his injury in the mine.

We could all go and...we could...

I stopped daydreaming as a faint hiss sounded from the east. The winds were on their way, and if I carried on like this then I'd never see another day to dream in. I packed up the stones as quickly as I could, eyes nervously scanning the wastes while I worked.

I was looking for blue dust. Years before, Uncle Res had given me makeshift survival lessons. All solaz workers used to get a full survival programme courtesy of the Company, but they'd long been cut from the budget. People are cheap and plentiful on Fellen's Moon, and the laws are company-made and few. Someone worked out that it was cheaper to replace us than to pay for the classes, so that was that. But we taught each other what we knew. Uncle Res, who was only vaguely related to us, left his living tube daily to make sure I was taught a whole heap of stuff.

"Mina - don't get caught outside the city after lock-up," he said, and then repeated it very slowly, staring into my eyes.

I nodded. I got it.

"But if you do, then wait until the pre-wind breezes start, and then look for lines of blue dust. You'll hear the breezes - " he made a hissing noise which turned out to be spot on " - before you really feel them, and you'll see the dust in the direction of the sound. Get it?"

I got it, nodding emphatically. He continued.

"That blue dust is elikium, and it comes from beneath the surface. If you see it then there are usually holes and craters about. You get to that elikium dust and find yourself a hole to hide out in. Don't fall in it - "

He grinned, and I grinned back.

" - just find one you fit in, if you can, with your head below the surface but not too much space round you. When the winds start that hole will fill up, and you'll be thrown around a fair bit, but at least you won't be blown into some rocks and killed. If your suit and your nerve both hold, then you have a good chance."

Which is why I was looking for blue dust as I packed the stones, and blessing Uncle Res in my head, and trying to keep my nerve.

Just as the hissing breeze was starting to frighten me I saw a thin bluish trail, like smoke. I raced towards it, then remembered about falling in holes and slowed down.

The first hole was tiny. The second was a cavern. The wind began to shriek, and dust and pebbles began to fly. I whimpered, I know I did. But the third hole fitted me like an extension of my suit. There was even a half-seat I could perch on inside, safely if not entirely comfortably.

So I lowered myself gingerly into the hole, and waited.

Dust poured into the hole. Being buried in the sandy debris and suit failure were the two most likely causes of death in this situation. Or losing my mind and doing something dumb. The suit blocked some of the sound and filtered harmful substances from what air there was, but I still felt deafened and stifled. I tried not to move, though it was painfully tempting to reach my arms up and check that I wasn't submerged in deep sand. But any piece of debris, flying at the speed of that wind, could have ripped through both my suit and the arm within it.

So I concentrated my mind on the stones and the joy they would bring. Living upgrade, and suit upgrades so that I could scavenge further afield. Better food and medicine to make us healthy. A chance to learn more, go somewhere else, even....the wind howled in frustration, wanting to tear me apart, but I sat it out with just my dreams for company.

***

I must have slept, though I don't remember dropping off. I came to with a jolt, my shoulders and neck aching with my cramped position, and I realised that I had gone deaf. The storm must have blown out my eardrums.

No! I would have felt the storm vibrating through the rock and felt the shifting of sand. I couldn't hear any sound because the storm was over and there was nothing to hear.

With some difficulty, a weight of dirt on my head, I looked up and saw nothing but more dirt. I raised my arms at last - and how good that felt. It felt even better when they broke through a fine layer above me, no threat at all. Shaking a little I climbed out of my refuge, and slowly made my way home.

Beeler was on gate duty - a company man, but one of the rare decent ones. When he saw me his face split into a grin.

"Mina! Good to see you! I heard you were lost."

"Sorry. I went too far last night."

"In more ways than one! Your folks'll skin you alive when they get hold of you! Well, after they quit hugging you, I guess. They came down here and made me check the records three times to see if you'd come in while I was on a break."

I smiled shamefacedly back at him.

"Oh go on," he said, and waved me in without making me fill in any official documents. "Go and make your family happy."

"Oh I will! Thanks!" I said. I will! I really will! I added mentally, grinning.

At the unit no one heard me let myself in, mainly because the babies were screaming. Merlys and Aled were as cute as buttons when they slept, but the rest of the time they spent bawling, eating, puking or filling their pants. And with twins, everything comes in stereo.

Mum and Dad had one each in first room, and were rocking them and singing to them in a vain attempt to shut them up. All four faces were creased and tired.

"Hey," I said during a brief break while the twins caught their breath for another round.

Mum and Dad spun towards me. Joy lit up their faces for a moment.

"Mina!" cried Dad. "Oh, thank the stars."

I was already unloading my pack onto the table, as I knew what the next line would be.

"Where have you been? What were you thinking? We've been worried out of our - OH!"

The predictable script was cut short as the stones spilled out in a great heap, heavy and unlovely.

Mum and Dad gazed drunkenly, and by way of miracles both twins shut up.

"I was just over the edge of the Rim, with just time to get back, when I spotted these. It took a while to get them all, but I thought it was worth the risk. I spent the night in an elikium hole. My suit might need an overhaul."

I stopped. Mum had nodded, but I didn't think that either was really listening to me.

"Eight k-weights according to my pack-scale," I added.

They heard that all right, and looked at me, and then back at the stones. And then they both smiled and cried and hugged me, and I smiled and cried and hugged them and the twins, who gurgled and dimpled sweetly, and it was one of the best moments of my life.

"Ah damn it, time for work," said Dad. He looked at the stones. "We'll decide tonight what to do with these."

Mum nodded agreement.

They kissed me, put the twins in their care spaces (basic food, lullabies and two diaper changes - the best package we could afford, but at least safe) and left, holding the bread pieces that they'd have for lunch. Stale bread because it was cheaper.

Fortunately scavengers make their own hours. I crawled on to my bunk in second room and was asleep in a moment.

I woke from a dream of being suffocated and having to pay for it. Hands were pushing grit into my mouth and taking money away from me. I was dying and going broke, and I opened my mouth to scream - and woke to find that the twins, maybe having the same dream, had beaten me to it and were screaming their heads off. There was nothing wrong; screaming is just what one-year-olds do.

I pulled myself up, bones creaking and muscles tweaking my nerve endings. After drinking a lot of water I washed myself all over at the sink. We had hot water three days a week, and it felt wonderfully luxurious as I soaped myself with a steaming sponge. I washed my hair and combed it until every last bit of dust, dirt or sweat was gone.

I think I was trying to be ceremonial - to mark this time, and make the day special in some way, with some sort of ritual. I could hardly look at the stones. They were too precious, and now that I was safely home my adventure beyond the Rim was freaking me out a little. I would never forget the sound of that wind - and if I hadn't found that hole...

I was shaking with either delayed shock or hunger or both, and ate some porridge and some bread. Soon I felt better, and played with the twins for a while.

"Mum. Dad. Mina," I said to them. "Come on, sweets. You can do it! Say Mum - Dad - Mina."

"Uh- ad," said Merlys.

"Ee-ya," said Aled.

I kissed them.

After dark my parents arrived home and we had broth. Then we all looked at the stones, which were still on the table, though I had pushed them out of the way of the twins in case they ate them.

Mum smiled at me.

"This takes all our worries away, Mina. I'm so proud of you."

"Yes, rent for years, plus the rent on the twins' care units, plus our tax. We can have a little treat each too," beamed Dad.

I couldn't believe what I was hearing, but I phrased my question carefully and politely.

"Mum - Dad - aren't we going to try to make things better at all? To upgrade? Two k-weights would buy me an elite suit, and I could stay out for days at a time beyond the Rim. You know how good I am at spotting the solaz. With a wider range I could get so much more, and we could live so much better..."

I trailed off as I saw them swap glances and then look at me seriously.

"Mina dear," said Dad, "You do understand that this find is a one-off, don't you? A better suit wouldn't get you more troves like this."

"I know! But you know that the elites get much more than we basics do. If I could go further for longer then I could get more stones, and we could have better lives, long-term."

Again they looked at each other and found confirmation there.

"Mina, there are more important things than a new suit. Do you know how hard we work? And how many accidents happen in the mine? As it is we have no security. We're always one broken leg away from losing this place and living with the cast-offs."

I thought of the cast-offs - beggars, buskers, thieves, drunks, addicts, prostitutes. The desperate, in other words. Few of them lasted more than a winter or two; the city kept out most of the killing winds, but not much cold.

"So we go on as we are?" I asked, my mouth dry.

"Yes, but with a wonderful safety net, thanks to you," said my mother, holding my hands in hers and stroking them gently.

"So we go on as we are, in joyless drudgery," I said, and took my hands away.

"Joyless," said my father coldly. "Really? You feel no joy in our lives together? No joy with your mother and me, or the twins?"

"When we see each other in the brief exhausted intervals between work and sleep, maybe," I snapped, "Though we're usually too tired and hungry for much joy, aren't we?"

"That's enough!" said Mum. "We're not getting the suit, and that's final. You may be classed as an adult in terms of being fit for scavenging work, but you haven't earned your fiscal and judicial rights yet. We decide money matters until you do, so there's no point in arguing any more."

I made one last effort.

"If not the suit, then how about an enhanced nutrition-education programme for the twins? Or we could buy a small transport and use it to - "

"Mina," said Dad, and it was a warning. I fell silent.

"We'll sell them first thing," said Dad, and then we cleared away the remains of the meal quietly. There were no leftovers.

Soon we all went to second room and our bunks.

Having slept much of the day I wasn't particularly tired, and I lay in my bunk feeling a mixture of anger and frustration. I could understand my parents' desire for a cushion between us and a cast-off life, but to use a haul like this for nothing but continuance felt like such a missed opportunity. The stones were worth more than a little security; we could improve things enormously, and open up a better life long-term. Why were they so short-sighted?

I answered my own question almost as soon as I asked it. They were short-sighted because their lives had been cramped down into narrow drudgery, any wider vision eroded. The best they could let themselves hope for was a slight alleviation of worry.

Well I wasn't ground down yet. And I had a plan.

I got up and crept through to first room. Quietly I packed my school record and ID, and three k-weights of the stones.

I left a message:

Dear Mum and Dad,
I've gone to get a better life. I'll be back when I have. Enjoy the stones and don't worry about me. I'll miss you all.

Love,
Mina.

I was thirteen, remember. At that age one is blunt.

Slipping through the door I headed to the night mart and bought an elite flight suit (not the scavenging suit I had coveted) for two k-weights of solaz. Then I headed for the port, and started talking to ship's captains.

Four turned me down out of hand, but the fifth - a short, quiet woman with grey hair in a long plait - listened to me, checked my record and equipment and looked at me with a frown.

"Your parents still have fiscal and judicial rights, don't they?" she asked.

"Relating to on-moon decisions, yes," I said. "But I'm classed as an adult for work purposes, and I can go off-surface if a ship contracts to take me."

She nodded.

"OK Mina. Why are you really going?"

I didn't try to lie. Instead I explained about the stones, and about the numbing disappointment of failing to use them to improve our lives. I told her how many I had taken and why, and showed her again my excellent nav and trading qualifications.

"I'll come back here with money, and get them all out of here, or at least into a better place," I finished.

"Running away to make your fortune, eh?" said the captain, but she didn't sound mocking. Then she nodded and sighed to herself.

"Minimum wage for the first year, plus a tithe of your personal trade tallies. Welcome aboard. I'm Captain Talli Keller."

I was trembling as I thanked her and stumbled aboard Ship F.O. 174 Harper.

I had pictured myself standing smartly in my new flight suit at the nav controls, and saluting. Instead I was provided with a set of ancient and tattered overalls.

"Wouldn't want to get that nice new suit all dirty, would you?" teased Tapman, the engineer and only other crewmember. Again, he didn't really sound mocking; rather he was testing me, so I gave a rueful smile and got changed.

About two hours of loading dirty boxes followed, and then I spent an hour cleaning the ship.

Captain Keller herself brought me a bucket of hot water, clean-gel and a towel afterwards.

"Still want to come?" she asked.

I smiled and nodded.

"Better get your flight suit back on then," she said, smiled back, and gave me a contract.

Test passed, I guessed. It all felt very right.

As we lifted off I could just see through a porthole, first the port and the city and then the whole of Fellen's Moon, pulling away from me and getting smaller and more insignificant.

I should have had a lump in my throat, right? I should have wept a tear each for my parents and the twins and Uncle Res. But frankly my main emotion was relief. I had been so afraid that something would prevent my escape, and I hadn't realised how heavily my old life had hung on me, weighing me down, until it slipped from my shoulders as I flew away.

My first meal on board was two kinds of vegetable, a spicy nut-bread and some sort of fruit preserved in syrup. I savoured every flavoursome mouthful. Now I know that the food was ordinary ship's rations and nothing special, but back then it seemed to fulfil the promise of my dreams. Mum, Dad, I thought to myself - I will bring all this back to you. You too will taste these tastes.

Seven years later I kept my word.

***

I spent all seven years on board the Harper with Captain Keller and Engineer Tapman - or Talli and Tap, as they were within a few days - and lots of that time was spent thanking the stars that I had been at the port when I had.

Our first trip was delivery of those dirty boxes to Nuovo Jupe, and it was simple enough. The rest of the time, except for meals, cleaning duties and maintenance, we talked.

Talli had inherited the ship from her sister Alix, who had died of an old heart problem that the medics couldn't fix. Her death had left them a crewmember and a lot of heart short - Tap had been Alix's lover - and a needy, naiive adolescent was an ideal project for them.

I didn't know that at the time, of course. For all I knew, all new crew on all ships were treated with bluff affection, and encouraged to learn as much as possible. On board the Harper I studied for and passed my pilot and mainenance exams as well as getting my advanced trader's licence, all at Talli's expense. She claimed at the time - and at first I was young enough to believe her - that it was an investment; I would be a more valuable crew member with the qualifications. When I had them, she raised my pay accordingly.

Maybe I was a touch dumb, but it took me a while to realise that the touchstone of the Harper crew was it's kindness. Even in trade Talli was fair and generous, which shocked me at first. To poor and struggling folk she gave better deals, and only ever took what she really needed.

Sometimes I'd sigh at the inefficiency. Harper was a ramshackle little ship run in a ramshackle little way, and part of me longed to be aboard one of the sleeker, faster ships. But then I remembered that those same ships had been too efficient to find a place for me. And Talli's behavious rubbed off on me; I traded more kindly and honestly than I might have done under a different influence. I can't claim credit for it, but I found that it made me happier to be kind rather than otherwise, though I never did make that fortune.

I'd just turned twenty when Talli called me to her quarters. We were on a lush garden planet with the sweetest, most invigorating air, and I was feeling energetic and joyful.

That all fell out of me in a nauseous lump when I saw Tap with his head in his hands and Talli looking at me with a sad little smile.

"What - what is it?" I asked.

"My heart," said Talli simply. "Same as Alix. I don't have long."

"You could get a transplant," I said, but she looked at me sharply.

"You know those hearts come from organ farms," she said. "I'm not giving money to people who farm other people."

"Of course not," I mumbled. "Sorry. Sorry."

"As I have friends here, I thought I'd stay here for the end," she continued as if we were talking about holiday plans. "It's a lovely place, so fresh and alive and I - oh sweethearts, it's OK..."

And she held and comforted us both while we sobbed.

We stayed for the four brutal and tender months it took her to die, and buried her, and planted fruit and flowers for her. And I raged against her choice of end, even though it was beautiful in some ways.

Talli had left us the ship jointly. I let Tap buy me out after we had argued over the amount - he wanted to give me more than my share, and I refused to take a jot over. In the end I managed to beat him down by getting him to take me to Fellen's Moon. My share of the ship plus my slender savings were no fortune, but in a place as poor as home it would buy a good-sized living unit outright, plus about five years' keep for the whole family. I would get Aled and Merlys the best schooling, and a chance at life.

I hadn't heard from my folks since I'd left. They had no off-world coms and anyway I was continually on the move. But I figured that just as the solaz stones had made up for a night's absence, so my nest egg would iron out any remaining frowns of disapproval.

I hugged Tap goodbye at the port.

"I'll be on Gef for the next couple of weeks, then on to Elkar. I don't know where I'll be after that, but I'll leave word for you at Elkar port. Any trouble here, you come find me and we'll go anywhere you want, OK?" he said.

I nodded.

"Are you sure you don't want me to wait for you now - just a couple of days?" he asked.

I shook my head. I was too near to tears to tell him to go, but he got the message.

"Good luck," I muttered and ran to the city gates. I was as clumsy as I had been at thirteen, though taller and healthier.

There at the city sign-in was Beeler, the decent Company man.

"Beeler!" I said happily. It felt like an omen - he had been there when I brought back the solaz, and he was here now.

He frowned for a moment and checked my documents.

"Mina!" he said with a sad smile.

"How are you, Beeler?"

"I'm OK. No promotion, though."

"You're too good to be promoted. So how are my folks? And the twins?"

" - I haven't seen them," faltered Beeler, and I felt cold as I heard the missed beat.

"What happened?"

Beeler sighed.

"Go find your Uncle Res. He'll be in his tube now, and he can explain things better than I can."

"Thanks," I gasped, and ran again.

The living tubes were just big enough to hold a sleeper on a mat, with blanket, and there was a shared sink/drain for washing, drinking and voiding. Res had always lived in his tube, but spent much of his time in our two-roomer, with the people he loved. His knowledge had saved my life when I found the stones, yet I had never said goodbye to him.

He exited his tube as soon as I showed my ID, and buried me in a great bear hug.

"Mina, Mina," he said gently, "So good to see you! You've grown! Look at you, a fine young woman! So where have you been? What have you been doing?"

"I'll tell you everything, I promise. But how are Mum and Dad and the twins?"

His face fell and my stomach went cold.

"Let's go somewhere we can talk properly," he said and I nodded dumbly.

In the end we went outside to the wastes as it was a warm day, with only a few scavengers in sight. The City was so crowded and dirty, and Res insisted on waiting until we were somewhere quiet. Later it occurred to me that he was simply putting off the moment of explanation.

We sat on the rocks and watched the dust blow.

"So?" I asked at last.

He sighed. "Your father died, Mina. He was never right after the accident, as you know. Your mother carried on but the heart went out of her. She was injured at work when a cartload of ore fell on her, and she was left with a broken collarbone and a twisted leg that never healed properly. Her chest was going, too, with the dust. The Company gave her minimum payout on some excuse.

The family ended up in the Cast-Offs, Mina."

"Oh...Aled? Merlys?"

"I don't know where they are. I tried to keep track of them all. I know your Mum is alive - I saw her in a bar a month ago, though she ran away screaming when she saw me. She can't bear anything that reminds her of the old days. The kids weren't with her and I haven't been able to find out where they are. The family changed location so often."

There was a moment's pause. I wiped my cheeks and blew my nose.

"I left them five k-weights of solaz stones," I bleated, pleading for forgiveness through a fog of guilt.

"Oh stars, Mina, it wasn't your fault!" Res seemed genuinely shocked. "You mustn't think that! They were proud of you, and so grateful for the haul. It helped them to keep going as long as they did."

"But if I'd been here then I could have helped them," I said.

"Maybe - or maybe you'd have sunk with them. Look, what is survival really worth here, under these conditions? You got out and succeeded at life, and your children will have a decent time because of it. Your parents would still be proud. You know, more than once your Mum said to me that she was glad you were out of it. It gave her comfort to think of you out there, exploring, happy, free."

I shook my head. I didn't know how to feel.

Res tried to persuade me to get on the next flight out, but instead I rented a small unit for a few months and went hunting for my family.

Much good it did me, or them. A barman told me that the twins had died of the Dust Disease, or the cold, three winters ago; it was hard to tell which, but there had been alot of coughing. My mother had broken down, and then become an addict. She was a prostitute now, though customers were few.

When I finally tracked her down, she refused to acknowledge me.

"You ain't Mina," snapped this coarse stranger lying in a filthy basement. "She's thirteen."

I showed her ID, told her things only I would know, and begged her to ask Res. She didn't believe me even when I gave her money, though that made her frown at me in confusion. I don't think many people gave her money without wanting something from her.

She spent it on a drug binge that killed her. I didn't know how to feel - more guilt, in part, but there was also a sense of relief. You'd understand if you'd seen her. I didn't want her to live like that, and I don't think she did either.

I went through the motions of life, dealing with documentation and paying the death fines.

I left shortly afterwards. I explained to Res that I'd go on the next ship that would take me, which most would given my qualifications and experience.

"Come with me," I said, but he shook his head, and wouldn't discuss it.

He said that Fellen's Moon was his home and that he would stay and try to make things better here. He didn't mean make more money, and I didn't really understand what he talked about. He said that he and some friends were working for real change - trying to change what the Company was and how it worked. It sounded like a drunken fantasy to me, and why would the Company listen to a grubby old lowlife like him?

I bought Res a unit and a tiny but sufficient income. He wept with a gratitude that I didn't think I deserved, and it made me uncomfortable. I just wanted to get the hell off the whole miserable moon.

I'd spent almost all my money. In the end I left Fellen's Moon for the second time with little more than I'd had the first time, seven years earlier, unless you count experience.

This time I was taken on as second engineer on a large ore freighter, and I learned how unusual Talli and her ship had been. The freighter was more conventional - everyone in his or her allotted place, doing designated tasks for maximum efficiency. In many ways I liked it.

And I've left behind most of that ridiculous guilt and sentimentality that I had when I was young. Res was right - none of what happened on Fellen's Moon was my fault. My parents were dumb to put up with the way the Company treated them, and a long life was no improvement on a short life there. They should have followed my example and left.

I found a man I liked when I was twenty-four, and we contracted to each other and had a child. He's a fine boy, strong and healthy, and we've sent him to the best school we can afford.

I know I've hardened. But I've also survived. Being sweet to other people didn't get me those solaz stones - strength, intelligence and luck all played their parts. My son will be brought up to be strong and clever. Of course I hope he'll be a good person too, but nothing is as important as his survival.

You want me to say that I miss him while he's away, or that my relationship lacks warmth, or that I miss my family? Maybe I should, but I don't, and I have no regrets. If I had stayed with my family then maybe their miserable lives could have been slightly extended - and mine deprived or destroyed. There is nothing wrong with seeking personal happiness, as long as you understand that there will be a price to pay. You don't get to be a hero, like Talli was to me when I was a kid, and be happy and successful too.

Right now I am happy and feel no guilt. I've worked hard for what I have, earned it all and done no wrong. I'm in our unit - two large rooms and our own bathroom! - on the ship. I've just drunk a warm, foamy cup of chettel - our allowance is three cups per week, raised from two last year, which is great. My man will be back from his shift in an hour, and we'll eat real set-meat with vegetables, and fresh gorda-fruit bars with added zelba, all the way from Gef.

I am so glad to be away from Fellen's Moon. I heard that there has been trouble there, terrorism, and fights breaking out. The Company will sort it out I'm sure, though they're taking their time.

We'll have two whole hours of leisure time tonight before lights out. Tomorrow my shift is only ten hours, and within six years I can expect promotion and an even better lifestyle. What more could I want? Yes, my life is rich in every way now, and I am happy. You can't put a price on that.

SMILERS

BY CAROLYN M. CHANG

People suck. Life sucks. Work sucks. It's a sucky world. Mays -- short for Maysing Volenda, which she thinks makes her sound like a circus act -- is a negaholic.

Mays ducks her head and slouches while walking home after another lousy day at work, hoping it makes her appear smaller, but only succeeds in making her look like she has no tits. Not that there was much to begin with. Still, it's hard not to notice a two-meter-tall-black-clad woman amidst a crowd dressed in the popular colour palette of the season: pastels. Revolting, she thinks. Or baby-butt-barf-ugly, to be more precise.

Mays barrels through the 24-hour advertising holograms lining a major street in the shopping district, wishing she could inflict real pain to the animations. Some are ridiculous animals, talking and gesturing like people. Some are sexy figures dancing to trendy, pulsing music. Others scream your name at you to shock you into noticing them.

One is new. She slows down to take a gander at the hologram:

a man that doesn't seem to be associated with any of the cheesy shops selling no-brand electronics or gaudy, pastel-colored clothes. He's dressed in soft white flowing robes, his serene face lined gently with age and wisdom. His hair and clothes ruffle in an unfelt breeze. Unlike the other holograms, he stands perfectly still. And he's smiling.

She hears his soothing voice say, "Do you seek peace of mind? Do you seek serenity and freedom from your everyday woes? Come to the Garden. We will help you discover your inner sanctuary."

"Shit," Mays mumbles. "So they've finally planted their jeezu-freaking' stakes in this dump of a town. Damn Smilers."

When she passes the robed figure, he turns to her, palm extended and facing upward. "What about you, young woman in black? Wouldn't you live each day filled with joy?"

She looks up at the shops, to see if someone is controlling the hologram remotely. Nothing. She trudges on.

"Ah…Such sadness. We could help you, lovely one," he says, his voice oozing with kindness.

Mays pauses. She doesn't recall anyone ever referring to her as 'lovely'. She turns to look at him with a momentary look of softness. Then she sneers.

"Piss off." She continues her way home.

***

Mays unlocks the door to her apartment situated next to a noisy beauty salon and rides the hydro-lift to her rooms painted in shades of grey. A high priority holo-mail awaits.

She places the small disc in the palm of her hand and watches the miniature holographic Smiler in pastel-colored robes recite its message: "...therefore, due to your consistent public show of negativity resulting in a potentially dangerous Positive Emotionality index, we have enrolled you in a local clinic. We are pleased to inform you that the Garden is ready to receive you tomorrow and --"

Mays pokes her finger through the hologram's belly, making the image jitter, interrupting the voice stream. She giggles. She removes her finger to let the message run its course while she half listens.

"Little phony-faced-do-gooder-freakos," she says to the tiny Smiler standing on her hand as it prepares to repeat the message. "I'm staying just the way I am and nobody's going to tell me otherwise."

It's 2059 and Mays has moved to this small hick town to escape the insanity around Positive Emotionality -- PE for short -- which has overtaken the bigger cities like a plague. She's sick of all the Smilers who continuously lick each other's arses; the Smilers who claim their way of life make them so incredibly-dorkily-retardedly happy. All that lifestyle would do for Mays is make her feel like a hypocrite. Or worse...happy.

After shutting down the holo-mail Mays tosses it into the trash bin. She saunters to the kitchen and says, "I wonder how they found me." Maybe someone complained about her. Was it her creepy, definitely-a-holo-penis manager at the Shaktomiso Art and Culture Center who hoped she would learn to 'get along with the invited artists'? If it wasn't for her being such an excellent art installation technician, she knows she would've been fired ages ago. Or maybe it was the owner of the beauty salon downstairs who greeted her the other day and Mays responded with: 'Get back to your dimwit-chit-chatty-uglies.' Or was it the man who asked her for directions and she answered, 'Find someone who cares about this stink-ass-creep-infested-hole.' She shrugs. Too many possibilities.

"Me, a 'threat to society'? Hah! Screw you, Smilers."

She grabs a low-cal-high-alc beer and slams herself down on the lounge bed.

"Stereo on."

A saxophone fills the room with mellow tones.

"No, something with more energy."

A pulsing rhythm with unintelligible female vocals in the background come on. She closes her eyes as the music and alcohol take over.

***

Empty beer cylinders tinkle as she stirs the following morning. She stumbles to the water closet and manages to flip open the hidden door before she retches pale yellow bile.

She reaches for the anti-bac-tartar-plaque spray while she peers reluctantly into a small grimy mirror. Greasy, black mud would be a good description of the colour of her hair, which is kept in a short, scraggly bob. She pushes her hair away to peer into bloodshot eyes, exposing delicate features and a nicely shaped mouth tinted deep pink. Her eyes are dark hazel -- a detail she often forgets. If only she took the time to care for her skin, maybe some of the blemishes would go away. But she doesn't see the point.

"Fugly," she mutters to her reflection. She shuts her eyes and grips her skull. "Oh..." She rummages in a small box cluttered with small containers brightly colored in alarm reds, neon pinks, and piercing blues. They look too damn cheerful.

Chimes ring. The front door comm. "Shit. Who could possibly be?" She staggers over and presses the touch pad. The security vid-panel lights up, the light stabbing her eyes, and she sees a pair of eager-looking male Smilers with glimmering, combed-back hair.

"Go away. Don't want any P.E. holo-books."

"Good morning, Ms. Volenda," says the one with a huge mole on his cheek. "We're from the Garden and it's time to start feeling hap-py."

"Go to hell, you freaky tooth-flashers!" She shuts down the comm.

Mays is about to spray painkiller into her mouth when she hears the hydro-lift whirring into action. A few seconds later, a knock on the door.

"Ms. Volenda? Would you please open the door? We're here to help you."

She stares dumbly at the entrance to her home. Then to her horror, there is a soft shuh sound. "They've opened the bloody door!"

Re-animated, Mays runs to the door and slams it shut only to have it jammed open by an intrusive Smiler shoe. Slowly and relentlessly, the door is forced open while Mays throws her weight against it. She jumps back as two muscular Smilers enter, both splitting open their lips to flash gleaming teeth.

"It's so nice to meet you in person, Ms. Volenda," says giant-mole-on-the-cheek. Grins are tattooed on both their faces.

Mays backs away, deeper into her apartment, towards the kitchen unit.

"Can we please do this the nice way? We want to help you turn your life around."

She turns and runs to the magnetic strip holding her sharp paring knife but the Smilers grab her and gag her. She is dragged downstairs to their vehicle through a sealed walkway which is jammed against her ground floor entrance, making it impossible to escape. No one notices her struggle.

***

The two big Smilers wheel Mays, strapped to the chair at the wrists and ankles, into her temporary home. The Garden looks just like its name, lush and green with the perfume of flowers punching her in the nose. Enthusiastic Smilers hustle about, their white robes fluttering like phony angels' wings.

The two Smilers escort her into an office where they remove her restraints. While she's rubbing her wrists, Big-mole-Smiler pats her on the shoulder and then they are gone.

Mays sits facing another Smiler perched behind a big white desk that looks like it could swallow him up. He is skinny with a large hooked nose and black eyes that belong on a crow. She would like to throw dried corn kernels at his face.

"Do you understand why you are here, Ms. Volenda?" His voice sounds kissy-kissy.

"Yes, because you Smilers are a bunch of compulsive-obssessive-positive-feely-junkies."

The Smiler shakes his head and puts on a small, knowing grin. He then launches a battery of tests.

"Fifty-five. *Tsk tsk tsk*," says the Smiler when they are done.

"Believe it or not, I've seen worse P.E. levels than yours. I hope you realise you're in for trouble if you don't change your ways, Ms. Volenda. It's all been documented. Severe health problems, most likely cancer, if not suicide." When he gazes at her with a concerned look on his face, Mays wants to punch him in that beak of his.

Her P.E. Life Change Programme is drawn up, along with a target P.E. growth curve with fixed points in time where her progress is to be measured. She's to start ASAP.

"What if I prefer to stay as I am?" asks Mays, the line between her brows deepening further.

"Ms. Volenda, that is simply unacceptable," replies the Smiler as he leads her out of the room. "Come. I'll take you to your first session. You'll be happy before you know it."

Mays follows numbly, her shoulders in their usual slumped position, her eyes focused one meter ahead on the floor in front of her.

***

Suzu's rambling is like the irritating buzz of a mosquito. No, you can at least squash a mosquito dead. Partner chat sessions are now a daily part of Mays' routine; a forced moment of bonding and sharing with a fellow Garden patient.

Mays looks bleary-eyed as she faces her partner's limp, dirty blond hair and pasty face, propped on top of a pudgy body. They both wear the same Garden-issued tunic and pants in pale green. Ugh, pastels.

Suzu requires rehab for a different PE disorder -- her self-denigrating attitude. It also didn't help that as a pharmacist she skimmed off many of her clients' more interesting prescriptions for personal consumption.

"So, Suzu, tell me what happened after you stuffed your face with that whole cylinder of ice cream." A robot couldn't have spoken in a more monotone voice.

"Well, I looked down and couldn't believe it was empty. I am such a pig." Suzu bites her lip and looks down at her sausage-link fingers clasped in her lap. "You know what it's like though, right? Where before you realise it, you've already done something bad?"

"Don't know…"

"But what about how you say all those mean things? Like yesterday in the cafeteria when that guy bumped into you and you told him he was a 'fatty-matty-fart-smeller.' I think I heard people do that kind of thing when they're afraid of having relationships. A kind of defense mechanism."

Mays glares at Suzu for a moment before her eyes lose focus again.

Mays has just turned twenty, single and friendless. She does remember a guy from some umpteen years ago -- Lesil Greenfield. She was twelve. So was he. He dumped her as soon as he got a dog for his birthday. It's better that way though, because inside she is nothing more than a pile of mush. But it's not her fault, it's her father's. You see, her mother left them as soon as she was ripped from the womb and papa's words are forever imprinted in her brain: *You were born to be a failure, Mays.*

"Well, that's just what the Smilers say," says Suzu. "I don't mind it, Mays. Really I don't."

Mays looks at the clock. They're everywhere, even in the toilets.

Living to a schedule is a 'way to fight depression' according to Garden guidelines.

"Yikes, gotta go!" Mays stands up. "Time for one-on-one time with picture lady."

"Okay. Same time tomorrow then? Hope you don't mind being my partner. I really appreciate--"

Mays is already out the door.

***

The Smiler who does the picture exercises is on a mission. Out of all the Smilers who provide P.E. treatments for Mays, she is the most cheerful and optimistic -- the most P.E. of them all.

Mays gazes wearily at the holo-picture of the man and woman sitting on a park bench on a sunny day. It's number 27. "Hmmm…I see two lovers who are in the middle of breaking up. He's telling her that she was a lousy lay. She asks, what do you mean? He says she could've at least made some noise instead of acting like a slimy-slippy-rotty-fish. She says, well, at least she doesn't have make-your-eyes-bleed body stink and --"

"Okay, Maysing. I get the idea." The Smiler's smile seems a little less smiley as she taps the holo-pad to send the picture away. "You know, your creativity never ceases to amaze me. Now if we could only channel it into a more P.E. direction." The Smiler leans back in her chair and gives Mays an appraising look. "Let's try something a bit radical to break this negative pattern of yours. What I'd like you to do is tell me one positive thing about one of these pictures. Anything, no matter how small. And you're not going to leave this room until you do."

"Is that right..."

"You heard me, Maysing." The Smiler grins. "Here we go." The Smiler taps the pad again and a holo-picture of a beagle puppy frolicking in a bed of flowers appears.

"That runt is about to get kicked by its master for taking a shit on the flowers and--"

"Next." It's a little girl and a woman holding hands.

"The woman is a serial killer and she's going to take the girl home, hack her into small pieces, then braise her with chopped tomatoes and--"

"Next."

It's been two hours and they are at holo-picture number 147. Mays sags in her chair and the Smiler's smile is but a whisper of what it was at the beginning of the session.

"Listen, Smiler-lady, I'm starving and dying of thirst. Can't we continue this charade tomorrow?" Mays rests her head back on the chair.

"You know what you need to do."

"This is a load of crap. I'm leaving." She gets out of the chair and tries the door. It's locked. "Let me out!"

"Not until you tell me something P.E. Sit down. Please."

"No."

"No problem. You can do this standing too."

The Smiler taps the pad. A single red flower appears.

"Some brainless florist left it behind so it's about to be dumped into a shredder and made into a poisonous tea for some unsuspecting old bag." Mays gives the Smiler a meaningful glare.

The Smiler sighs. "I'm sorry, but you leave me no choice, Mays." She taps the pad and Mays arches her back and screams. It lasts no longer than a split second. Mays falls to her knees gasping for breath. A moment later she vomits. She can't help but observe it's flecked green -- the green leaf salad with soy-and-rice-wine-vinegar dressing served at lunch.

"How…?" Mays wipes her mouth and then hugs her arms around her bony frame.

"It's my little Smiler secret. I preferred not to do that, but you weren't responding. So can we try again? I'm going to give you another chance on this same one."

Mays opens her mouth, then closes it again.

"It's pretty," mumbles Mays.

"See, that wasn't so bad, was it?"

There's a click. Mays stands up and tries the door. It opens. She turns to look at the Smiler who beams at her. Mays scowls and leaves for her evening dietetic meal.

***

"--so I figure it has to be in my genes or something," drones Suzu. "I practically lay on the kils just from inhaling the smell of candy. I'm so weak-willed that I…ummm…Mays? Are you okay?"

"Whuh?" Mays' complexion is grey, her greasy hair grazes her shoulders now, and the circles under her eyes are at their widest. She is a skeleton draped in pastel-green cloth.

Suzu leans towards Mays and whispers, "You're finally losing it for real, aren't you?"

"Who isn't?"

"I've been here longer than you so I've seen it plenty of times."

"Yeah, well, this place is killing me. And picture-lady is the worst. I would do anything for the chance to take that holo-pad and jam it up her ass."

"Yeah, she's a real bitch of a Smiler, isn't she?" Suzu attempts a smile, but it fades quickly.

"These Smilers…Why are they obsessed with changing us? Why can't they just let us be?" Mays shivers.

"There is a way out of sorts. But it's, well, permanent."

Mays lifts her head slightly. "What do you mean?"

"Because you end up kinda, umm…dead."

"Oh." Mays looks down again. After a moment, she says, "Tell me."

Suzu lowers her voice. "I've been keeping an eye on the meds they use around here, and I happen to know that a particular combination is deadly. But you have to take them within a few hours of each other." Mays doesn't respond. "One is Ferilak. That's for vomiting and nausea. And the other is a sedative -- Sintaline. I've seen them give that one when one of us got out of control. So if you get both of these in you, you'll be out in a flash." Suzu snaps her fingers for emphasis, making Mays jump.

"How do you know this?"

"I used to be a pharmacist, remember?" Suzu's smile confident for a change. And it actually makes her look rather attractive, thinks Mays. Oh, dear. Was that a P.E. thought? No. She stomps the thought out of her mind.

Mays considers Suzu's idea. A part of her is terrified, but another is fascinated. She decides to push it away for now. She has to shore up some energy. Picture-lady is still to come.

***

Another month has passed and Mays is a ghost. Her skin is dry and scaly and she shuffles because it is too tiring to lift her feet. She whispers most of the time. But with her P.E. levels finally improving and stablising, the Smilers push even harder.

"Your current P.E. level of eighty-seven is a positive sign. You will be embracing Smiler ways before you know it," says the picture-lady at the end of one of their sessions. Her hopefulness makes Mays want to vomit.

She has been considering Suzu's idea. She closes her eyes and imagines herself a cold, inanimate slab of meat, Smilers scuttling about her lifeless form. She cringes.

"So, let's get started. We haven't had to use the pain method again for two weeks now. That's progress!"

***

The next day when she enters picture-lady's office, Mays sits in the chair and attempts a smile. It is strained and tight, her facial muscles weak from lack of use, but there it is, as visible and painful as a puss-filled, infected wound on one's forehead. The Smiler's eyes are nearly popping from enthusiasm.

"Shall we get started?"

Mays nods as enthusiastically as her scrawny neck will allow.

A holo-picture of a forest with rays of sunlight breaking through the trees appears.

Mays licks her dry lips. "Nature…Animals live there. They mate and make more animals."

Picture lady tilts her head. "Nice, Mays. I like it."

Now it's a clown.

"He's going to a party for children and makes all kinds of P.E. jokes. One of the children cries so he pulls down his trousers to reveal a pair of polka-dotted underpants. The child laughs."

"Lovely."

Mays looks at the picture of a boy with a red ball.

"The red ball belongs to his big brother who told him, 'Go ahead and play with it. I was going to watch some holo-vids anyway'."

"You're doing great, Mays. You're going to be one of us before you know it." The Smiler beams at Mays. She then hesitates before tapping the pad to call up a young woman with dark hair.

Mays studies her own scowling face from her Garden photo ID.

"That's Mays. She…wants to be a Smiler." She looks at picture-lady and attempts another withered grin.

The Smiler is overjoyed and stands up to embrace Mays.

***

"You've been here five months now, Mays, and just look at your P.E. chart!" The male Smiler with the black, crow-eyes behind the big desk points at the vid-screen with his metal pointing stick. The curve has made an impressive ramp upwards. "According to this, your P.E. has elevated to a very healthy level of ninety-two. You're going home soon. Isn't that good news?"

"Why yes, it is. But I'll miss the Garden with all of the Smilers running about, my pastel green clothing and all of the inspiring individuals here." The smile on Mays' face is rather plasticy now. In fact, it is a rare moment when she is without it now.

"We'll miss you too. You've been quite a challenge, but well worth it." The Smiler escorts her back to her room. "I'm sure the next time we see each other will be farewell." He winks at her and walks away.

Within three days Mays is released after making a new personal record on her P.E. tests. Ninety-five. She leaves the Garden amidst a flurry of warm embraces and vigorous handshakes. They let her take her pastel green tunic and pants home as a souvenir.

When she arrives at her apartment, the first thing she does is paint her home yellow. Bright, Smiler, big-and-happy-flowery yellow. She tosses out her entire wardrobe and buys the trendy pastels of the day. The woman at the shop tells Mays how becoming she looks in a flower-petal-pink dress.

"I do look goody-candy-sugar-sweet, don't I?" She spins around in front of the mirror as the shop keeper smiles.

***

The opening party at the Shaktomisto Art and Culture Center is in full swing. Well-clad guests in pastels mingle and admire the art installation amidst music consisting of crooning vocals with a backdrop of string instruments and light percussion. Everyone sips politely from funny-shaped glasses with cocktail sticks topped with a miniature of the artist's head alongside an accompaniment of small pastry puffs filled with something cheesy and fragrant. The event is for the featured artist of the season -- Ray Halisin.

Mays was happy to provide cheerful and enthusiastic assistance to the artist in setting up his art installation, *Street Fight Alley*. She didn't even complain about his bad breath and eye-watering musky cologne. Ray has done nothing but praise Mays' work and her wonderful P.E.-ness. Mays is up for a promotion as a result: <u>Senior</u> Art Installation Technician.

Mays stands on the black-rubber floor tiles, admiring a mass of black tubes with a red, wet wobbly mass on top. She hears a voice next to her.

"Boring as hell," mutters the man, just loud enough for Mays to hear. "Standing around here like a bunch of juveniles on this big rubber playmat. And can you tell me what the hell that thing up there is? Something a homeless guy puked up?"

She considers his comments for a moment, drawing upon memories of herself only a few months ago. "Well…that cute, red, wiggly thing represents the 'heart of the street fighter'. I would know since I put it up there myself under the guidance of the artist."

"You mean you actually helped the idiot who came up this collection of crap?"

Mays turns her head so fast her bleached-blond hair slaps gently across her cheek. She inspects the flushed and sweaty-faced man standing next to her. He is frowning and dressed in dark, drab brown.

She speaks in a fierce, bitter whisper with harsh emotions camouflaged with pastels and too-white-teeth. "Don't be such a middle-finger-up-the-ass. You don't want to end up at a place like the Garden, do you, Mister Dung-for-brains? Take it back. Replace it with P.E. things. Otherwise, you'll regret it." She spits on the floor between them.

The man's mouth drops open. Then he laughs derisively and walks away. "You stupid Smilers. Always trying to brainwash people every chance you get."

Mays shakes her head and scowls as she watches the man leave. Then the deep line between her pale eyebrows smoothes out. She adjusts her pastel blue jumpsuit and walks over to the next piece of art, smiling.

CRACKS IN THE CONCRETE

BY FRANK ROGER

Ross cast a glance outside, and his first impressions were promising. The cloud-covered sky was grey, not a single streak of blue could be seen. It was quiet. Most people were still asleep, but soon they would be out on the streets, rushing off to their offices and factories. Yet he would have enough time to inspect the area that fell under his command.

He quickly scanned the pavement, then the concrete road. There appeared to be no trace of any of the dreaded "wrong" colours. This might well prove an easy morning. For a while there had been no unwelcome "invaders", and he could only hope it would stay this way. It would make his life easier, and everybody else's too for that matter.

He dutifully did his tour of inspection, not missing a single crack between the pavement stones or the concrete slabs. Then he did his tour again, this time checking the facades. Everything looked fine. The colour grey was all-pervasive, nothing stood out. The situation was under control, allowing him to breathe more freely. He went back inside to have breakfast in the privacy of his small three-room house, a privilege coming with his level D Inspector function, just before the workers were preparing to leave. As an Inspector, Ross had to put in fewer hours at the office, just enough to file his reports. His inspecting duties were considered to be of prime importance.

As he was nibbling his nutritious breakfast tablets, washing them down with filtered water, he heard whispered conversations and hurried footsteps, the usual sounds of people leaving their homes. With a bit of luck it would be an uneventful day.

Until noon everything went smoothly indeed. He did his second tour of inspection, went to the Bureau to file his report and have lunch (fortunately the only "public" meal of the day) in the mess-hall. He nodded to his colleagues, and they greeted him in the same way. As usual the droning electronic music was so loud people were unable to talk to each other. This was as it should be. City workers came here to eat, not to engage in pointless conversation, during which perhaps subjects considered unacceptable such as the quality of the food might be raised. He handed his ticket to the mess administrator, got his food tray and looked for a place to sit. The broth and the yellowish lump of paste were pretty tasteless, but at least they had a high nutritional value. Should one ask for more?

He finished his meal and waited a few moments before he got up again. At times Ross found his life lacked excitement, but he found comfort in the thought that he was a lot better off than those with "regular" jobs, toiling away in offices and factories. The pounding music made it difficult to stay in a reflective mood for longer than a few seconds, so he put away his tray and left the mess-hall.

As he went back to do his next shift, he noted the cloud cover was breaking up and patches of blue sky became visible. This was not a good sign. As he was halfway on his tour of inspection, one third of the sky was uncovered. The moment he heard the startling buzzing sound he knew his premonition had been right. Irritated at this disruption of normal life and all it would entail, he tried to locate the origin of the noise.

There! An insect! He hadn't seen one of these despicable creatures for some time. It flew in circles, back and forth, appeared to drift off on the breeze but came back, as if looking for something. How had it come here? What had attracted it? Was it alone, an individual cut off from its nest, doomed to perish? Or was it the vanguard of an entire army of insects, preparing to invade the city? He took his communicator and notified the Administrator of the Cleaning Squads that he had discovered a problem. They shouldn't take any chances. Anyway, it was his duty to report this kind of incident.

When the Squad arrived, mere minutes later, the insect was nowhere to be seen anymore. Yet Ross knew he had done the right thing. Thomas, the Squad Leader, thanked him for his quick action and congratulated him for taking his responsibilities so seriously. They would scour all the neighbouring districts, get in touch with local inspectors and check every square inch. They would not rest until they had found their prey. This city was built for man, and for man only. There was no room for any intruders. The City Council was adamant in this respect. The insect and the ones possibly following in its trail didn't stand a chance.

The rest of the day was calm, deceptively calm. The cloud cover dissipated completely, leaving an even blue sky. This was an unhealthy situation. The workers would be notified that they would have to protect themselves against direct sunlight as they returned home.

They knew very well they should avoid harsh sunlight hitting their skin. Anyway, the City Council's recommendations were not open to debate.

After his final tour of inspection, Ross went back home for his supper and retired for the night soon after, deciding to skip the socialising hours at the Level D Pub he was entitled to. He was not in the mood for small talk. After barely a few hours of sleep it became clear the tranquillity had been the proverbial calm before the storm. The sound of the rain that came pouring down and the howling wind kept him awake for most of the night. How would he find his area of inspection tomorrow? What would the storm have littered the streets with? He shuddered at the very idea, and whatever sleep still followed was too disturbed to have its full effect.

The next morning he got up at his usual hour, and unsurprisingly he didn't feel too well. He needed several more hours of sleep, but he had a job to do. He stepped outside, saw that the sky had reverted to its even grey colour. The wind had died down, the heavy downpour had dwindled to a faint drizzle. The night's storm had left its legacy all over the place. Ross's heart sank as he saw everything was covered by a layer of sand and dirt, and a lot of debris was strewn about. To his horror he even noted a fair number of insects and other creatures, most of which appeared to be dead. This would be a hell of a mess to clean up. He called the Squads immediately, told them the condition was critical in his quarter, and probably all over the city. Other inspectors would undoubtedly confirm this. Then he hurried back inside for a quick breakfast, as he wanted to be present when the Squads were active.

Mere minutes later he watched as the Squad was doing what it could to clear the street. The Squad Leader told him it was indeed like this all over the city, and the Council considered proclaiming an emergency situation. The drizzle finally stopped, the cloud cover broke and the wind started blowing again. Ross cursed as he saw the countless fluffs of pollen that were carried on the breeze. If any of these took root in a handful of dirt the Squads failed to remove, the city would run the risk of a "green invasion". All the inspectors would have to intensify their rounds so as to make sure no pollen had seen an opportunity to develop into a plant. The City Council would not take this matter lightly.

The Squads and the inspectors worked themselves into a sweat until well into the afternoon. Then the wind picked up, the sky turned a darker shade of grey and a new storm hit the city. Ross cringed when he heard the sound of thunder. Heavy rain started coming down. The Squad Leader turned to him and said:

"We can't work like this, Inspector. We must take cover. We'll continue as soon as we can."

Ross nodded as the men went for shelter in their vehicles. Had all the day's unrelenting work been in vain? Would they have to start all over again tomorrow morning? And what if the weather remained inclement, what if they would prove unable to perform their duties as expected? Ross shook his head, fighting back the despair. He had a bad feeling about this. He decided to go back home when he could hardly see the Squad's vehicles through the sheets of rain. By the time he had reached the safety of his house, he was soaked through. This was no ordinary shower; it was a deluge.

The weather remained bad for the entire week, and normal life in the city was seriously disturbed. In between the downpours and the fierce winds, there were quiet periods, with sunshine and a barrage of pollen washing over the city. Also there were more and more reported sightings of insects and even lizards. It was obvious the Cleaning Squads were unable to cope with the situation.

At one point Ross and his Squad were even asked to offer help in the Women's Quarters, where they were not allowed to set foot, unless requested explicitly and exceptionally. Over there the Squads were too overworked and demoralised to perform at the required level, so a selection of Men's Squads had been sent for. Unfortunately they only had the time and energy to clean up the worst.

The City Council kept spreading messages meant to boost the morale and to incite everyone to stick to his daily duties as best he could. The bad weather wouldn't last, so a Council spokesman claimed, and soon enough life in the city would be back to normal.

Ross's daily schedule basically didn't change. He got up, called the Squads and told them his area was a disaster, and supervised the cleaning operations. He realised they were all fighting a losing battle and working under tremendous strain. Then he filed his report at the bureau, had lunch, and continued his job. At one such occasion, he had a conversation with the Squad Leader as they had taken shelter in their vehicle when another downpour descended onto the city. They had worked together for quite some time now, and did engage in conversation when there was an opportunity.

"We can't go on like this, Inspector. Why does the City Council send us off under these conditions? Why don't they wait until this bad spell is over? Wouldn't it make more sense to start cleaning then?"

"I see your point, Thomas," Ross said. "But the Council seems to think it's better not to take any chances. If we wait to start cleaning until the weather improves, the city may already be infested with all sorts of life-forms. Eradicating all that might be well impossible. Our living conditions here might be jeopardised already."

"A few patches of moss and grass, some insects and harmless creatures, how can they threaten our way of life?"

"Don't say that," Ross exclaimed, horrified. "There are no such things as harmless creatures. The problems we faced in the past are well-documented. The epidemics, spreading like fire and decimating mankind. The infections, crippling man's existence. As if you don't know all that. I must say you disappoint me."

The Squad leader sighed, shook his head, as the rain kept pounding on the vehicle's roof and windows. "I know the City Council's position. I'm not criticising it, and it's certainly not my intention to disappoint you. The Council's views is what we were taught, and what they keep telling us. Man should take his survival into his own hands."

"Remove himself from the food chain linking all other life-forms," Ross joined in. "Isolate himself in a city built for man, and for man only. Where all intruders are denied entry. Thus avoiding all contact that may lead to health crises and survival problems."

"I suppose the Council knows what it's doing," the Squad leader said. "But they appear to be so extremist. Keeping men and women separate. Allowing young and healthy men a fortnightly sperm donation to ensure procreation. Feeding us indefinable stuff. Regulating and controlling every aspect of our lives. Holding us in a stranglehold."

"Uncontrolled contact between men and women allowed lethal viruses to decimate mankind. Our food supply does not depend on the food chain, is free of health hazards and highly nutritious. This so-called stranglehold may be the only way to keep things going. Isn't our survival, without any major problems for a long time, proof of that?"

The Squad Leader shot him a wary look. "Well, the Council seems to have your full support. And you're obviously right. It's clear this is the only way. I apologise for venting these unorthodox views of mine. I suppose the bad weather and the strain of the hard work are getting to me. Please forget what I said."

The rain showed signs of abating, and the men climbed back out of the vehicle to continue their jobs. Before they parted company, the Squad Leader told him: "We should talk more often."

"Whenever there's an opportunity," Ross said. He didn't mind some conversation, even if it veered into dangerous waters at times. It was a welcome addition to the official socialising hours in the evening, which were often boring and limited to contacts with people of his own level at the designated Pub. And these last few days the only topic raised in the Level D Pub was the terrible weather, and he preferred not to be reminded of that in his few spare hours.

After ten days the weather finally improved. The wind and rain stopped, but the grey cloud cover wasn't restored completely, sheltering the city from the sun only intermittently. Now the Cleaning Squads could begin the real work. The City Council encouraged everyone to make sure life reverted to its former situation as quickly as possible. "Everyone should take up his responsibility," the Council's spokesman declared. "No one should rest until the City is back in its pristine state. Only this way will you all be able to live safely and comfortably. Keep in mind that this City was built for man and for man only. Not any contamination will be allowed. No cracks in the concrete will be overlooked, each sign of wear or tear will be spotted, reported and repaired. The Council counts on your unwavering commitment and drive."

Ross shook his head in despair as he noticed, on the first "normal" day, what was awaiting the Squads. He did his tour of inspection in his area, and made a note of everything he saw. Small patches of moss had appeared on the pavement and on some facades. Blades of grass could be seen, tiny green intruders hoping to pass unnoticed. Several insects crawled or flew around, ants, bugs, wasps, flies. One small lizard scuttling away as he approached completed the picture. The entire city must be soiled to an unprecedented degree. The Squads would have to work around the clock to eradicate all these life-forms. And the faint breeze carried yet more fluffs of pollen, those tireless messengers of death.

At the end of the first day, Ross had a short conversation with the Squad Leader. "My men can't take it any more," Thomas said. "They're exhausted, and some even claim this harrowing work is virtually pointless."

"I hope the Council doesn't find out about your men's subversive ideas. Such views aren't exactly encouraged, and I'm putting it mildly."

"I know. People should be more cautious. But don't you think the Council is going too far at certain moments? Their reasoning is so rigid, so harsh."

"The Council prefers not to take any chances. They haven't forgotten the lessons from the past."

"Neither have we. But we can get rid of all these critters and weeds without taking things to the limit."

"You're underestimating the enemy, my dear friend. One mosquito infecting one single man may unchain an epidemic. One plant may spread into a green tide, attracting many more animals and vegetation and insurmountable problems. Zero tolerance is the only way."

The Squad Leader shot him a weary look. "I can see you're a hard-liner. Just like the City Council."

"It's the hard-liners who survive," Ross rebutted. "You know the saying. No cracks in the concrete will be overlooked…"

The Squad Leader nodded. "Of course. Will you tell the Council now that my men are growing disgruntled?"

"I will pretend I never heard your words," Ross said. "I understand your men are under enormous strain. It's only natural that they show weakness at a moment of crisis like this. Tell your men they have my full support. I'm sure the Council will be behind them, especially in these difficult times."

For several days the Squads put in many hours, removing all traces of vegetation and killing all the insects and other creatures they could find. Ross did round after round of inspection, checking if the Squads had not overlooked something and if perhaps any new intruders had arrived on the scene. A lot of progress was made, but each time Ross was about to conclude a particular area had been cleared, he noticed an alarming presence. A small spider, scuttling away, glimpsed from the corner of his eye. A minuscule patch of green, almost hidden from sight, having taken root in an unlikely place.

Ross was convinced that everything would be back to normal soon, when on the fifth day the City Council spokesman announced some devastating news. Cockroaches had been found in the City's food supplies. The matter was being investigated, and measures would be taken as quickly as possible. No more details were given.

At the first lunch break after the announcement, Ross noted that his colleagues were discussing the matter. They shouted loud enough to drown the pounding music filling the mess-hall.

"What they usually do is destroy the supplies that have gone bad or been soiled," one man said at the top of his voice. "But can they do that now?"

"If there are cockroaches all over the supplies, they must destroy everything," a second man concluded. "But then what will people eat?"

"What are we eating now?" a third man joined in, pointing at the food on his tray. "Can someone tell us what this is we're getting?"

"This is not the moment to complain about the food," Ross argued. "What will the Council decide? Will we have something to eat at all? Will there be famine? How will the City survive?"

The mess-hall administrator must have understood a heated discussion was being held, as he turned up the music's volume, rendering all conversation impossible. The men ate, their thoughts concentrated on what they would find on their trays the following days – if there would be something at all. It was the first time Ross had seen his colleagues engaging in an argument over lunch. The entire City's population must be on edge.

After his last round of inspection, Ross had supper in the privacy of his small house. He nibbled his tablets, wondering if these were perhaps the last he would eat. A week's supplies were usually handed out on the first day of the week, which was tomorrow. He assumed he was not the only one anxious to find out how the City Council would cope with the crisis.

That evening he went to the Level D Pub, and found a surprisingly high number of people in attendance. The conversations dealt invariably with the hot topics of the last few days, the bad weather that had opened the gate for so many creatures and plants, and the food crisis. While some people were convinced that there was basically nothing to worry about, others claimed the Apocalypse was about to descend onto them. Both parties had strong arguments to back up their theory. Ross didn't stay long. He had come here to get away from the pressures of work, not to be reminded of them.

The next morning he did his first round of inspection, and was happy to note everything was as it should be. For the first time in many days, he would not have to call the Squad. A smile appeared on his face, and he was about to return home and have breakfast when he noted a flotilla of pollen sailing past on the breeze. Almost simultaneously, he heard the typical buzzing sound of an insect, but didn't see it. Would this never end? He scanned the sky, patches of blue among the grey clouds, and to his horror he saw a bird, high up there. The situation was degrading rapidly. He called the Squad, informed them of the problem, and went back inside to have breakfast.

He had almost finished as he got a call. It was the Food Administrator, who told him that the City Council had decided to ration the food supplies, but Inspectors and other key personnel would get slightly bigger rations, so as not to impair their capacity to work, considered vital for the City's security. In order not to publicise this, he would not receive his week's rations along with the rest of his area's population, but during his lunch break. Ross acknowledged the message. Having a Level D job did have its advantages.

He could only hope that the City Council would ensure the food production was speeded up, so that the population would not suffer overly much. Social unrest would only make matters worse. It was clear to him that the City was heading for its biggest crisis in recent times, and he shuddered to think what would happen when public dissatisfaction reached its boiling point.

The rest of the day was unusual in various ways. The Squads came around, but there was little they could do apart from catching fluffs of pollen. The thought struck him that these uniformed men seemed to be playing a merry game, rather than safeguarding the survival of the City.

"I hope this constant flow of pollen will stop soon," the Squad Leader told him. "We must look like fools. We're supposed to kill and exterminate, not to jump around like children."

Instead of telling him they were indeed making fools of themselves, Ross replied: "Every bit of pollen is a potential clump of vegetation. So in a sense you are exterminating. You're doing what's expected of you. Concentrate on your job and get those degrading ideas out of your head."

"Of course, Inspector."

During his lunch break he received the week's food supplies, an amount that appeared modest but that should be sufficient. He wondered how much workers in the lower levels were entitled to. The deafening music in the mess-hall irritated him. This had never happened before. It was an indication of how he was buckling under the strain he had endured. No doubt it was true for every inhabitant of the City. For how long could they go on like this?

For a long time they had lived comfortable lives in the City, and no one had questioned the Council's authority. There had been occasional problems, which had always been solved quickly and efficiently. Life in the City might seem extremely rigid and regimented, with men and women living separately and a strict set of rules and regulations to stick to, but it had been free of the medical, social and criminal upheavals that had struck humanity in the past. Now that period seemed to draw to a close. Would chaos and epidemics make a triumphant return? Would the City built for man and for man only crumble under the onslaught of aggressive invaders?

Late in the afternoon he received a call from the Justice Administrator. Ross was told his inspection duties for the day were cancelled and he had to attend a public trial in a neighbouring district. The Administrator gave him the specific place and time where the trial would be held. When he arrived there at the scheduled hour, he noted most of the district's inhabitants were there, and a vast number of Inspectors and Squad Leaders from all over the City.

A representative of the Justice Administration welcomed everyone. "Superb work was done by this district's Inspector," he said. "Yesterday this dedicated City worker discovered an irresponsible citizen, living in this district, had caught a lizard during the period of bad weather the City suffered, and kept the animal alive in a make-shift cage, thus exposing all the City's inhabitants to an incalculable risk. It goes without saying that this district's Cleaning Squad has already dealt with the issue. Now it is up to the Justice Administration to pass sentence on this citizen."

The crowd looked how two uniformed security officers hauled a man out of an apartment block for level B workers. The man tried to hide his face, realising both what crime he had committed and what ordeal was awaiting him. A roar of cat-calls rose from the audience. The Justice representative addressed him directly.

"Citizen, you have exposed the entire City to great risk. You have jeopardised the safety the City Council has painstakingly managed to maintain. Your despicable actions are unforgivable. The Justice Administrator has decided all traces of your activities in this district must be erased. So it will be. I ask five law-abiding citizens from the district to empty this man's apartment."

Several men raised their hands, and five of them were selected. They hurried into the building, removed all the criminal's possessions and spread them out on the street. The Justice representative then sprinkled a liquid onto the goods, and put fire to the stack. Cheers went up as flames devoured the furniture, clothes and personal items of the victim, while the audience chanted "Cleansing fire, cleansing fire." Soon there was nothing left but a small mound of cinders. Then the criminal was led away, and the crowd dispersed. These people had all been dismissed from work to attend the trial, but were now expected to resume their jobs.

Ross returned to his district too. What had possessed this unfortunate soul to keep a living lizard in his apartment? He must have known it would be discovered one day, and what fate would be in store for him. He would now have to serve a term in the City Prison, from which only the strongest men returned. Ross shook his head, failing to understand why some people chose to disobey the rules in such a foolhardy way. They simply did not deserve to live in this City. The punishment for this sort of crime might be harsh, but it was justified.

Ross was not surprised he was given special orders the day afterwards. All the City's Inspectors were supposed to do a thorough check of every house and apartment in their area. If one man had managed to keep a lizard, others may have had similar ideas. The

Council would not take any chances, and urged all citizens to fully co-operate with the Inspectors who would visit them shortly. Any suspicious behaviour would be interpreted as an admission of guilt and be punished accordingly.

In the morning Ross did his usual inspection, then had breakfast. It was just one tablet, a meagre ration, but still more than what most people had left. Still feeling hungry, he began his full inspection tour of his area, which would last an entire week at least if he was to do it thoroughly. He might not run into many people as he carried out his duties – most people would be at their factories or offices, apart from workers with special hours or exceptional schedules.

His first inspection run didn't yield anything. He hadn't expected any spectacular results. The man with the lizard had probably been an exception, and it would surprise him if he stumbled onto any other creatures or plants hidden in someone's apartment. Afterwards he went to the Bureau to file his reports. As he was about to finish, one of his colleagues at the desk next to him whispered:

"Inspector?"

He looked up. "Yes?"

"We should talk. Do you have a minute? Can we discuss something while we go to the mess-hall to have lunch?"

Ross nodded. This was unusual, but not against the rules. "Fine with me."

A few minutes later they were on their way to the mess-hall and his colleague said: "I've received information. I think we all should know."

"Information about what?"

"Haven't you noticed that social unrest is brewing? People are no longer happy with the way the City Council is running things. The food rations, the strict obedience of the regulations, the endless clean-ups, the sanctions. The unrest runs through all the levels. It's not just A and B, but even the higher levels, up to E. Many Squad Leaders and Inspectors like ourselves share these feelings."

"The City Council isn't taking these actions for no reason. Every measure is taken in the City's best interest."

"I know that. Still, people would like some more freedom, the possibility to socialise with women, even to raise children. Wouldn't you say that's a justified demand?"

"If people were free, they might make the same mistakes that caused so many problems in the past."

"That's a direct quote from our history lessons. I know all that, and I'm not denying it. Still, many people are convinced the Council is taking its views a bit too far. I was hoping you might share that opinion, but you seem to be firmly on the Council's side."

"Why were you hoping it would be otherwise?"

The man shook his head. He seemed to be glad they had reached the mess-hall, where the music, played at a higher volume than before, made every discussion impossible. Was the man trying to rally supporters for his cause? Was he planning something? Would subversive or even revolutionary forces take advantage of the social unrest and try to seize control? Was the City Council aware of this alarming evolution? Should he warn the Council?

Or was this colleague working for the Council, posing as a revolutionary to discover who might be receptive to subversive messages? Maybe the Council had got the air something was afoot and was gathering information. In that case it would be wiser not to react. It was a difficult situation. It so preoccupied him that his appetite was spoiled, although the meagre lunch ration did not require a lot of appetite.

The following days he continued his inspections. The first three days did not yield anything. They were marred only by fairly inclement weather, spells of bright sunlight alternating with showers. This was far from ideal for the City, considering its current problems. The Council preferred overcast skies, with no rain and only a light breeze. Such weather was said to keep the City's population more subdued, while sunlight and rain raised the risks of "invaders" meeting with success, and wind only brought more pollen and consequently more problems. Powerful as the City Council was, it could exert no influence on meteorological conditions, however. On the fourth day of his district tour he unexpectedly ran into a man as he entered an apartment in a building for level B workers.

"Good morning, citizen," Ross said, surprised. It was highly unlikely but not altogether impossible for someone to be home in the morning, but he would like to know why.

"Good morning, Inspector," the man replied. "I assume you come to check my place."

"Yes, indeed. I hope there will be no problem. And could you perhaps explain your presence here at this hour?"

The man shot him a worried look. "There should be no problem. But there is something I should tell you. It's about my garden. That's why I chose to stay here today." The man smiled sheepishly.

"Your… garden?" Ross asked, astonished. What was this man talking about? There were no gardens in the City, the very notion of a garden was supposed to be unknown, especially among level B workers. What was going on here?

"Please come with me," the man said. Ross followed him into the back of the twin room apartment. The man turned around and pointed at the window sill. Ross saw a crudely made pot, made with shards and all sorts of debris, and from the pot emerged a small green plant sporting a red flower. The bright colours almost hurt his eyes. These colours were not supposed to be present in the City! What the hell was this?

"Here it is," the man said. "I call it my garden. Don't you think it's beautiful, Inspector?"

Ross could hardly believe what he saw. "Beautiful? A living plant in full bloom! This is a severe violation of the City law."

"I know that," the man said. "But please, Inspector, take a closer look. Can you honestly say this flower represents evil? That it poses a threat to us all? You know what it represents, Inspector? It symbolises freedom, the possibility to live as it desires. It has a capacity that we lack. We are not free. We live as the Council desires. We are not allowed to get in touch with each other. Men and women are separated, procreation is controlled by the Council. We donate our semen at the Medical Centre and that's where our involvement ends. This is not a society. It's a collection of isolated individuals, ruled by a merciless Council. We are unable to erupt into full bloom, like this flower. We need to break free."

Ross let the man talk. If he didn't interrupt him, he might supply more information.

"I'm not the only one who favours such views. There are more of us, and we're trying to organise ourselves without the Council noticing. But we need to be stronger yet. We should have more supporters among the higher levels. We need people like you, Inspector. Look at this beauty. Let its smell convince you. Join us."

Ross looked him in the eyes, then shifted his gaze back to the flower. Had he indeed stumbled onto a member of a subversive movement? Were there others like him in the City, as this man claimed? Would they all approach Inspectors and other higher level workers, was this part of their plan? Was a wide-scale revolution brewing? Had this man really neglected his professional duties and stayed at home intentionally, expecting the visit of an Inspector, in an effort to enlist him? How would his fellow level D workers react? Would they join or denounce the revolutionaries? Ultimately there were only two possibilities. Either the rebels were successful and grabbed power, in which case the Council and all its loyal supporters would bite the dust. It would be the end of the City. Or the Council would prevail, and all its enemies would be wiped out. So in fact there was only one wise move.

"This flower," Ross said. "Did you grow it in just these last few days, when the City was swamped with pollen?"

"Oh, no," the man replied. "These plants don't grow that quickly. I've had this one for quite a while now. Look, there's a wasp. A fascinating creature."

To Ross's horror, an insect indeed came in through the open window. It flew in circles round the plant, hovered in the air for a moment, then seemed to notice him and went straight for his face. Panic welled up inside him, and he hit the insect before it could come near.

"Don't do that," the man cried out. "It's attracted by the flower. It means you no harm, unless you attack it. In that case it will defend itself."

"That's enough," Ross snarled. "I will report you. This flower, the insect, your subversive ideas, your efforts to win me for your despicable cause. You will pay a high price for your treason, citizen."

"Your hand, Inspector. Look at your hand."

Just as he grew aware of a throbbing pain, he looked down and saw his hand was swelling. The pain quickly exploded, setting his entire arm aflame, driving all thoughts out of his mind, until it filled every square inch of his body and short-circuited his brain. He yelled, thrashed and flailed, felt how he hit the plant, the man standing next to him and the wall. He must have hurt himself, but the added pain was lost in the agony that held his entire body in its grip. Then everything faded into blackness, and his consciousness dimmed.

When he awoke he understood he was in the City Hospital. His hand was bandaged. He moved it, but there was hardly any pain anymore. How long had he been here? Had his condition been serious, perhaps even critical? What had that goddamned insect done to him? As he got up a doctor entered his room.

"Good afternoon, Inspector. I can see you're up and running again."

"Doctor, how long have I been here? Was my condition serious?"

The doctor shook his head. "You needn't have worried. You were stung by a wasp, a relatively harmless incident, if treated correctly and timely. You must have overreacted for emotional reasons, or perhaps you suffered an allergic reaction. You also bruised your hand by smashing it into a wall. It's all been taken care of. In a few days you'll be able to use your hand again. Until then you should take it easy."

"Doctor, that wasp… There was this man… He was hiding a

flower…"

"I know. I was told. Several colleagues of yours are taking over your inspecting duties until you're fully recovered. The man you mentioned has already been sentenced. Several similar cases have been denounced. A small rebel movement, you might say. Your superiors will undoubtedly give you a full report and briefing. Be assured that the situation is under control."

"Thank you, doctor."

A few days later Ross was already back in shape and had resumed his old routines. The special inspection run was in its final stages. The incident with the flower and the wasp had made him even more unyielding than before. He reported everything he saw that did not belong in the City: the tiniest patch of moss, a dead bug on the street, a minuscule spider scuttling away in a dark corner of an apartment. This City was built for man, and for man only. No invaders would be tolerated, no crack in the concrete would be overlooked. His briefing, after his dismissal from the hospital, had merely urged him to continue his inspections even more rigorously. He was also told a nice promotion was a definite possibility if he performed his duties flawlessly. A Level E function might well be within his reach.

In one of the very last apartments to be checked in his district he discovered a box holding what looked like dried up remains of plants and seeds. He had found the box in a cupboard that clearly hadn't been opened for years, and the man living here probably didn't know about the box anymore. Its contents had virtually fallen to dust. For a moment Ross considered what to do. Would it be justified to denounce the owner of the box for possessing illegal organic material, even if he might have forgotten about its existence by now and it hardly posed a threat anymore? After all the man would perhaps hardly understand what he was being accused of.

A number of memories came flooding back. The flower with its bright red petals, the wasp that had stung him, the blinding pain setting his arm aflame. The briefing, telling him the City relied on men of his moral stamina to keep life going under difficult circumstances. The spectre of a revolution rearing its ugly head, a menace that had to be stamped out. It was clear what he should do.

The man who had kept this box, even if he might have forgotten all about it, must at one point have been prone to deviant behaviour. In the current climate, with social unrest brewing and a rebel movement trying to organise itself, one should not take any chances. If this man was approached by subversive elements, there was a possibility he might yield and throw in his lot with the rebels.

Ross took his communicator, convinced he was doing the right thing. This man should pay for his crimes. His sentence would be an example to others. Without him and others of his ilk, the City would be a safer place.

In the afternoon he received the news that the public trial was scheduled for tomorrow. He finished the last inspections on his round, which did not reveal any suspicious behaviour. Later that night, he went down to the Level D pub, as he felt the need to socialise. Instead of engaging in conversations that might ease his mind, strained by the incident, the medical treatment and the heavy inspection schedule, he was immersed in heated discussions that were on the verge of erupting into violent arguments.

The City Council failed to deal efficiently with the food supply problem, some claimed. The overly restrictive rationing only served to stimulate the social unrest. The prison was filling rapidly with convicts, and the staff were not equipped to handle the situation. The City had been free of serious problems for a long time, and the Council's reaction to a limited presence of small animals and vegetation was exaggerated. Most of these views were heavily contested, and even more fiercely defended. Ross was too tired to take part in the attacks and counter-attacks. Why couldn't level D workers content themselves to doing their jobs as best they could and leave the rest to the Council? If there hadn't been any serious problems in a long time, wasn't that proof that the City Council's strategy worked perfectly?

The following day he woke up and noticed it must have rained during the night, but the clouds had already made room for an even blue sky and sunshine. This was not a good sign. It was the day of the trial in his district, and he had a gut feeling it might not go entirely as planned. The very moment he arrived at the scheduled place and time, he knew something wasn't right.

There were way too many people out on the street. It was unthinkable the Council had invited all these people to a simple trial. He looked around and noted there were a fair number of level B and C workers among them, even a handful of A levels. This was unheard of! Who had given these people permission to stay away from their factories and offices? Why were they hanging around here?

Just before the trial was about to begin, the representative of the Justice Administration approached him. "Inspector," he said, "many of the spectators here have no right to be here. Security forces are on their way to deal with the situation. The trial should go as scheduled."

Ross nodded. So he had been right. Something was afoot.

The trial began with a short delay. The security forces had pushed back the unauthorised onlookers, and the Justice spokesman addressed the others. "This district's Inspector has performed superior work. A citizen living in the building behind me proved to be in possession of illegal organic material. This man jeopardised the safety of everyone living in the City. There can be only one sentence for such behaviour."

Uniformed men appeared, dragging along the man responsible for this crime. Before the speaker could continue, the man struggled free of one of the guards, raised his arm and shouted, "Freedom! Freedom!" Within seconds the guards held him in a stranglehold and forced him to silence. However, the crowd picked up his cry and started chanting, "Freedom! Freedom!"

"These people have no right to be here," the Justice representative shouted. "They're disturbing a trial. I want that crowd dispersed."

The moment the Security Forces charged, the crowd came rushing forward. As the latter largely outnumbered the former, Ross and the other higher level workers were quickly surrounded by angry workers, yelling unintelligible insults and threats. Ross managed to run off, but saw how the Justice representative was beaten up badly by a few workers, and how others tried to liberate the criminal. As Ross fled to safety, he noted that Security reinforcements were hurrying to the scene of the trial.

The riots lasted for a few hours, and a lot of damage was done. Several official vehicles were overturned and set aflame, and two City Council buildings were completely thrashed. A large number of people were injured, but ultimately Security managed to regain control of the district. Although many of the protesters escaped, a fair number were arrested and sent to prison. No more public trials were organised, as the Council considered a "swift and efficient administrative procedure should temporarily be sufficient in these times of crisis". The City Council issued a warning that no one was authorised to be out on the streets except for official business, such as going to or returning from work. Any infringement would be punished instantly.

The fear that the riots would spread and the rebels might grab their chance to seize control proved wrong. There were a few more isolated incidents in various districts, even in the women's quarters, but Security forces managed to re-establish law and order all over the City in a matter of days by brute repression. The Council issued a statement to all citizens, reassuring them that a rebel movement had tried in vain to overthrow the authorities and unleash the reign of chaos, but that there was no danger anymore.

For a few more days an almost tangible tension hung in the air. In the morning, as Ross went out for his first inspection round, he expected to see people out on the streets, ready to wreak havoc, but everything was as it used to be. The City's Security Forces had demonstrated they had the power to deal with any crisis. The revolution had been nipped in the bud. The City Council was still the supreme ruler of the city, and would evidently remain in power for a long time.

Several days went by and life in the City returned to normal. Grey clouds dominated the sky, and the rain was at a minimal level. Inspection rounds as a rule did not turn up any "invaders". The food supplies had been cleared of "undesired contaminants" and the rations had been lifted. The only place which still suffered from a food shortage was the overflowing prison, densely overpopulated since the recent events.

No official statements were given about the living conditions in the prison, but from hastily whispered exchanges from colleagues in the Bureau and rumours spread in the Pub, he could puzzle together how the Council must have solved this delicate problem.

Apparently the Council had decided not to raise the total food supply allocated to the Prison. That meant that as the number of convicts swelled exponentially in a matter of days, the amount of food given to each prisoner diminished accordingly. Consequently, the overpopulation problem had ceased to exist as the majority of the convicts or perhaps even all of them had perished for lack of sufficient food and water. Among the higher levels, this was considered an "elegant solution" that had left the City "purified".

A week went by, without any disruptions of normal life in the City. A fair number of apartments in his district, and probably all over the City, were now uninhabited, which could only mean that those people had been unmasked as subversive elements and sentenced. In the mess-hall where he went to lunch too, there were fewer people than before. It was clear the revolutionary feelings had penetrated into the higher levels as well, an extremely ominous evolution that had fortunately been stopped short.

One morning Ross got up and noticed that a light rainstorm had left its stamp on his district. It was nothing serious, just bits of sand and dirt swept by the wind into corners. Still, he decided to call the Cleaning Squad. After breakfast, he went out to greet the Squad Leader who had just arrived.

"Good morning. I'm glad you came quickly."

"Good morning, Inspector. What exactly is the problem?"

"Didn't you take a look around?"

"Yes, but all I saw is a bit of sand here and there. Honestly, Inspector, that doesn't look like an emergency situation that requires instant action from an entire Cleaning Squad."

"Just a bit of sand here and there. It may look harmless at this stage, but if more sand and dirt are blown this way, vegetation may start to take root before we realise what's happening. We cannot take any chances. You know what troubles we've recently been through. And you know the City Council's stance."

"Yes, of course, Inspector. This City was built for man and for man only. There can be no other living creatures here. Each intrusion of other life-forms is an infection, a menace for man's survival that should be stamped out. Man is the crown of creation, and the City is his, and his only. We've been taught all that, Inspector, as you well know. But this is just a handful of sand. It's not as if there's an immediate threat."

"You appear not completely convinced of the City Council's views," Ross said. "That's not an attitude expected from a Squad Leader."

"Come on, Inspector. You know very well that I'm a dedicated City worker. We've known each other for how long now? How many frank and open-minded discussions did we have? And have I ever failed you?"

Ross just shot the man a cold, hard look.

"Do you remember the difficult times we had a few weeks ago?" the Squad Leader continued. "Do you remember how my men worked around the clock until the crisis situation had been completely taken care of? How then can you doubt our commitment?"

"I will not doubt your commitment as soon as you've cleaned up the sand and dirt soiling my district," Ross said. Then he turned away his gaze, making it clear the discussion was closed. The Squad Leader returned to his men and gave them their orders. Moments later his district had been cleared and the Squad left.

When he was at the Bureau to file his report, he let his thoughts roam for a few minutes. Should he mention the Squad Leader had shown some reticence in doing his job, had appeared somewhat doubtful of the City Council's views? It was true that he had known the man for a long time and that he had a flawless track record. At least, until now. Admittedly, the last few weeks had been harrowing and now that the situation was back to normal, it was perhaps understandable that some people loosened up a bit.

On the other hand, the Council's views were not open to discussion, and City workers, especially in the higher levels, were supposed to show unswerving support and dedication. This was of utmost importance. Life in the City had been prosperous for as long as most people could remember, and that was largely due to the Council's uncompromising reign. It was only logical that all the City's inhabitants, and in particular the higher level workers, would hold the Council in the highest esteem and apply its directives unconditionally. In that respect the Squad Leader had failed. Even if there were extenuating circumstances, there was too much at stake in this post-revolutionary period to allow for any weakness in a higher level worker.

Ross noted in his report that the Squad Leader of his district had turned into a liability, and that the Justice Administrator should take the steps he deemed necessary. Then Ross leaned back in his seat, convinced he had done the right thing. The City's guaranteed security relied on men like him.

The following days brought nothing special. The weather was quite normal, mostly overcast with an occasional sprinkle of sunshine, no rain, and just a light breeze. He did not spot any intrusions in his district, even if he checked everything with renewed rigour. It appeared this kind of weather indeed rendered living conditions easier and the population more subdued. It was true that there was no trace left anymore of the revolutionary atmosphere of a few weeks ago.

One day there was a small incident after the public lunch in the mess-hall. Since the contamination of the food supplies, their lunch consisted of an indefinable clump of grey material that lacked taste and looked pretty unappetising. Still, most people were glad they were back on regular portions. As a group of workers prepared to go back to their districts, one man held up his hand and said:

"Wait, please. I need to ask something. Does anybody know what we're eating? Does anybody know what that stuff we're served is made of?"

"Does it matter?" someone replied. "It's safe and hygienic. It's healthy and nutritious. What else do you want?"

"I just need to know what it is made of. It can't contain meat or vegetables, as there are no animals or plants in the City. So it must be synthetic. But how does synthetic food attract cockroaches, as they said? How do you explain that?"

"It may be synthetic, but it's edible, right?"

"Are you sure it's edible? Have you tasted that stuff?"

"This discussion is leading nowhere," another man said. "We should be happy we have sufficient and adequate food supplies again. No more questions need be asked."

"I'm not calling for a revolution," the man said. "I just want to know what we're getting to eat."

Nobody bothered to reply, and they all went their separate ways, eager to go back to their jobs. Ross was neither surprised nor unhappy to find out the man was no longer among them the following day. It could only mean one of his colleagues had taken up his responsibility and passed on the information about this case of socially unacceptable criticism to the authorities. As a matter of fact, he had considered doing so himself.

A few days later he spotted a bird at the edge of his district on his early inspection round. The animal was sitting in a portico and did not fly away when he approached. Upon closer inspection he found the bird was injured, perhaps even dying. That explained why the bird had landed here, as in principle there was nothing in the City that might attract birds or any other creatures. This animal must have been too weak to continue its flight, and had come here to die. He called for the Cleaning Squad, adding that this was not an emergency requiring the full Squad.

Shortly afterwards a handful of men arrived, led by his district's new Squad Leader. It was the first time they met in the field. He had of course been informed of the "replacement" of Thomas, thanks to his report, but his successor had not yet been officially presented.

"Good morning, Inspector. How can we be of service?"

"There's an animal over there. I'll show you. It's a bird, and it's dying, or maybe already dead. This should not be difficult."

"A bird." The Leader's face had abject horror written all over it. "An animal, in our city. How disgusting. We'll deal with this, Inspector. Give us a moment and this district will no longer be soiled."

Ross was satisfied to see the men carry out their duties flawlessly. As they clambered back into their vehicle their Leader walked over to him.

"Mission accomplished, Inspector. Is there anything else we can do?"

"No, thanks. I'm sure we'll have a long and fruitful professional relationship," Ross said. "The City needs more men like you."

"Thank you, Inspector. I'm proud to live and work here. In a city built for man, and for man only. Freed of the presence of lower life-forms. Unsoiled by vegetation. This is where we belong, where we can live without fear of infection. Where no cracks in the concrete are overlooked, and each sign of wear or tear is spotted, reported and repaired. A City of bricks and mortar, a landscape of unspoiled concrete, without a strip of the colour green to be seen. It's a dream come true, and we'll do whatever is in our power to keep that dream going."

"I'm glad to see you're a firm supporter of the City Council's views," Ross commended him. "It will be a pleasure to work with you."

"I will never fail you or the City," the Squad Leader assured him. "I believe we will see each other regularly. The City Council has issued this new directive, as I'm sure you know."

"Yes. It's part of their programme to raise the security measures in the City. They learned their lessons from the recent upheavals. Of course I'm fully behind them."

"So am I, Inspector. Goodbye."

The City Council had indeed decided to reschedule and intensify all security measures. He was glad that the Cleaning Squads had been given new responsibilities. Especially with a Squad Leader like this new guy in his district, things would move in the right direction. The Units that sprayed all the City's streets and squares with disinfectant every fortnight had been disbanded, and their personnel added to the various Cleaning Squads active all over town. From now on the enhanced Squads would spray the City twice a week, so as to make sure not even the tiniest life-forms, including those too small for the eye to see, would stand a chance at surviving in the City.

This City was built for man, and for man only, Ross thought. We'll do everything we can to ensure our survival. There would be zero tolerance for any other life-forms that might threaten the City's security, and for any citizen not fully in line with the City Council's doctrine. Too much was at stake. No crack in the concrete would be overlooked, as the official slogan had it.

One of the following days he ran into the Squad Leader as his men were spraying the streets.

"Good afternoon, Inspector," the man greeted him. "You should forgive me for not having a complete Squad right now. A few of my men have been sent to prison and no replacements have been appointed yet. I'm sure we'll be back in full force soon."

"Fine," Ross said. "What was the problem?"

"They questioned the City Council's food policy," he explained. "They complained they were getting unpalatable stuff, wondered in public what it was made of, and accused the Council of needlessly going to extremes regarding the food supplies. It goes without saying that such views cannot be tolerated from men directly involved with the City's security. I'm happy to say they were removed from my Squad and duly sentenced."

Ross nodded approvingly. "I must say I witnessed a comparable case recently," he said. "A fellow level D worker voiced similar complaints after lunch in the mess-hall. He wasn't seen again."

"You denounced him as you filed your report?"

"A colleague of mine must have done so. It's good to see people take up their responsibilities and commit themselves to maintaining the City's security."

"You're absolutely right, Inspector. Now, I must return to my duties. Good afternoon."

Later that evening, as Ross had finished his inspection round, he considered going to the Level D Pub after supper. He had just taken out the food tablets he was entitled to as the door of his place was brutally shattered and a group of Security Forces stormed inside.

"What is this supposed to mean?" he exclaimed, totally taken by surprise.

"You are relieved of your duties," the Forces' Leader replied. "You must come along. You will be imprisoned according to City Council decree. There will be no public trial, as the Council still applies its swift crisis procedure."

Ross could hardly believe what he heard. "This must be a mistake," he stammered. "I'm a loyal level D City worker. I'm fully behind the Council's views and committed to carrying out my duties to the best of my capacities."

The men paid no attention to his words. He was handcuffed and led away. As he was dragged along on the street, the Forces' Leader said to him:

"This district's Cleaning Squad Leader denounced you in his report. Apparently you confessed to him having witnessed a case of unacceptable behaviour. A colleague voicing protest against the City Council's food policy. You admitted not having mentioned this incident in your report."

"Someone else did," Ross said in his defence. "That man was sentenced."

"But you failed to take up your responsibilities. For a Level D worker that is unacceptable. You have become a liability. The City Council prefers not to take any chances. Too much is at stake. Now, follow us in silence."

Ross followed the Security Forces without one further word. The City Prison awaited him. He had reached the end of the line, and it was entirely his fault. Why hadn't he realised that? Why had he mentioned his failure to act to his new Squad Leader? He knew the man was a hard-liner who would take up his responsibility. As he should have done. After all, there was a lot at stake.

As they reached the City prison, he thought: No cracks in the concrete are overlooked, each sign of wear or tear is spotted, reported and repaired. That's official City Council doctrine, Ross. You of all people should know that.

SYSTEM ERROR

BY JAY FAULKNER

"Betrayal isn't something easily overcome, but..."

"Betrayal," Advocate Deaver Banning interrupted, his hand hovering motionless over the lightly rippling information screen. The images displayed on his side of the holographic projection showed the man in front of him from different angles, each image framed in various hues and colours. Lines traced his biometrics, alongside the images, as everything that could possibly be diagnosed about the man, was.

Banning stared intently at the terabytes of information, streaming constantly across the infonet to his fingertips, before flicking his gaze up to the man across from him. "Is that why you did it?" he asked, trying hard not to stare at the angry looking scar that throbbed, in staccato rhythm with the man's displayed heartbeat, on his temple.

Doctor Morgan Black leant back as far as the electro-statically charged Chair that held him in place would allow, and eyed the jittery man sitting across from him. "It?" he asked, a small smile belying the innocence of the question.

"… erm … is that why you killed them?"

"Come, come, Advocate Banning," Black tutted. "You really have to phrase your questions more stringently, you know, if you want to get a definitive response within the accepted percentile for judgement."

"I know that …"

"You don't, obviously!" Black interjected. "If you did then you would frame each question in such a way that it ensured that my answers could be interpreted correctly by the Scanner and thus the validity of my statements proved, or disproved, accordingly."

"… but …"

"It is all well and good having me in the Chair, Deaver, but unless you ask the right questions there is no way for the Scanner to pick up the nearly infinite amount of electromagnetic responses that my mind and body will put out. You will simply be wasting both of our time!"

"You got somewhere else to be, Mister Black?"

The baritone voice, softly spoken yet full of strength, brought both Black and Banning up short. Banning looked past Black's shoulder and he leapt to his feet with a short, sharp salute. Black, held as he was in the grip of the Chair, simply smiled.

"That is Doctor Black, please," he quipped. "I didn't work hard, all those years, to be called simply 'Mister'."

"I see, Doctor Black," the speaker replied, as he moved into view and sat down in the chair that Banning had vacated. The younger man stepped back to stand impassively behind him. "Well, I am Jacob Rusch …"

"Chief Magistrate of the World Judiciary, I know," Black

interrupted. "I am honoured; who would have expected to get the head of the Judiciary himself dealing with something like this? I have to say, though, that I do hope that you are a little better at this than young Deaver here – no offence, of course."

"Well, Mister …"

"Doctor."

"… Doctor Black." The Chief Magistrate corrected himself with a dismissive wave. "The reason that you have garnered my attention is no doubt the same reason that you have Advocate Banning here so flustered."

"Really?"

"Of course," Rusch admitted, steepling his hands in front of him as his gaze flickered across the information displayed on the screen. "You are a celebrity, after all; the first person to commit murder in seventeen years!"

"Has it really been that long?"

"Yes, Doctor Black, it has," Rusch nodded as his hands danced across the moving images. Banning, from his position behind the older man, stood in awe at the skill being displayed as images and information wove together in a lattice of light and data. "The twenty-ninth of April, in the year two thousand and forty-eight."

"Mercedes De Souza," Black stated. "A failed actress who made her real fame by being caught in that Senator's bed, before his wife took a kitchen knife to her face. Horrible business, really, but from a personal point of view I have to admit that her death was a sort of silver lining, for me."

"What!?" Banning blurted out in shock, and then blushed as he glanced at the Chief Magistrate. "Oh, sorry sir."

"Remarkable memory," Rusch ignored the young Advocate. "But then I suppose that, for someone involved in the development of the technol …"

"Involved in?" Black choked out. The display in front of Rusch changed dramatically as the colours around the images of Black's face darkened into hues of red and purple and the biometric lines – heart rate, blood pressure, brain activity – all peaked closer together. "I wasn't 'involved in' anything, Rusch; I single-handedly revolutionised the criminal justice sector and brought crime to near extinction! "

"It says here …" Rusch started, glancing at the information running in front of him.

"I know what it says there …" Black interjected, sharply, biting of the words. At the tone in his voice Banning took a step forwards, putting himself between Black and Rusch as he pulled a cylindrical object from a holster at his side. Black's laughter, and Rusch's raised hand, brought the younger man to a halt and, with embarrassment evident on his face, he stared sheepishly at the high backed chair that kept Black statically held in stasis.

"Don't worry, Advocate," Black laughed again, watching as Banning placed the device back at his side. "I am pretty sure that you won't have to use your Pacifier; I am no threat 'tied up' as I am. It would take a molecular bolt cutter to free me from the chair without the proper access codes and, even then, it would probably take more skin than I would care to part with!"

"How do you know this stuff?" Banning asked, his voice rising.

"As I was saying," Black continued, non-plussed, "and despite what I know it says in the official records, I know 'this stuff' – I know about the Chair, the Scanner and the Pacifier – because I ***created*** them.

In a way I created you as well because, if it weren't for those devices, then there wouldn't be a Ministry of Justice for you to be part of. "

"C'mon!" Banning argued, reaching out and, with a single touch of his finger, allowed Black to see what was displayed. "Even a second grader knows who invented those things! We all learned about the people who brought a new age of peace and prosperity to the World and, believe me, your name wasn't even a footnote!"

"Oh, I do believe you, my dear Deaver," Black smiled, no humour reflected in his eyes. "Though, actually, you are wrong – a footnote is *exactly* where my name was."

"I don't understand …"

"Well then let me make it simple for you, boy," Black bit of the words through clenched teeth. "Everything that you think that you know about this so called 'Golden Age' – everything that you think that you know about the brilliant and wonderful people who supposedly ushered it in – is a lie; I know because they stole it – they stole everything – from me!"

"Doctor Black," Rusch interjected, running a hand across his tired eyes. "According to our records you were a lab assistant at Queen's University's IllumaDyne Futures, working with Diane Rodgers and Daniel Kline – the people actually credited with the creation and development of the technology that you claim to be your own – and then, two years after that, you dropped off the radar until tonight … until …"

"Until you found Diane Rodgers-Kline and Daniel Kline," Black smoothly picked up from where Rusch's voice had trailed off. "The blissfully, happily married couple – the double Noble Peace Prize winners – the 'should have been sainted, walk on fucking water

Messiahs' - shot dead?"

"Yes, Doctor Black," Rusch's face blanched as the crime scene images of the bodies – vacant eyes staring as small entry wounds in their foreheads exploded into gaping gore at what remained of the read of their heads – flashed in front of him. "I find it quite a coincidence that you walk into this facility, murder weapon in hand, asking to speak to one of my Advocates, about a crime involving people that you obviously claim you had some involvement with …"

"You asked me," Black suddenly interrupted, staring at Banning, "if I had done 'it' because of betrayal, Deaver, didn't you?"

"Yes, I did."

"Ask me again," Black prompted, smiling, "ask the question properly."

"What?"

"I said ask me the proper question!"

"… I don't understand."

"This technology was created so that there would be no need for the suspect of a crime to admit his guilt; the Chair would hold him in place, electro-magnetically bonding with his skin and reading every story that his body had to tell while the Scanner translated the electrical and chemical messages from his brain into visual information," Black recounted in a bored tone, as if instructing a small child. "As long as the right question was asked there wouldn't even be a need for words; the body and mind would speak for itself and my technology would confirm the truth of the matter!"

"You missed out an important part!" Doctor Black," Rusch pointed out, staring at the man across from him. "The fact that the Chair has a secondary function – the fact that, once guilt of a crime is proven – the verdict is transmitted to the World Judiciary mainframe, and sentence is carried out immediately. The Chair rips those electro-magnetic bonds to shreds and disperses each, single, atom to vapour."

"Oh, no, Rusch," Black laughed. "I didn't miss that part out at all. I am very aware of that fact but, still, the real fact of the matter is that unless you ask the right questions you won't get the right answer and so judgement cannot be carried out; really, all we are doing here is wasting time!"

"Fine." Rusch decided, suddenly. Leaning forwards he ran his fingers across the display, focusing the Scanner squarely on Black's face, calibrating the sensors and ensuring that every detail was being picked up by the Chair before taking a deep, steadying, breath. "Doctor Black, did you kill Diane and Daniel Kline?"

"Ah – now that's the question, isn't it?" He smiled as the halo of colour around his face turned a light blue and the biometric readings all turned the same colour. "And, not that it's needed, the answer is yes."

"Doctor Morgan Black," Rusch intoned, formally, his hand touching the screen and transferring the finding of the trial Worldwide. "In accordance with the McGuinness Act 0f 2023 I hereby find you guilty of the crime of …"

"Don't you want to know why, though?" Black interrupted.

"I don't need to know why …"

"But you ***want*** to, though, don't you?"

Rusch's hand paused, inches away from the movement that would enforce the summary judgment. He stared intently at the screen in front of him and, as he took in all the information, his eyes tightened.

"Mister Black," he finally decided. "You have five minutes and then this is finished; I am not wasting any more time on you …"

"Five minutes is all I need," Black smiled, his teeth flashing. "Whether you believe it or not – no matter what the records show – it ***was*** my ideas and discoveries that led to the creation of your Judiciary. Though I will admit that it was actually because of Diane Rodgers herself that I changed the World."

"Oh come on …" Banning interrupted with a bark of laughter.

"Shush, Deaver," Black said without taking his glance from Rusch. "Bear with me, child, there is not long now. You see the three of us were at College together, back when Queen's was still an institution of learning rather than the center for worldwide, totalitarian, judiciary; we were – at one time – the best of friends. Diane, though, was more than that to me. I wanted to prove this to her and, with my scientist's mind working with my idiotic, romantic heart I stumbled upon the way to actually show her my feelings."

"What?" Banning asked, interested despite himself.

"Back when I was a child, my great-grandmother …"

"Is this actually going anywhere, Black?" Banning asked sharply. "Is there any point to all of this other than you just wasting our time?"

"Yes, Deaver." Black stated, simply. "I am not *just* wasting your time and, if you would stop interrupting, I may just be able to finish what I started."

"Go on, Doctor Black." Rusch said, waving Banning back. "Your five minutes are running, though, and after that judgment will be carried out."

"My grand-mother told me about this toy that she'd got in Smithfield Market ..."

"Smithfield, what's that?" Banning asked.

"It's long gone now, along with most everything that made this place unique rather than sterile," Black continued, staring into space. "The ring though, that was just small piece of jewelry, made out of cheap metal and coloured glass but it had the ability to read the wearer's mood; it changed colours as their emotions did."

"Like the Scanner!" Banning couldn't help but blurt out.

"No, not really," Black chuckled. "You see it wasn't doing anything other than reading temperature changes of the wearer's body but that didn't matter – people still believed in them."

"Let me guess," Banning laughed. "You gave Diane your grandmother's ring and declared your undying love for her?"

"It was my great-grandmother," Black said, icily. "And don't be stupid; I already told you that the ring didn't actually work. What I did was invent the early prototype of the Scanner and *showed* Diane how I felt."

"What?"

"I took the basic precept of Kirlian photography and combined it with my own specialist research area of the body's electromagnetic energy," Black continued. "The first iteration of the Scanner filled half of my lab but, it worked – I hooked myself up to it and showed Diane how I felt about her. I showed her my love!"

"… and?" Rusch prompted.

"And she laughed!" Black shouted. "She laughed and told me that I was 'sweet'. I had already come up with the basic concept of the Chair – and how it would bond, electro-magnetically, to any living being – as well as the Pacifier – which would allow the police, as you Advocates were known back then – first the RUC, then the PSNI, then finally Advocates - to cause a synaptic shockwave and incapacitate anyone, quickly and easily; it took another two years of my life to develop the Scanner – allowing every human being to be read as easily as a book – two years to lay my heart open for her, almost literally, and she chose Kline over me!"

"Ah," Rusch sighed, softly.

"What?" Black barked out.

"I see now," Rusch nodded. "It makes more sense, but I don't understand why you waited so long."

"Waited?"

"To kill them," Rusch pointed out, simply. "They betrayed you so you killed them."

"They didn't just betray me!" Black bit off through gritted teeth. "They took everything from me … you say that I dropped off the radar, all those years ago. That is what they did to me! When they realised what I had discovered, what I had invented, they saw the potential quicker than I did!"

"… and?"

"And by the time that I realised what they were doing," Black sighed, "it was too late! They had taken my work and made it their own. They had spread rumours and lies to discredit me. They ruined me, they took everything that should have been mine and made it their own. They laughed at me!"

"And so you killed them," Rusch repeated. "You were angry and you took your revenge; you killed them – but why wait so long? Why wait so many years?"

"Oh no," Black laughed, suddenly. "You don't understand. I killed them, yes, but not because I was angry – at least not *just* with them. I tried to get my life back, you see, I tried to convince people that they had taken everything from me but while they were being lauded and given the Noble Peace prize I was being laughed at and ridiculed … even now a moron like Deaver here knows **their** name but hasn't got a clue who I am!"

"… why is that so funny?"

"Because this was never about killing Diane and Kline," Black admitted, the colours on the image of his face showing the truth of his words. "This was about ensuring that my name is known - that it is ***never*** forgotten. You see there is something about the way that the Scanner reads the electro-magnetic energy of the human being that was overlooked by Diane and Kline, something that I have spent the last few years working on …"

"… what?"

"It is simple, really," Black admitted, calmly. "The Scanner is nothing more than a glorified receiver and if something can receive information it can also transmit it – broadcast it, if you will."

"You can't …"

"Actually," Black grinned, the scar on his temple pulsing. "I can. You see I implanted a chip, with an override code and a manufactured super-emotion, inside me that is capable of corrupting the system from the inside out. All I needed was access to the Scanner network itself … and what better way to ensure that I had all the time that I needed than by putting myself under its scrutiny and ensuring that the network was focused on me for the time that it needed to upload the virus and ensure that it couldn't be stopped; and keeping you talking gave me that time."

"… no," Rusch breathed, flicking his hands across the sluggish and non-responsive screen.

"Killing Diane and Kline, while satisfying, was never an end goal; it was simply a means to an end," Black stated. "For all these years the crime rate has fallen because technology read their emotions and kept them in check; now I am going to use that same technology - MY TECHNOLOGY –to send one, pure emotion across the infonet that connects every living, breathing person. To every receiver, every Scanner, every cell, every uplink … everything! I am going to make them feel what I feel every minute of every hour of every day; anger!"

"It will be chaos; anarchy!"

"I know ... you've become the peace-keepers of a sterile World, with my stolen technology but now – a thousand years after they last used the term – I'm going to remind the World what the word 'Troubles' really means."

"Are you mad?" Rusch whispered, watching in horror as the readouts on the screen in front of him showed a burst of activity as millions of connections were made Worldwide.

Black didn't answer; he didn't need to. Before the infonet fell, and the Scanner went black for the final time, it showed his smiling face framed in the glowing blue of truth.

MICHAEL'S GATE

BY LESLIE J. ANDERSON

The hospital was stunningly white. The tile was white. The walls were painted white. Even the stretchers and equipment was made from white, enameled aluminum. On my first day the head nurse, Julia, explained that Michael's Gate Hospital went to a lot of trouble to keep it this way, spotless and light, so that it always seemed clean and hopeful. She gestured around her as she gave me the tour and beamed at the whiteness. She was so proud to be there, and so was I.

I loved Julia. She had thin, pink lips that always smiled and large, almond colored eyes. She was always moving, sweeping in, then out of the office, hovering around patients like a humming bird, then zipping into the hallway, dancing around Doctor Clemens like he was the curtain of her stage. Sometimes though, when she slowed a moment in her dance, you could see how tired she was. She was older than me, maybe 30 or 35, but there were creases at the corner of her eyes and on her forehead that a young woman shouldn't have yet, and she had a persistent cough that she tried and failed to hide. I wasn't surprised. She had lived a hard life and she worked hard to stay in her new one, where everything was clean and full of hope.

Like me she was not a doctor, not even a nurse, she was one of the first Medical Assistants to receive her certification. We were trained and stationed by the Rising Angels Association, a group that recruited from the worst neighborhoods to find kind and intelligent women to care for a rapidly ageing population, mostly the people who could afford a place like Michael's Gate. They came here to buy a little more health, a few more years, and a safe place to pass away. We were gophers. We carried, we tucked, we handed, we smiled and assured. We never looked at charts or knew full names.

We were trained in basic medical knowledge, given two starched uniforms, and sent to live in dorms at places like Michael's Gate and Saint Francis and Our Lady of the City. We worked for our room and board and a few dollars more, which was always sent home to our families. No one even asked if I wanted to send my extra money to my family. There was simply a forwarding address on the sheet. Of course I filled it out.

And yes, we were proud to be Medical Assistants. When I was recruited I was 19, one of the few girls to graduate from high school. Most had children already. Most of the boys who graduated with me were fathers, headed off to the army or navy. There weren't a lot of ways to move up in the world, so when Sister Sarah knocked on my door and asked my mother if I would be interested in the Rising Angels, she said yes. Of course she said yes. She would be proud to have her daughter wear a white uniform and walk down white hallways.

It was the month of May when things started to change. I woke up to the sound of the bell and a light rain against the window. The dorms where we lived were not white. They were pale blue and green, soft colors that reminded me of a child's nursery from the magazines.

Julia told me they once had bunk beds, but some of the ladies had trouble getting in and out of them. Now there were white army beds along both walls. Julia slept next to me, and sometimes we would talk before we slept, or when we got ready in the morning.

Every morning I pulled the wires from the port in my chest and the heart monitor made a little frantic beep, before realizing I was only getting up and hadn't died, and going into sleep mode. The ports were an easy way for the hospital to pipe in our daily vitamins. Because most of us had grown up without proper nutrition they tried to make up for it at night. During the orientation, when the port was put in, Doctor Clemens explained that it was a necessity. They had given each Assistant a handful of pills, but it made them sick to their stomachs, so they did this instead. I was fine with it, though it was itchy.

I changed into my uniform and ate breakfast sitting on my bed. We walked in a line to the hospital, which was right next door. The two shared a wall. In the front door we pressed our hands to a scanner that flashed our names. We had our own entrance, just for us, our little white-uniformed parade. I went to check on my first patients, a distant, polite old heiress named Rose, and an army veteran named Stevens

"I feel so much better today." Mrs. Rose said as I cleaned away her oatmeal. I smiled, but didn't say anything. It was best not to talk while the doctor was in the room.

"Miss. Take away the other tray. Now, Mr. Stevens, is that arm improving?" Doctor Clemens said. He was a small man whose clothing was made to fit a younger, fitter body. He had small, wet eyes and short, mustard hair. His impatient authority filled the room like a gas.

"You bet doctor!" Mr. Stevens said.

Then something happened that had never happened before. The red alarm light above the bed sprang to brilliant life. A buzzing noise filled the room. The patients looked at me, confused, but I didn't know what to tell them. There were never any emergencies here. The intercom, usually silent, crackled to life.

"Doctor Clemens, please come to Ms. Marie's room immediately."

The doctor pushed his clipboard into my hands and almost ran from the room. It made sense. Ms. Marie had paid for half the hospital, or so the rumors said. She was important, and any emergency involving her would be worth running for, and breaking protocol. I looked at the clipboard in my hands. We weren't supposed to see the clipboards. We weren't even supposed to handle them. I knew I should have just put it down or given it to Julia or something, but I was curious. I read some medical textbooks when I was a student, maybe I could make out something from the doctor's notes. I slipped out of the room and went to the bathroom. It was empty, thank goodness. I ducked in a stall and leafed through the packet, my heart beating in my chest. I could read it! There was the heart rate, blood pressure, blood work.

It was all normal, perfectly normal. I looked at the next sheet. Mrs. Jeffers. All the same. Slightly elevated cholesterol. Slightly. But that was all. A few of them reported complaints upon arriving that, on the current sheets, had disappeared. They were all healthy. Why were they in a hospital? I would ask Julia. I was sure Julia would know.

I realized I left both trays in the room. The cooks expected them in the kitchen so they could clean them for lunch. I dropped the clipboard on Doctor Clemens' desk and rushed into the room to grab the trays. Mr. Stevens looked up from his book and offered a worried smile.

"Jane," he said softly, "how are you?"

"A little tired, actually." I admitted, trying to cover my guilt. What I had done was very against the rules. "I guess I get worn out keeping up with you!" He laughed. I picked up his tray and scurried out.

I almost ran into Julia, coming out of Ms. Marie's room. Miss Marie had two rooms actually, all to herself. She was Julia's assignment and took up most of her time. She looked exhausted, and I knew she would always put Ms. Marie's health before her own.

"Well good morning, Miss Julia." I said, carefully, aware that whatever she left in Miss. Marie's room must have been an emergency.

"Good morning, Miss Jane!" She answered, but it deteriorated into a cough.

"Please ask the doctor about that." I frowned at her. "Is Miss Marie all right?"

"I don't know." Julia said. "Everything the Doctor says is gibberish to me. They want me to grab a defibrillator, though, just in case." She coughed again.

"I need to talk to you." I said and dropped my voice to a whisper. I had to get it over with. "I saw the patients charts and they're not right."

"Shhh!" She hissed at me. "You're not supposed to do that!"

"I know! I'm sorry."

She nodded as if I'd repented enough. "I have to get back quick. We'll talk about it tonight, okay?" I nodded and she swept back to Miss Marie.

But she didn't come back to the dorm with us. I waited up all night, fiddling with the itchy port. Finally she snuck in, closing the door quietly behind her. A few of the other girls murmured in their sleep.

"Julia!" I hissed at her.

"Shh!" She hissed again. "I am only here to change my uniform. I can't stay."

"What's going on?"

"Ms. Marie isn't recovering. Doctor Clemens told me if she doesn't get better he's going to try something highly experimental. He needs help so I'm going to go back." She sounded almost excited as she buttoned her clean, white shirt.

"How are you going to get in? The scanner won't let you."

"The technician turned it off. I can get in. Now go to bed. I'll see you tomorrow."

She coughed into her elbow then took a moment to ruffle my hair. I could see her white uniform glide past the beds and out the door. She turned the knob so the tongue wouldn't make a noise as it closed.

The next morning I got up and disconnected my port. The machine beeped and then was quiet. I rubbed my eyes and groaned. I felt even more tired than I did when I went to sleep. I guess all the excitement from the night before got to me. As I stood up the door opened and one of the nurses walked in. Everyone froze. You would have thought a tiger had appeared in the door. It might as well have been. No one came to the dorms but us. She held the door open with one hand, as if she didn't want to be completely in the room with us.

"Ladies," she started, as if she had to get our attention. Her red uniform stood out like a spot of blood in the pale room. "I am here to inform you that Miss Julia passed away last night. The stress of caring for Miss Marie was too great and affected her heart. We have truly lost a great healer and our hearts go out to you. Those closest to Julia may take a day to grieve. Miss Jane?"

I looked up, surprised. "Yes?" I tried, but my throat had completely dried. I coughed and tried again. "Yes? I'm here."

She turned her red attention to me. "You will be reassigned to Miss Marie, beginning today. That is all ladies, thank you."

When the door closed the room began to move again. Any conversation was done in whispers. A few women cried. I did not follow them to get my breakfast. I slipped out and headed to work. What else could I do? Stay in my bed and cry all day? I couldn't face it, though I kept running the words through my head. Surely Julia was just in the next building, somewhere in the hospital. It was a hospital after all! Couldn't they save her?

The morning was cold and damp. The lawn, as always, was empty and well kept. The place had once been a public hospital and emergency room, but now the parking lot was mostly empty. No one really came or went. Those who were already here stayed here. The road was always empty too. No one lived out in the country anymore. They grouped together in the city, like bugs around a light, or at places like Michael's Gate. It seemed like everyone was either very old or very young these days, either in the city or in the hospital.

I held my hand to the scanner inside the door. It beeped loudly, too loudly – a long, drawn out error message. I looked around nervously. My name flashed on the screen and I walked to Miss Marie's room. I had to keep my mind busy. There was no way I could process the events of the morning. I couldn't even begin to feel the things that filled up in my chest like tumors. I found the doctor inside. He was checking the machinery, and didn't look at me when I came in.

"You gave us quite a scare." He said to Miss Marie, his voice glowing, like a favorite son. "We haven't had something like that happen in a long time! I think everything's under control now.

Her room was bigger than my past patients', but fairly similar. Still there was an extra bed, just in case of overflow, all set up with IV and port and all the other machines. There were tall, clear glass vases full of flowers on the window. I wondered if Julia died here, maybe passing out on the floor, and the thought made my body ache from my chest to my spine. I put a smile on my face and picked up Miss Marie's food tray.

She smiled at me, a tiny woman with the faintest cloud of white hair. I could see the veins under her thin skin. "I feel so much better today." She said.

"That's wonderful." I answered.

And life went on. I fell into my new routine. My workload was much lighter with only one patient, but life seemed to wear me down faster without Julia. I felt tired and depressed. I developed her cough, as if I missed the sound of it. I lost track of time. I no longer dreamt of a life beyond Michael's Gate. For my short breaks I drank coffee in the Nurse's room, alone, and thought nothing at all. A new Medical Assistant came, Jessie, to fill Julia's bed. She seemed so young, I tried to help her where I could. She told us about her son, his father dead in the War. What choice did she have? The little money she sent home might even get him through school. She came up to me one afternoon, during my break.

"Jane? I thought you might want to know. Mr. Stevens is

checking out today. I thought you might want to say good bye."

"Oh. Thank you." I said, forced a smile, and walked past her.

I found him standing by the door, a box of his belongings in his hands, reading the plaques beside the door.

"Mr. Stevens." I called out and he turned to smile at me. "I am so sad to see you go."

He scoffed. "I bet you are."

I held my smile. "I can understand why you'd want to leave. Everyone was so shocked by Julia's death."

"Oh I'm not shocked by death." He said, smiling a little. "I fought in the War, you know, before my uncle made his fortune and I came home to work with him. No, death is just the thing that happens at the end of life."

"Well you're a lot tougher than me." I felt a frown pull at the edge of my practices smile, but the smile remained

"Death doesn't do a thing to you, Miss Jane. Life. Life is what wears you down. Life makes you old and tired. Life continues on when your teachers, your parents, and finally your colleagues and friends die."

He walked over to me, his cane making a dull, thunking noise on the clean floor. He put a hand on my shoulder. "I am sorry about Julia." He said. "I really am. She was a good girl. She didn't deserve that." He looked at me as if he might say more. He looked at me like he was seeing me, completely, for the first time. He licked his lips and frowned. "You be safe," was all he said, and turned to walk out the front door.

I wandered back to the break room and looked out the window at the steady rain. I should leave too. I could walk out into the pouring rain and just keep walking. I hadn't stolen anything from them, except the clothes on my back. I didn't keep my crappy clothes from my old life. Would they come after me for a white shirt and pants? White shoes? Probably. I couldn't go home. They knew where I lived, where my family lived.

They used us. I suppose that if you spread the suffering out enough, no one would notice, except sometimes something went wrong. Like Miss. Marie. I wondered if my extra pay ever made it to my family at all. Maybe there was no extra pay for me at all, or Julia, or Irena, or Claire. For some reason this made me the angry, when nothing else did.

The red light sprung to life in the break room. Everyone jumped and turned to stare at it. A buzzing filled the room and the intercom crackled to life.

"Doctor Clemens, please come to Miss Marie's room immediately."

The nurses and Medical Assistants turned to look at me. They watched me take a last sip of my coffee and they watched as I walked out of the room. I paused to cough into my elbow. Miss Marie's room was in chaos. Three nurses were around her bed. She was having some kind of seizure and Doctor Clemens was injecting something clear into her IV. Someone had knocked one of the flowers off the windowsill. The vase was broken across the floor and the daisies had been crushed underfoot. I worried that someone might slip in the water, but I didn't go for the mop. I closed the door softly behind me.

Doctor Clemens looked up as Miss Marie stilled on the bed. "Ah. Miss. Please come in. We need your help." He raised his hand to take my arm, to guide me into the room.

"I know." I said. Doctor Clemens stopped and looked at me with his small, wet eyes. He looked at me for a long time.

"You know?" He repeated. The nurses slowed and looked over their shoulders at us. They looked afraid.

I knew the empty bed was just to my right, with its port and its machines like hungry infants. I could still walk into the rain. I could walk into the other room and scream until the windows broke and the foundation shook. I could take a needle from the tray and stab the doctor in the eye. I could. I could do any of these things. I am powerful. I am so much more powerful than them, the pathetic doctor and nurses, looking at me like I am poisonous or explosive. I have defeated the army of secrets and death. My mind is clear and powerful.

"Yes." I say.

FIRST HEAD

BY H.S. DONNELLY

Murmur ... Four more CC's ... Mr. Kamil? ... He is doing fine ... Yes, increase the levels ... Mr. Tilson? ... No, same schedule ... Yes, Doctor ...

Senses dull, fuzzy. Temples throb faintly. Tongue feels like a lump of liver; teeth (lifting tongue up to touch them) are clean, freshly scrubbed; throat—*hack-hack*—raw.

In the background, a '*throb-throb-throb*' vibration. Eyes open warily. Dimly lit room. Vague, oval shapes on a row of night tables opposite. "Huhhh—" he utters hoarsely.

Swuck—Light.

To the left, double doors slide open. Man clothed in glowing white fabric enters silently. Weird blue-white globe hovers over him. White Ghost stops at the first table, bends down, then straightens up and moves to the next table, and the next, and—

"Uhggg!" A row of severed heads! All along the opposite wall.

Pad, pad, pad. White Ghost stops in front of him. "Ohhh, you're the one. Time for some extra juice." He peers down at him and double-clicks on something. "There, better?"

"Uhggg." Tingle of relaxation spreads from the back of his head.

The horror recedes.

"Happy days, bud," White Ghost whispers. "You're alive now."

"Uhggg?"

But White Ghost has vanished.

***

Awake.

"Uhaaa!" An object is stuck in his throat.

"Shhh!"

He stops.

The object retreats and, now he can see a man standing in front of him holding a metallic device. "There. That takes care of the Vocalotomy," the man says. The fellow, white shirt, black curly hair, places the object onto a tray to the left and then picks up a green rectangular pane of glass and taps on it.

Click, then *wheeze*—A breath of air comes in through his nose, stops and then—*Wheeze*—reverses. Odd sensation, yet everything still feels ... detached.

"Okay," Curly Hair looks at him, "do you remember your name? Blink once for 'Yes' and twice for 'No'."

Wheeze ... Name? Strange, he should know that. But everything—*Wheeze*—feels vague, lost.

"Do you know your name? Once for 'Yes'; twice for 'No'."

Timidly, he blinks twice.

"Do you remember your past life?"

His *past life*? Okay, he woke up to those ghastly severed heads. And before that there was ... nothing. Frustration and fear. Two quick blinks.

"Good," Curly Hair continues. "Okay, let me explain." He looks down at his tablet device and begins, "You've been successfully revived, so welcome to your Second Life."

"Uhaaa—" Second Life?

"I'm your Revivologist, Doctor Huter. And your name is Jim Tilson."

Jim Tilson? Pause. Is that right?

"You died three hundred and fifty years ago."

"Uhaaa?" Died? God, he thinks, blinking rapidly, what sort of place is this?

"Don't worry." Dr. Huter looks up at him. "Normally you'd prepare for your re-awakening as part of your prior life. But you are so old, standard preparation protocols were not in place when you were interned. Fortunately, however, they were smart enough to perform a decapitation."

"Uhaaa?" My God! Those heads!

"Please, Mr. Tilson. Decapitation is a standard procedure." Dr. Huter returns to his green tablet. "Your life functions are now being maintained via tubes that draw nutrients from the reservoir tanks in your Head Cart."

Head Cart, Jim wonders, looking down. He can just see the black edge of—gulp—*his* table top. He imagines the tubes below him throbbing like arteries. And what if—No, he doesn't want to think about that.

"Now that you've been stabilized, we'll begin your evaluation process to determine your future net worth to society. Assuming a favorable outcome, you then move on to be re-attached to one of the headless bodies that are grown on our body farms."

Headless?

More taps. "Final activity for today is for you to review your prior life. Life Catalogue on," Dr. Huter calls.

A square of blue words, *Jim Tilson. First Life*, floats in front of him—

Beep! Beep!

Dr. Huter touches his tablet device. "Yes, I'm just about finished here. I'll be there in two minutes." He looks back over to Jim. "You can do this yourself. Just make a sound to activate things. I'll be back tomorrow."

Prickles go up Jim's neck as he watches Dr. Huter leave. God, he thinks and puckers his lips as air starts wheezing out. Quiet now, save for some clinks and shuffles coming in from the hall outside. The blue words hang there waiting.

"Uhaaa," he squeezes out when an exhale comes.

The title vanishes, replaced by a block of words:

Jim Tilson: *Never married. No descendants.*

Revival Rating: *Restricted revival classification.*

Potential emotional problems.

Current Status: *Revived via investigative protocol.*

Life Items: *Item One: Revivology History.*

"Uhaaa."

Item One: Revivology History.

Underwent vitrification. Pioneer client of Revivology.

"Uhaaa."

No more words.

***

Sunlight through the window.

Birds chirp.

Morning? No idea.

From the hall come faint noises of people talking mixed with odd knocks and clinks. Underneath, the machinery gurgles.

Strange not knowing what time it is. Or who he was.

Jim Tilson, he tries again. It still doesn't feel right. Edginess creeps into his jaw muscles.

Huh?

A man stands motionless by the door. The fellow is average in height and build. Short brown hair. Healthy pinkish complexion. Brown jacket and pants. Tan colored open collar shirt. Staring outward at nothing.

"Hu—llo," Jim tries.

No response.

Once more, "Hu—llo."

Nothing.

Footsteps.

"Mr. Tilson," Dr. Huter sweeps in. "How is your voice today?"

"B-heh-ter," he manages.

"Wonderful. You're making excellent progress. Today you get your own Personal Robot Assistant, or P.R.A." He points towards the man in the corner. "He will be your 'legs' for the next little while. And the first thing we're going to have him do today is take you to your Indoctrination Session. Do you have a name you'd like to call him?"

Name? He tries to remember some names. Come on, think!

Think!

"Okay, maybe we'll call him 'Bob'," Dr. Huter says. "Control, initialize P.R.A. to client Jim Tilson with I.D. 'Bob'."

The robot straightens to attention.

"Good. Bob, come here."

Robot Bob's body emits a soft hum, rotates and then turns and faces Jim.

"Bob, say hello to Jim Tilson."

"Hello Jim Tilson." Robot Bob echoes and smiles.

"Good, Bob. Now take Mr. Tilson to the Indoctrination Session." He glances towards Jim. "You're coming along quite nicely, Mr. Tilson."

"G—hood." Jim tries to sound confident as Rob-o-Bob steps behind him and starts unhooking various unseen connections.

Dr. Huter frowns as Rob-o-Bob turns him around and heads towards the door.

***

P.R.As and Heads roll through the door ahead of Jim. The Head in front of him appears normal with smooth olive-colored skin and short, thick black hair. But the next one has pale skin with blotches and almost no hair. God, he hopes he looks better than that.

The other P.R.A.s are like Rob-o-Bob, from height and slim build to the measured way they walk. Half have the same brown jackets and pants, while the rest sport longer female-looking long hair and curves. Most have olive colored skin, though a few have black or pinkish-white pigment.

The room opens up into a great semi-circle with white curving walls that arch together. The blue carpeted floor slopes downwards towards a stage lit by floodlights ringing the perimeter.

He feels a slight bump as Rob-o-Bob maneuvers the Head Cart into a set of metal rails recessed into the carpet.

Click–Click

From behind, Rob-o-Bob announces, "Head Cart anchored." —*Swuck*—Then, "Replenishment tubes re-connected." Then, "Jim Tilson, do you require anything?"

"W-a-ter?" He's not thirsty; just craves the sensation of cool water in his mouth.

Click—Click

A water bottle appears with a drinking tube hovering near his lips. He snags it and awkwardly sucks at it with his cheeks. Water, fresh, wonderful water, gushes into his mouth. He swallows,

Whirrrr

Does it matter that some little pump evacuates the water from the bottom of his neck into some sort of receptacle? No, water in his mouth still feels good. Finally he releases the tube and Rob-o-Bob withdraws the bottle.

"Jim Tilson, do you require anything?"

"N-oo." He feels the last bit of liquid in his mouth. Good Rob-o-Bob, he thinks.

"Shutting down," and the faint hum from Rob-o-Bob is gone.

Sweet dreams, Rob-o-Bob.

Whispers and clicks drift over. Three dozen other Heads sit clamped onto their carts facing the stage with their P.R.A.'s standing motionless behind them.

"Oh, hi! How you doing," a chirpy man's voice asks.

To his left, Jim can make out a vague shape. "F—ine."

"Name's Steve."

"J-im."

"Still getting your voice back?"

"Y-ah."

"You'll be good in a couple of days. So what revival is this for you?"

"W-un."

"Ohhh! Must be pretty exciting, eh?"

"Yeah," The real answer is much longer, but saying, 'Y-ah' is easier.

"Better than being frozen, eh?"

"Y-ah," Feels good to talk to someone.

Suddenly there is a muffled Thump – Sloosh noise off to the left. Ahead, two rows up and three over, a replenishment tube from a Head Cart snakes free and sprays a stream of brownish-red liquid into the air and then onto the carpet.

"Help, help," a female voice shouts, terror creeping into her voice.

"Leak! Leak!" The cry echoes around the room.

As the liquid sprays onto the carpet, her P.R.A. revives, grabs the tube and reconnects it. A human female dashes over. "Sweet Fotheringham," she exclaims as she unconnects the floor tubes, reconnects her Head Cart tubes and then quickly pushes her towards an exit. The P.R.A. strides after.

Mutters echo around the room.

"Okay, everything's under control, people!" a tall man wearing a dark sports jacket announces, stretching his arm up in the air. Some cheery background music fills the air. Two other humans with little vacuums move in and clean up the carpet.

"Wh-aaa a—bout my t-ubes?" Jim asks. He can see them throbbing away, just waiting to burst.

"Don't worry, she could have leaked for five minutes before anything serious happened."

Is she really all right, Jim wonders.

"This is my second." Steve continues, "Originally I was frozen for thirty-two years; this time it was for fifty-two. Still don't have hardly any frost damage. Boy, the first time, I was so nervous I wasn't going to get a body!"

"*G-et a bo-dy*?"

"Yeah, you know? *Lots of Heads in the fridge, but only so many bodies*. They revive you every so often just to check that you haven't turned into a mush-ball. So there's usually more heads than bodies."

"M-ush b-all?"

"Sure. Cell damage from freezing and thawing. Sometimes happens when the antifreeze pools in a funny way."

"Wh-aaa d-oes it f-eel l-ike—"

But the lights flicker, cutting off the rest of Jim's question.

A thin man wearing a long flowing robe shuffles out to the center of the platform. He has a smooth bald head and hooked nose. Gold chains hang around his neck. He squints around the room, then clears his throat and begins, "Welcome to this Indoctrination Session. I'm Reverend Hancock, a minister in the Revivalist Religion."

There are tongue-clicking sounds around the room.

"Thank you. I'm sure you're all glad to see me."

Scattered titters.

"Now, I would like to offer a short dedication to the very first revived Head, Ernest Fotheringham, beloved Green Grocer from Manchester, England.

"Lord, praise be Ernest Fotheringham for his courage and bravery. And thank you Lord for giving us His example, for giving us the miracle of Revivology that we all may indulge. Through Revivology, the promise of Eternal Life has been achieved. And Lord, give us the goodness to use our New Lives in ways that You would approve. And Lord, when, at last, all of our New Lives here on Earth are finished, make us welcome in Your House. Amen."

"Amen."

"Revivology," Reverend Hancock continues, "is the final medical procedure. And through the evaluation process, we optimize the benefit to society by evaluating the net worth of each individual. All of us should every day ask of ourselves, 'How can I best use this new life of mine?'"

More tongue clicking.

"Now I would like to conclude this short service with a hymn, *Lord Cherish My Body and Let Me Not Do Ill with It.*"

Lights dim. Soft soprano voices begin singing,

Oh Lord cleave my Head

From my Body so that

In the Eternal Fridge

I may dwell, Awaiting

That rapturous moment when . . .

High above a dozen holographic Heads float, all singing the hymn. Faintly, voices around him join in. He moves his lips too, though he doesn't know the words.

***

A woman enters, flicks on her tablet, taps a few things, and then says, "Mr. Tilson?"

"Yeah."

She makes a few more taps on her tablet and then frowns. "Your happy levels are low today."

His answer comes out slowly, "I w-ill work at be-ing happ-y."

She stares at him for a moment, her expression uncertain. But then she returns to her tablet device.

Click-Click-Click, and he can feel the starting tingle of happy drugs starting to circulate. He looks toward the window with its never changing breeze and bird songs. There must be a lawn of green grass out there. "Out-side," Jim says, "I wanna to go out-side.

"Sorry," she glances up momentarily, "that's not on your schedule. But I'll notify your Revivologist."

And then she leaves.

Sigh. Green grass. But he's stuck. What if he could detach himself from the Head Cart? Be free to roam? He tries wiggling just a bit. Nope. Clamped down tight.

Birds continue chirping in the background as the happy drugs creep into his brain. Just beyond the horizon, sadness is lurking. Or is it anger? He tries to relax and let the drugs do their job. Outside, he can still hear chirping.

Dr Huter enters. "Okay, Mr. Tilson, you can go outside to Paradise Garden tomorrow."

"What?" Outside! Outside!

"That's the spirit, Mr. Tilson. Think happy!" Dr. Huter breaks into a smile.

***

Revivologists cluster together, none looking at them, as Jim and Rob-o-Bob roll down the corridor. Here and there, other Heads sit outside their rooms, some with open eyes, others not.

One Head shoots Jim a pleading glance. Another gives him an impish smile as if to say, *Don't we look ridiculous being wheeled around in these silly carts*? The Head has a fuzzy layer of hair; a smooth, small face suggests female.

Jim smiles back as Rob-o-Bob whisks him by. Should he have ordered Rob-o-Bob to stop? But what would he have said? Is this your first revival? Have you been evaluated yet?

He imagines her laughing, *What a colossal joke, huh? You're dead. But then you wake up and find all these jerks running around deciding what's best for you. Makes you want to get a body, then come back and kick the crap out of someone.*

Concentrate on happy, happy, happy. More dopamine, please. And he mustn't be angry.

Swuck.

Double doors slide open and they roll into an atrium.

Sunlight floods in through tinted octagonal shaped glass panels that stretch upwards to a canopy of converging metal beams. Green leafy plants overflow large red clay pots at the base of each window. Birds chirp overhead.

Wonderful to see the sun casting pools of light intermingling with shadows on the floor.

Run, run, run. He wants to feel the ground bang against the bottoms of his shoes as he lifts his knees as high as they will go and leave Rob-o-Bob far behind. Goodbye Rob-o-Bob! Stupid machine—No, Rob-o-Bob has been good to him.

Another set of double doors slide apart and they roll outside out onto a terrace four meters above a garden.

"Arrive. Paradise Garden," says Rob-o-Bob.

The garden stretches off. In the distance, a flat lake sits with three triangle-sailed boats floating motionless and then after that, a range of purplish mountains. A reddish sun hovers above the mountains.

To the right is a set of marble stairs, while on the other side, a Head and P.R.A. descend along a ramp towards a garden crisscrossed with chalk white paths radiating outwards. A half dozen Heads are being pushed along the pathways.

So, does he want to descend into the garden like all the other Heads? No. Just wait for a moment. And talk to someone. "What to talk to some-one," he says.

"Specify who."

Sigh. "Turn left, and go."

Rob-o-Bob moves them along the terrace.

Falling–Falling–If he can't run, maybe he could fall? Funny, yes? Wickedly funny. Dead. He lets the word echo about in his mind. Strange, it doesn't frighten him.

They turn a corner and another Head is sitting there with its P.R.A. standing behind.

"Turn me to face him," Jim says.

The other Head blinks as Jim is placed in front of him. Behind the other Head are the sloping mirror-like walls of the Revivology Facility.

"Hell-o. I'm Jim."

"Oh, hi." Pause. "I'm Lassal." There is only a wisp of hair on the top of his head. And his sunken eyes seem tired.

"How are you?"

"Fine." Lassal licks his thin lips and stops. Even his skin looks worn out. "What's with you?" he asks.

"Wait-ing for my e-val-u-ation."

"You aren't supposed to be out here until you've been evaluated."

"Why?"

"This is Paradise Garden." Lassal gestures with his tongue towards the garden, "That's where they put us Reject Heads; you know, the ones that don't get reattached."

Jim feels the muscles in his jaw tightening. "Maybe I should leave you alone."

"No, no." Pause. "That's Okay."

Now he doesn't want to talk to this fellow. But what can he do? "Why didn't you get a body?" he asks.

Lassal pauses, collects some air into his cheeks, puckers his lips and then makes a spitting motion towards the railing. "Long story stort. In my past life, I got caught up documenting my previous life's work. All very important stuff. But I didn't give myself enough time plan my future life. So I got all screwed up in my evaluation session.

"It's a real knock, you know?" Lassal continues, "But you can't let it get you down." Lassal's expression hardens. "It's the guy with the good attitude and perseverance that ends up with a body the next time."

Jim stops, frozen. So what will he say about *his* future life?

***

"Bob stop," Dr. Huter says.

Faint whirling sounds end as Jim's cart halts. Before him five people with neck chains sit behind a curving wood-grained table.

Dr. Huter clears his throat. "This is Jim Tilson."

"I have him now," the middle fellow frowns as he peers down into his tablet. "I see ... Mr. Tilson is very old."

"So why hasn't he submitted a curriculum vita," the woman next to him interjects.

"That's explained in note three," Dr. Huter replies.

"Oh yes," Scowl agrees. "And his memory isn't working?"

"No, his memory is functioning. However he doesn't remember his past life. That's in note one."

"Oh yes," Scowl looks over to his left. "What about the rest of you?"

A thin-faced man with snow white hair and similarly sour expression responds, "Even if he doesn't have a Future-Life Statement, does he have some idea as to what he wants to do with his future life?"

"I think he just wants to live."

"Live," Jim agrees.

"That's not much of a plan."

"I want a body!"

"Please, Mr. Tilson," Scowl glares at him. "No interruptions!"

"Sorry."

“Mr. Tilson is a special case—” Dr. Huter begins.

“Yes, yes, everyone is a special case,” Scowl waves his hand, “and there are only so many bodies. Now, you have completed your research, correct?”

“Yes.”

“So doing an attachment doesn’t really add much, does it?”

Long pause, then, “No.”

White Hair glances at Jim and then turns to the others. “Mr. Tilson is rather old, so we could have approved him because of his historical memories, except of course, he doesn’t have any. So I suggest Mr. Tilson be rehabilitated as a Head, and then in two years, he can be re-vitrified and apply for a body in his next life. His prospects will be much better. Thank you.”

“Body,” Jim mutters.

Scowl looks at Jim. “Sorry. Study-up and work on your attitude and the next time you should have better luck.”

Why, he thinks as Rob-o-Bob wheels him out.

They arrive back in the room.

Rob-o-Bob clicks Jim into place.

“Why?” he asks.

“I’m sorry,” Dr. Huter touches Jim’s head, “we all don’t get bodies.”

“No. Why did you take my memories?”

Silence. “You were a suicide. Suicides aren’t usually revived as they are depressed to begin with and almost always don’t adjust. My new technique removed the memories associated with your suicide. But I couldn’t untangle them from everything else as you were depressed most of your previous life.”

Jim sobs. "Body."

Dr. Huter looks at him. "You're upset. Let me give you—"

"No! Leave me be!"

There is silence for several seconds. Then Dr. Huter says, "You're not going to get a body, but at least you're alive."

Alive.

Alive to wheel about in a little cart with Rob-o-Bob always there watching. And with no memories.

"Jim?"

He looks at Dr. Huter. The man must be disappointed that his experiment was ruined by such a poor subject. "Do I have to live? Aren't you finished?"

Dr. Huter looks startled. "No, no. It's not that bad. You can learn and start planning for your next life. It doesn't have to be as," he hesitates, "unsuccessful as this one."

Oh. He gets to try again. But what if he doesn't want to?

Dr. Huter is fiddling with his tablet. "Based on your suicide note, I honestly thought you were a good candidate for my procedure. Here, let me open it up and you can read it."

Jim Tilson: Suicide Note is floating in front of him.

"I'm sorry." Dr. Huter looks at him, this time softly. "I'll leave you now."

Sigh. "Go."

Item: Suicide Note.

To all and sundry,

Alas, with the recent cessation of my inconsequential day job, I am now at a crisis point. But before my fiscal capacity dwindles away, I have decided to execute my escape plan to a better world while still having the wherewithal to do so.

I left a message with one of the many acquaintances I've met over the years at SF Conferences. As he declined my dining invitation tonight owing to other commitments, he won't receive said message until I have expired. However I expect to be found within time for my planned cryogenic freezing.

Please sell my apartment and place all moneys into a trust fund dedicated to maintain my frozen body. And also please investigate getting my novel published as my spectacular demise may make publishers more interested in said story.

Finally, I wish mankind Godspeed in perfecting the revival protocol.

***

They are sitting out on the terrace as the sun turns red and sinks towards the horizon. What if he had been able to remember something? Would that really have made any difference? Or would they have still said, *Sorry, you're life was not worth remembering. Work hard, then come back and try again.*

"Scheduled Paradise Garden time finished," Rob-o-Bob says and starts wheeling him back towards the Revivology Building.

They pass the marble stairs when Jim suddenly knows what he wants to do. "Bob," he says, "stop here and turn me to the right."

Rob-o-Bob stops.

Jim looks down the twenty eight steps. He grits his teeth. So how bad can the fall be? Maybe he'll be lucky and be knocked out as he hits the first step? Sure, he has to start getting lucky at some point, doesn't he?

"Bob," he finally whispers, "push me forwards."

Rob-o-Bob stops. "Potential harmful action. Cannot comply."

"Bob!" he shouts, then stops.

No use. Rob-o-Bob is a robot.

And robots don't have emotions.

***

"I was trying to prevent this," Dr. Huter says.

"Didn't mean to cause trouble," Jim mumbles. Good old Rob-o-Bob. The whole incident was recorded in real time on the Rob-o-Bob-cam.

Rob-o-Bob, the ever present, reliable informer.

"This is a difficult choice," Dr. Huter continues, "I can up your dosage or return you to the fridge and wait for a better protocol. Unfortunately, a higher level of drugs could make future revivals problematic. So the best solution is to return you to the fridge."

"No," Jim protests. "Why can't you just let me die?"

Dr. Huter looks shocked. Then his expression hardens. "We'll take good care of you." Then his eyes dart down to his tablet and his fingers begin clicking away.

"No..." Jim tries again. But it is too late. Sleep is reaching up for him; a long dreamless sleep that will only end sometime in the future, in another room with another Revivologist.

GUARDIAN

H. DAVID BLALOCK

He couldn't see anything through the hood, but the uneven flight of the aircar told him they had left the main settlement and were headed into the surrounding countryside. He again tested the cords holding his hands together behind his back, but they refused to budge. A cramp threatened to form in his right arm. He ignored it. He was more concerned about what they intended to do, and who they might be.

"Settle down, Krandall," the muffled voice of one of his captors barked. "You'll just hurt yourself."

"No loss," another said from slightly farther off, probably in the front of the vehicle. "Just another Guardian gone. Why are we letting him live, anyway?"

A thrill went through him at that. He tried not to show his nervousness. He didn't mind dying. He just wanted to go down fighting, not trussed up like a sacrificial animal.

"Shut up!" the first voice snapped. "You know as well as I do we don't question orders."

Krandall relaxed as best he could. Better not to draw any more attention to himself, cause any more tension. Even the best soldiers could forget themselves if they were put under too much stress. He knew that from personal experience.

During the war, he'd been assigned to a front-line unit. One of their first objectives was to take the colony here on Beta Epsilon IV. It wasn't much of a settlement, but its position afforded strategic advantage and He wanted it taken, He being Emperor Helion II, Scion of the Royal Line of Mavon, Protector of the Faith, Luminary of the Three Suns, etc., etc., etc.

The Empire had formed order out of the chaos of the Dispersal, no mean feat in itself. Humanity had just begun to use FTL technology when the killer asteroid appeared inside Jupiter's orbit. Those that could, left Earth before it hit, a giant rock 350 miles across plummeting into the Asian continent, rendering the entire world uninhabitable in minutes. The greatest achievements of humanity destroyed and mankind itself forced into ships, orphaned, doomed to wander the spaces between systems until dying in the cold void or becoming lucky enough to find a place to eke out an existence. Human beings might have become completely extinct if not for the genius and determination of Mavon. Born on the colony of Sigma Eta III, he was the first of the second generation to believe humanity could once more rise from the ashes.

It became an honor to be part of that effort, and Krandall was humbled by the privilege of becoming a Guardian of the Empire on his graduation from the Imperial University on ΣΗ III. He had served faithfully for almost nine years on ΣΗ III and then here, on BE IV after its liberation from the enemy, for another three. There had not been any evidence of enemy presence since then, at least, not until now.

The vehicle slowed. Krandall heard the man nearest him shift his position.

"What's going on?" he said.

"Roadblock."

The man cursed. "Have they seen us yet?"

"Don't think so."

"Spin. We'll have to find a way around."

Krandall felt the vehicle lift and turn as it headed in a different direction.

"Pursuit?"

There was a moment's pause. Krandall didn't let himself hope the men at the roadblock had noticed the vehicle's behavior and decided to investigate. He knew how even his own unit had come to believe BE IV was secure.

"None."

"Good." Krandall heard the man settle back beside him. "Your friends don't know it, Krandall, but they almost rescued you there."

Krandall bit back a sharp reply. Best not antagonize the man while his hands were tied.

"That's one thing in our favor nowadays," the man went on. "The Guardians don't believe we're still here." Krandall grunted as the man poked him in the ribs. "But you do, don't you?"

He made no reply and the man eventually stopped goading him. The rest of the trip went quietly, Krandall going over the events of the last few hours, trying to figure out what was going on. It was hard to think, nearly as hard to breathe, in the blackness of the hood. He remembered being thrown into the back of the aircar and before that...

* * *

Guardian Krandall signed out his weapons at the duty officer's station and checked it for proper charge before tucking it away. He didn't really expect to need it. The colonists were becoming used to their presence, although Krandall suspected it would take some time before they would forget the bloodshed and realize the Empire only meant to help them, to bring them the best available from the far reaches of the systems. The Imperials put them to work building schools, roads, and hospitals. BE IV went from a backward settlement to an important military outpost. Couldn't they see how much better they had it now?

True, once in a while the odd criminal had to be handled. Attempted vandalism of the military installation was still a nuisance, but after the last incident the public execution of five of the conspirators seemed to have made an impact. Order had been restored and the colony had been quiet for nearly a year. The population was increasing, the schools provided the necessary education in the Imperial curricula, and the local constabulary had actually begun to adhere to the uniform standards.

He made his way out of the Command Center and walked down the main road, turning toward the rear of the compound past the troop barracks. BE IV's sun was setting as he walked by the mess hall. The smell of the night meal was just starting to waft out of its chimneys, reminding him he hadn't eaten since breakfast. Well, he'd check on the guards at the ammo dump and then run back for a bite.

There are very few things more boring than guard duty on a munitions depot. Krandall found the main entrance guard nodding against the wall of the building.

"Crowley!"

The man snapped awake and yanked himself to attention. "Guardian Krandall!" he yelped, saluting.

"I assume you were patrolling and noticed something on the ground just now?"

"Uh... yes, sir!"

"Have you checked the perimeter in the last hour?"

"Yes, sir."

"Check it again."

The other scurried off and soon disappeared, occasionally glancing nervously over his shoulder. Krandall forgot about him almost as soon as he dismissed the man. Crowley was a local colonist, part of a conscripted detail used for the more mundane duties. The Guardians, imperial elite soldiers, were the officers and commanders.

He started his own patrol circuit around the depot. There were four other stations to check, all manned with the locals. One dozing might be overlooked, but if he found another one shirking duty there would be consequences.

The structure was a simple design, rectangular with one story above ground and two below. The entrance was secure and armed by autoguns. Anyone approaching the front without the proper subcutaneous implants would be eliminated without warning. He walked around the building clockwise, checking the walls for an evidence of breach, not really expecting to find anything. The colonials kept well clear of everything on the military compound anyway, mainly because there was nothing civilian-friendly there.

It was his lack of expectations that gave them the opening.

Of a sudden, everything went dark as the hood dropped over his head, then totally black as something crashed into his head and consciousness fled.

He woke in the back of the aircar.

* * *

They arrived.

Two of his captors grabbed him and hauled him from the vehicle. Krandall did his best to keep up as they half-shoved, half-carried him along. He heard crowd sounds come and go as they moved. Probably down a long hallway in a big building. He was surprised no one challenged them, two men escorting a hooded third. Just how large was this organization, anyway?

They stopped briefly as a door opened and he was shoved through. Krandall stumbled, fell, skidded on the floor, tasted blood as he bit the inside of his cheek on the impact.

"Shut the door and lock it behind you," first voice said.

"Want anything else?" The second voice was the driver, apparently more than a little annoyed.

"Just do it."

The hood came off and Krandall flinched at the sudden light. It took a few moments to adjust, but the room wasn't much to look at anyway. Barely more than a six by six cell with a single door, a military cot, and a metal sink moulded into the wall. His captor sat on the cot, looking at him with a dour expression. The man couldn't have been more than twenty years old. Krandall was startled to see he wore the uniform of a local conscript.

"What do you want?" Krandall managed, struggling to sit up.

The man scowled at him for a moment, watching him finally get into an upright position. Slowly, he rose, placed his foot on Krandall's chest, and pushed him back down. Krandall grunted in pain as his head bounced on the hard floor. The other looked at him for another long moment, then returned to the cot. Krandall lay partially stunned.

"Three years ago, the land where this building now stands was a farm," the man said. "It wasn't large. It didn't produce tons of crops. It belonged to a single family who subsisted off what it gave them. Do you know what happened to them?"

Krandall shook off the headache and struggled into a sitting position again. Once more, his captor knocked him down and returned to the cot.

"You and your kind came, burned down the farm, murdered the parents, and then pressed the children into your work camps," he went on.

"I had nothing to do..." Krandall started to protest.

"Quiet!" He waited until Krandall's mouth closed, then spoke. "Since you lot came, life has been hell. We came here to live the simple life. We were happy."

"The colony was failing," Krandall growled.

"So *you* say!"

"So said the colony organizers," Krandall countered.

"Imperial collaborators!"

Krandall started to try to get up again, but abandoned the attempt when the other raised an eyebrow. "You've bought yourself more trouble than you can handle, you know. I'll be missed soon."

"That's up to you," the man said. "We brought you here to see something."

"Nothing you can show me would make any difference. You've signed your own death warrants."

The man smiled grimly. "We'll see." He went to the door and knocked twice. As the door opened, he turned back. "I just want you to know, the only reason you're still alive is because of one of those children. Think about that."

He left and two other men came in. So did the hood.

Krandall stumbled and staggered blindly between the men, cursing under his breath at each lurch. They seemed to navigate an endless number of doors and rooms, bouncing left and right off door jambs and thresholds. His escort remained silent and unforgiving, pushing and shoving whenever he felt as if he might recover his balance.

Fresh air. They were outside now, crossing a hard pavement. There was the sound of a large door opening. He was hustled inside an echoing building, heard the door shut behind him. The hood lifted to reveal he was standing in a storehouse filled with chemical containers. Above the containers, attached to the ceiling, was a structure Krandall didn't recognize.

"It's a machine to disperse the chemical into the atmosphere," his captor said from behind him. Apparently the man had followed them, because Krandall didn't remember hearing the door open again. "Those containers are filled with the same nerve gas you lot used against the colony when you pushed our defense forces into their last stand. In a single battle, without even one casualty on your side because you were all huddled in your ships in orbit, you slaughtered more than 50,000 of our able-bodied men and women. People who, until you came, had been simply farmers and merchants, craftsmen and wrights.

"There is a very ancient proverb. Perhaps you've heard it. 'What goes around, comes around.' At an appointed time, bases like this one all over the colony will simultaneously release their charge. Everyone unprepared will die within a few minutes of exposure."

"You're insane!" Krandall said, shocked. "You would kill your own people?"

"Our people will be safe. Shelters are prepared and the plans spread to the faithful. Only the Imperials and their collaborators will die. Beta Epsilon will be free again."

Krandall stared at the man in disbelief. "Why are you showing me this?"

"Because I want you to take the word back to the Empire once the deed is done that Beta Epsilon will not concede to Imperial tyranny," the man replied, his face dark. "You will be held here until it is done, then released. We know you will scurry back to your masters and bleat everything you've seen here. It will make them think twice about coming back."

Krandall shook his head. "You really don't understand, do you?"

"Understand? What is there to understand? You are invaders, murderers, tyrants. You deserve no better than death."

"We may be that in your eyes, but we certainly are not fools."

An explosion knocked them all off their feet as the door flew inward. As the Imperial Guardians poured into the building, Krandall looked at the dazed face of his unnamed captor.

"Guardians are implanted with subcutaneous transmitters," he told the man. "The moment I was missed, they activated its locator. It was simply a matter of time." He smiled at his captive. "Love Live the Emperor!" he shouted as the conspirators were gathered together.

HOPE UNKNOWN

JASON CAMPAGNA

Sooner or later, the other girls were going to try and take the last thing Hope had from her mother. She was one of eight girls crammed into a ten by ten foot cell stacked high with two columns of bunk beds. At one point, she thought she heard one of the starship's crew refer to the trip as the "orphan run." The air inside the room smelled of recirculated despair and left a stale taste in Hope's mouth.

She thought about curling up into a tight ball, but the bunk on top of her own left no room to turn on her side. Hope stared at the smooth white underside surface inches from her face. Someone had scratched into it, "If you can read this, then you're fucked." At the age of twelve, Hope understood the phrase, "fucked," quite well. She never knew her father, but her mother had done her best to raise Hope on the street level underside of old New York City. Hope tried not to think about the man who took her mother's life. He left the young girl alone and starving in a city with an insatiable appetite for victims.

While the police were still wrapping up paperwork involved in the murder, Hope scaled the back wall of the children's shelter and lost herself in the labyrinth of streets. Her single possession was a two-inch Statue of Liberty figure that her mother had given her.

Hope slept in alleyways and abandoned buildings for months. She learned to beg for handouts and stole food from anywhere she could manage. Her meals often involved a trash can. Eventually, the police caught up with her and brought her in. Before she knew it, she found herself bussed off to the starport.

On the ship, she felt like a rat stuffed into a cage. Part of her wanted to lash out at the walls and bunk above her. To calm herself, she would look at the figure her mother gave her and memorize the details in the metal work. Hope wondered why she was wearing a crown.

As for the other girls, no one talked, lest they draw the attention of Regulator. Regulator was a floating gray-ball shaped robot who administered a nasty shock to unruly little girls. It gave the orphans the rules when they had first arrived aboard the *Wayfar*. The sixteen girls had been lined up shoulder to shoulder in the terminal at the spaceport. All the girls wore identical gray jumpsuits with nametags over their left breast. The machine circled around the group like a shark testing its prey.

"I am Regulator," the floating ball said. "During the trip you will stay in your beds except when otherwise instructed. There will be no talking except when otherwise instructed. Failure to comply will result in electric shock or sedation. Are there any questions?"

Beside Hope, a girl with long curly brown hair and the name Tiffany Spring on her jumper spoke up. "I don't listen to machines."

"That was not a question," Regulator replied. A small prong popped out of Regulator's sphere and the robot shifted in front of

Tiffany. A burst of electricity arced out at Tiffany's right arm. The girl dropped to the floor crying while she held the appendage.

Hope held her head forward pretending not to see. Growing up in the city had taught her that making eye contact could draw unwanted attention of others. She clutched onto the statue figure in the palm of her hand. Regulator turned the prong to face her.

"Unusual," Regulator said. "Hope Unknown, your heart rate remains normal." The machine paused for several seconds. "You are carrying a metallic object in your left hand. Show it to me."

Hope brought up her arm and opened her fingers, "I won't give her up," Hope said, "and I won't let you take her."

A blue light emitted from the sphere and it swept over the statue. "Do you know what the object stands for?" Regulator said.

"No," Hope said, "But it's the only thing I have left of my mother."

The electric prong on Regulator slid back into the sphere of its body. "Your failure to comply will have consequences for you later. This incident has been noted in your case file," Regulator said.

***

The door to the quarters slid open and Regulator addressed the girls. "It is time for the evening meal. Disembark your bunks and line up single file on the red line in the corridor. Everyone will line up behind Hope Unknown."

Hope slid out of bed and then maneuvered her way through the mass of girls. She knew they were glaring at her. Tiffany bumped into her from behind hard enough that Hope had to catch herself on the bulkhead.

"Give it to me," Tiffany said. Hope squeezed the tiny statue in her hand and kept moving.

Outside the cell, the corridor was ten feet wide and bustling with crew members going in both directions. Except to maneuver around the children, the crew ignored the orphans. The ship *Wayfar*'s duty was to transport the children. It was the cadre of robots' job to tend them. Regulator conducted the girls to the mess hall.

Cafeterias in space looked like cafeterias everywhere. Long rows of tables were bathed in the unappetizing smell of low quality food. Regulator lined the girls up along the wall as was customary every meal. As was also customary at every meal, Hope was singled out.

"Hope Unknown," Regulator said, "You will eat your meal first while the other girls watch. They can eat with you, if you surrender the statue."

"I can't," Hope said.

"Then as usual," Regulator said, "they must pay the price. Hope Unknown, do you not care for the other girls?"

"I won't eat," Hope said. "They can eat in my place."

"Hope Unknown, that is unacceptable. If you do not eat, none of the others will."

"Please," Hope said.

"The consequences are of your own choosing. No one shall eat until you surrender the statue."

The other girls stood in line glaring at Hope. Tiffany's right hand was balled into a fist. Silently she mouthed, "Hope, I'm going to get you."

"Hope Unknown, I believe it is time that you met my counterpart

Arbiter."

The door to the cafeteria slid open and another gray ball entered the room. The ball headed directly toward Hope.

"Hope Unknown, I am Arbiter. I will review your case file and decide accordingly. Follow me." It led Hope out of the cafeteria and down the corridor to a nearby elevator. The elevator door opened up to a rather peculiar level. The corridor seemed to be sized for the dimensions of a kid. Hope had to pay particular care not to hit her head on low hanging pipes as she followed the robot. She wondered if the crew even ventured into this part of the ship. It also made her wonder what went on here that needed to be done away from the human crew.

After several minutes of walking, Hope found herself in a large circular room. The room was awash with white light that seemed to emanate directly from the walls. Nothing was there except for a child-sized metallic chair that sat in the center. She was directed to the center of the room. "You may be seated if you wish," Arbiter said.

"Why am I here?" Hope said. She stood rather than taking the chair.

"The other girls are being transported because they are orphans," Arbiter said. "You stand apart and will not share their fate. Your fate must be different because you are both an orphan and a murderer."

Hope bit her lower lip and felt her cheeks warm.

"It is true," Arbiter said, "that you had a justifiable defense for your actions. The security cameras, in the alley, produced enough evidence in your defense. Law enforcement has determined you were lucky to have survived the encounter. It was fortunate your mother's attacker ignored you after the initial assault. It was also fortunate you noticed the brick you employed to cave in the back of the man's skull. Review of the footage has determined your mother was already deceased by the time of your blow."

"She was all that I had," Hope said.

"Why did you run from the authorities? They would have helped you."

"I don't know," Hope said. She looked at the floor and squeezed the small statue in her hand. The question had been one that had bothered her since she ran. "My mom had been saving up so that we could go to the park on the upside of the city. She wanted to take me to the zoo they have there. I realized that it meant more to her to give that to me. I thought about her dying sad because she will never get to take me someplace that was special to her. I felt like I couldn't breathe, so I ran. I needed to be lost."

"And now you are here," Arbiter said. "Your time for being lost has ended. Now, it must be decided how to deal with you. You are an extremely complex case. It is uncommon for a child to have dealt with the level of trauma you have experienced and still function in normal society. There is some concern as to your physiological well-being; yet, observation depicts a strong level of emotional control. We will try and salvage this trait when we wipe your memory."

"What?" Hope said looking up from the floor.

An iris opened on the spherical surface of Arbiter. A crystal blue eye formed in the opening. It gazed at Hope. "Your short life is plagued with misfortune and you carry an excess of emotional baggage."

"You can't," Hope said.

"The courts of the United Planets of Earth have determined, in your case, it would be merciful to relieve you of these experiences.

It is why we refer to your last name as Unknown. Your future is in question."

"But it's my life," Hope demanded.

"Will you try and hold on to it like your statue?" Arbiter said.

"I have to," Hope said.

"Hope Unknown, why would you do this?"

"Because it's who I am," she said. "I have a name!"

"That is an acceptable answer," Arbiter said. "Individuality is paramount to society, but society cannot exist without people willing to defend it. If we let you have your mind, would you be willing to pay the cost?"

"What do you want?" Hope said.

"First you must understand your situation," Arbiter said. "The United Planets of Earth is currently in a depression. The government has created a policy of shipping undesirables off world to other colonies. Understand, you are deemed as undesirable by your own people. Three years ago, independent colonies started purchasing orphans from Earth."

"I'm a slave?" Hope said.

"No," said Arbiter. "But Earth has treated your citizenship as a commodity to be sold. This helps Earth to supplement its failing economy. After it was determined you were a ward of the state, it was within the government's right to adopt you out. The Constitutional Empire of Cornet has laid out a substantial amount to adopt you. You now have two options. Your memory can be erased and you will be adopted out to loving parents who will raise you-"

"What's the option where I get to keep my mom?" Hope said.

"Agoge," Arbiter replied. "It is an ancient Greek term used in reference to training children to become soldiers. The Cornet Empire has adopted it to ensure a progression of highly talented individuals in the service of the Empire. The point of the Agoge is to be tough on children so that they can handle the difficult task of building and defending a new society."

"I'm not afraid," Hope said. "I want to keep my memories."

"Rash girl," Arbiter said. "You do not even know what is involved. It is a painful process. Perhaps you would be better off submitting your fate to those who are more enlightened than yourself.

"Everything in my life has been painful," Hope said.

"Do you know what the statue in your hand represents?" Arbiter asked.

"To me, it's my mother," Hope said. "It's the only thing I have left of how things were before."

"It is interesting you feel that way, Hope Unknown. The figure is the Statue of Liberty. It represents a way of life and symbolizes freedom. Historically, it was the first glimpse of America immigrants would see when migrating to the old United States. It is ironic that you carry this symbol as an immigrant. Tell me Hope Unknown, do you consider yourself to be a free person?"

"I don't know," Hope said. "No one told me what to do when I was alone. Is that what freedom means?"

"Yes," Arbiter said. "That is part of what it means to be free. As an orphan we have restricted your level of freedom, but not entirely."

"You haven't tried to take my statue," Hope said. "I know you could have taken it, but Regulator has made the other girls hate me for it. Why do you want me to give it up?"

"It is hard to take freedom from someone who will not surrender it herself," Arbiter said. "Yes, it is by design that we have made the other girls hate you. You have been allowed to show them that you have something they do not. Humans have a tendency to desire and at the same time despise what they do not have. We have highlighted this by giving you special treatment, and punishing them."

"I don't understand," Hope said.

"Hope Unknown, I am disappointed that you have not figured this out for yourself. It is for your education. Freedom must be understood before it can be defended. In old America, it was once said that eternal vigilance is the price of freedom."

"You've wanted me to fight," Hope said.

"Good," Arbiter said. Arbiter's eyes shifted to red.

"Because it is now time to put theory into practice. The other children have been informed that they will not eat until you surrender the statue. They have also been informed if they do not compel you to surrender the item, Regulator will shock all of them."

The door behind Hope slid open. Hope turned her head at the noise. She saw that Tiffany stood in the doorway with the other girls behind her.

"One last thing," Arbiter said. "If you surrender your statue to them, we will be obliged to erase your memories."

Arbiter floated away from Hope, abandoning her to angry faces. Tiffany strutted into the circular room and the other girls fanned out to either side of her. "Give us the statue, or we will take it from you," Tiffany said.

"I can't," Hope said. "They'll erase my mind if I do."

"We can't eat until you give it up," Tiffany said. "We're sick of being punished for you."

Tiffany and the other girls closed in on Hope.

"It's mine," Hope said. "I won't give it to you, and I won't let you take it."

"I'm going to hurt you," Tiffany said.

Tiffany reached out to grab Hope's jumpsuit. Hope stepped away from her and bumped into the metal chair. Hope reached down and felt the cool metal of the chair's upper back brace on her fingers. Her hand curled under the edge of the brace. Tiffany continued to move forward, closing in on Hope.

Her grip tightened on the chair and it felt weightless in her hand. Suddenly, Hope felt like she was back in the alley where her mother died. She felt fear and rage all over again. Hope locked eyes on Tiffany and swung the chair. The chair smashed into the side of Tiffany's face and the girl dropped to the ground. The other girls grabbed at Hope trying to stop her.

Hope swung the chair again. She brought the weight of the chair down on a girl's arm that was grabbing onto Hope's shoulder. The girl's arm snapped.

The chair bounced off the ground and Hope used the momentum to swing it in a wild circular arc to catch anyone else close by. She felt the chair bash into yet another girl. The girl toppled over, grabbing her knee. The other girls ran.

"That will be enough," Arbiter said.

Hope dropped the chair and noticed Tiffany on the floor and bleeding from the head. Tiffany looked unconscious or dead, a pool of blood was expanding underneath her. Another girl was crawling out of the room while she tried to cradle a limp leg. Her jumpsuit was torn at the knee and a patch of red soaked the leg.

Hope's scalp tingled in muted pain. One of the girls must have managed to pull her hair. Her lip felt puffy and numb, she tasted something of tang in her mouth.

"It is time to leave, Hope Unknown," Arbiter said. "The crew of the *Wayfar* will tend to their wounds. The injuries sustained on the other children only appear severe. I believe congratulations are in order. You have earned your cherished memories."

"I don't want your congratulations," Hope said. "You're a cruel and evil little machine."

"I am a reflection of my creators," Arbiter said. "I operate strictly within mission parameters that your kind endowed me with. Though, in defense of humans, there are far worse things that exist in the galaxy. Things you will face soon enough."

"That doesn't make it right," Hope said.

"I am not programmed for ethics," Arbiter said. "I am programed to expedite the acquisition of resources to ensure the survival of the human species. Ethics are a luxury of those not facing annihilation. Enjoy your victory."

Hope took the small statue from her jumpsuit pocket. She held the object in her hand examining it shape. She committed the Statue of Liberty to memory and let it slip from her fingers to the deck. It bounced twice before it settled to a stop. The statue stood erect.

"Explain," Arbiter said.

"I don't need it anymore," Hope said. "I've paid the price for the girls to eat."

"The others were scheduled to eat no matter the outcome," Arbiter replied. "Again, why would you leave the object you have so cherished?"

"Because I have my memories," Hope said.

UNDER A POMEGRANATE SKY

BY MANDI M. LYNCH

YEAR NEW 643

"In the year M257, a large ship carrying reinforcements of every kind – food, people, medicine, supplies – encountered a series of problems that led them to an irreversible fate. They crash landed here, just up that rock face," Mynerva stopped and pointed to a few old growth trees at the top of a seemingly sheer cliff before continuing, "on a planet they hadn't noticed, without communication. In other words, they were stuck.

"Axl and Abel, twins onboard the ship, set out to do a search of the island and went off in the opposite direction. There, they found sloping land, numerous habitable caves, and a large source of water. Once satisfied that this would be their new home, everyone grabbed what they could carry and set off through the woodlands and into the city they would call Topan. When they woke from their first night's sleep, they gathered together to make the rules for the new lands. By the time the meeting was over, the year was 1, and the city was called Utopia, for this was their opportunity to have the world they wanted to have, and everything was going to be perfect."

In front of her, a group of children squirmed in their seats but otherwise gave her their full attention. Unlike many of the adults in Shellaghey, these children hadn't been raised with the old stories and the iron fist of precision that they would have had in Topan. When adults told the stories, it was a rare treat. "But, My-"

Mynerva cast the child a look and kept talking, pulling bits and pieces of her story from her memory. "There were two islands off the coast, and one was set up for government, with room to watch over, but to send a point – government was separate from everyday life. That's how they wanted it, and that's how it would be. The other island stayed empty for many years, but as time turned, it became The Manor. They set it up as a utopia, and even called it that, although the name ended up as Topan.

"The year was New 314, and the area that had been able to withhold a population of up to 5000 people without much issue was feeling the pinch of a population of almost 17,000. A poorly prepared batch of seeds in New 299 had left them with an inadequate harvest, and a slew of health problems that they hadn't faced before. People rioted. The government response was to build, and the planet got its first construction projects – the formal school, the residential buildings for the government employees and their families, boats for those set adrift, and The Manor took life. On the eve of the fourth full moon set, Georg, Ayja, and their four children made their way across the bridge and onto the island. Here, the children were free from the stares of people who didn't like their misshapen bodies. It wasn't long before a number of other people and families started joining them as well. They were allowed to in the beginning – families – but as The Manor took on more residents and the government took more control, all of that changed as well.

"The same inspectors that were going around and welcoming new population were also checking for unwanteds. By New 320, citizens that were sent to The Manor were stricken from the life record, blacked out in a way that prevented anyone from seeing who they had been, instead of merely being crossed out at death with a line that left their name still readable. They were taken away as if they had never been, and the bridge back and forth had become a one way walk of shame, full of screams and tears. The citizens of Topan acted as if they didn't know that anything was on the other side, but the people of The Manor got their news whenever a new arrival joined them. New additions to the population were always greeted with love and attention, and in many ways, they found The Manor to be more of a paradise than their former utopia had ever been…"

***

Year New 588

The grey clouds were dissipating, and Eirene sat at the front of her cave, looking out at Topan and rubbing her huge swollen belly. A cart rumbled past her, full of goods and trash, forcing itself through the muddy ruts left in the ground from carts that came before.

"Good morning, Miss Eirene. Do you have any trash today?" the garbage man asked, forcing the cart to stop for her and her immediate neighbors.

"It's in the can with everyone else's," she said, pointing at the neighbor's doorway. "Bad day for pickup, isn't it?"

"Hard to run this through the mud, but I'll make do. You know the law, pickup every ten days. Gotta do my part."

Eirene stared at the city around her. "Almost looks like the law should be changed so you can come more often."

"That's true, ma'am. But for now, it is what it is. Just do your part and pick up what you see laying around." He tipped the contents of the can into his cart and then grabbed the handles of the cart again, exerting great force to get the cart rolling again through the thick mud.

She watched him work his way downhill. Behind her, a crash startled her out of her thoughts. Wax puddled behind her on the floor, the candle extinguished by the force of the landing. Its holder was broken into dozens of pieces. She surveyed the scene. Her children were out of sight, but certainly not out of hearing range. Clearly, they were the culprits. Now to find them. There were nine rooms in her cave, shared between herself and a long list of extended family, the back three rooms devoted mostly to the small children of the family. She passed her sister's room and gave a wave through the open curtain. Her sister was also pregnant but having a much worse time of it. The noise of the children was doing little to alleviate her illness.

"Garricke and Ursule! Get out here right now!" Eirene waddled quickly into the back room. "Both of you! When I call you, you come to me imm…" She stopped suddenly, mouth agape.

"He won't take it off, Mother." Ursule looked at her brother and continued. "I told him to take it off and he told me no. I tried to change his clothes and he wouldn't listen to me!"

Eirene continued to stare at her children. "Garricke…"

"Mynerva. My name is Mynerva. Don't call me Garricke. That's a boy's name," the small child said.

"You're a boy."

"No. I'm a girl. My name's Mynerva." There wasn't disobedience in his voice, but an absolute, yet quiet, assurance that this was the right way, the only way.

Eirene didn't know what to say. "I don't care what you say you are, I know for a fact that you are a boy. You have boy parts. Take off that dress immediately." She reached for him, but he pulled out of her grasp.

"NO!"

"Garricke Davys!"

He opened his mouth and let out a scream that could wake the dead. "I DON'T CARE WHAT YOU SAY, I AM GOING TO WEAR THIS AND YOU CAN'T STOP ME!!!!"

"What the hell is going on back here?!" Gaylen bellowed, entering the back of the cave. He brushed past his daughter, tousling her hair as he did and joining his wife at her side. He didn't need an answer, just followed her gaze to the back of the room, to his four year old son, who cowered behind the bedroll in the dress his cousin had just outgrown. "What's the meaning of this, son?"

"I'm not your son. I'm a girl and my name is Mynerva." Now the child crossed his arms and pouted. "I'm a girl. I want to be a girl. You can't make me not be a girl."

"I most very well can make you not be a girl. You are a boy. Boys have penises and pee standing up. Don't you do that?" He didn't know what else to say to him.

"Nope. Never 'gain. From now on, I'm going to pee sitting down like Ursule does."

It was hard to argue with a young child's determination, no matter how wrong the child was. Still, Gaylen knew better than to let this continue. "You will not, do you understand me?!" Now it was his turn to reach for his son. The child bit him and forced himself under the bed, having to completely flatten against the ground to fit under the slats of the furniture.

"Mother-"

"Stop, Ursule. Go clean up the mess you left in the living room. You broke the candle plate," Eirene replied.

"Sorry, Mother." She put her head down and worked her way to the front of the cave, taking care not to step in the wax that dripped from the wall sconces.

Gaylen and Eirene went into an adjoining room, taking time to light the lantern as they entered. The light sputtered as it filled the dark space, casting a shadowy glow on everything.

Gaylen took a bundle of textiles off the nearby chair and offered his wife a seat. She accepted without argument or discussion, more than happy to rest her weary body. The silence was interrupted only by the crackle of the candle wick and the sound of their breathing. Gaylen sank to the floor and massaged his wife's legs. "Tell me what happened."

"I don't know. One minute I was talking to the trash man, the next I heard a crash behind me." She went on to recount the scene and the following argument. "You heard and saw what I did, honey. Garricke shouted that he was a girl and we must call him Mynerva. Imagine!" Her anguish showed on her face.

"We'll get to the bottom of this."

"The inspector comes through soon!" she wailed and hung her head on her husband's shoulder. "What if he's still determined by then?"

"It's okay, sweetheart, everything will be okay."

***

"I'm glad your child is well, Prisca," inspector Avrom said, handing the baby back to Eirene, who passed it again to her sister. "And you, Eirene? When for you?"

"Forty days, I believe. I'm hoping for another boy, since Prisca had one." Eirene looked at the sleeping child. "I'll settle for healthy."

"Yes, well, where are the other two?"

"Garricke is down for a nap," she said.

"But I can get Ursule for you." Eirene tried to beckon her eldest child without the inspector following, but he followed too closely behind. They entered the back room on each other's heels.

"Who's child is this, Eirene?"

"Just a playmate," she lied as her son greeted the man.

"I am Mynerva, daughter of Eirene and Gaylen."

Eirene's face went ashen. She cast a look at Ursule, glaring at the girl. The inspector had control enough to banish him to the Manor without any thought. Because of this, she had given her daughter one task – quiet her brother and stop any talk about Mynerva until the inspector had left their cave. Law was law, and once the inspector left, he wasn't allowed back in for a number of months. Now, however, he had cause to take her son or come back unannounced whenever he felt the need to.

"Eirene?"

"Yes, Inspector?"

"Is this," he consulted his clipboard, "Garricke? Your son? Why is he in a dress?"

"QUIT CALLING ME GARRICKE!!!" The child was dressed head to toe in girls clothes and took quite a bit of pleasure in raising a booted foot and kicking the inspector in the shin.

Inspector Avrom cursed and glanced at his leg. The heel of the boot had ripped his trouser and cut his skin. "Eirene, how long has this been going on?"

"This morning, sir."

"Eirene, how long has this been going on?" He repeated the question, absolutely sure that it had been happening for more than a day. "I won't ask again."

She understood the repercussions of what was being said to her, and she didn't want to answer. She knew what the ultimate result was going to be.

"Come with me, son." Inspector Avrom grabbed at the child and missed, falling to the floor. Now he'd have bruises and a concussion to add to his list of ailments.

"You can't take him! He's four! It's a phase!"

"Eirene, stand down." Cautiously, he pushed past the pregnant woman, unwilling to lose the child in the system of caverns. As inspector, he knew of the two tendrils of cavern that snaked backwards into the ground. Avrom was much too large to fit down them, but there was ample width for a four year old to get quite a ways in before getting stuck. He grabbed the child again, this time receiving a bite on the arm. He yelped in pain, but tightened his grip on the squirming child anyway.

"You can't take him! Not like this! Don't!" Eirene tried to run after him, but her huge belly hindered even normal slow movement.

Avrom spun, swinging the child's legs like a broken pendulum. Garricke's foot connected squarely with his mother's belly and she fell to the ground in pain, a gush of water coming from her almost instantly.

Gaylen was torn between his wife and the inspector. Ursule appeared at her mother's side, waving her father on without word.

He ran after Avrom and his son, stepping into the inspector's path. "You can't have him. This isn't right!"

"This is the law, the way it is supposed to be! You know you're wrong here!"

"Consider my wife. She's already lost so many children, and now you're taking this one?"

"Sir! I am not telling you again. Stand down, or I will take you in as well!"

A scream came from within the cave, and Gaylen's hair stood on end. "If your actions have cost my wife this child, too, I will have you sent to the Manor, do you understand me? Unhand my son, right this minute!" He reached for his child, but Avrom swung his free hand, hitting Gaylen square in the face. Blood immediately spurted out of his nose. Avrom walked down the hillside, the squirming child kicking harder at him as he walked.

Gaylen knew it was futile to follow him, so he turned back into the cave and to his wife. The look on his daughter's face said it all. Ursule was now all he had in the world. He fell to the ground with his daughter and cried on the cold stone floor until he could cry no more.

***

Down the hill, Avrom had crossed the kilometer and a half to the bridge in record time. After crossing words with the sentry, he was granted pass of the bridge. The evening was already darkening, and the oil lamps were casting an eerie glow on the wooden planks of the bridge. It felt to Avrom like six kilometers, but in reality was only three hundred and twenty-nine meters long – he knew the number for sure because he not only helped build the bridge, but also was assigned to inspect it every year.

The walk across never got easier. In his years as inspector, he had brought dozens if not hundreds of people across the bridge and deposited them in the confines of the Manor. Anguished people, those like Eirene, were a dime a dozen, but the law was law and he had sworn to uphold it. They were in place for a reason – sworn to protect people from the degradation of society because of undue burdens placed on them because of problems. He didn't know what caused them, sometimes it seemed to be a freak thing. Other times, like in Garricke's case, he wondered if it was a case of a bad combination of people. Maybe if Eirene and Gaylen had been looked at more carefully, the union would have been denied. He wondered if the issues – Eirene's seven miscarriages and now this – would still have occurred if she had been partnered differently.

"Hello, Avrom." Bryor stood at the doorway, standing as tall as she could with her bowed legs. "What is the problem with this one?"

"You'll find that the outward appearance doesn't match that underneath. This is, in fact, a boy."

Bryor shook her head. Now that they were in the Manor, it didn't matter anymore. If this child wanted to bang his – her? – head against the wall in the corner all day, Bryor didn't care to correct the situation. Garricke was no longer citizen number gee-four-seven-nine-six-two-eff, a solid black bar obliterating him from the citizen record. He was a memory, a ghost, and as a ghost, Bryor saw no reason to make him conform to the rules of society. She reached out a gentle hand and took the child from his abductor. "We are done with you now, sir. You can leave us now."

"I need a count."

"One, two, three." She said. "There, a count. Would you like a count of five, perhaps a count of ten would be better?"

Avrom was always taken back by her attitude towards him. "I need to know how many are here, Bryor."

"How would I know that?" She looked down at her deformed legs, bowed out to the point she had to walk by swaying. "I'm not created like you. I lack something. Surely you can't expect me to count correctly and understand how many are here. I'm much too stupid to understand that."

Avrom never understood her opposition to him. The Manor gave her the ability to breathe air a little longer. If it weren't for the island, weren't for the system of care that she had been allowed, Bryor would have been eliminated as a small child, certainly before her second birthday.

"I said that we were done."

"I can give you a fate worse than death, there's a boat ready as we speak, if you'd like it." He sneered at her, dared her to challenge him.

Bryor scoffed at the idea. That was the government's big

punishment. Putting a citizen in a boat, tethered with a rope that would dissolve in two days' time, leaving them to float off to nothing with no food to sustain them. It was the unknown that they threatened, but everyone knew the truth. They never came back. But she'd never come back anyway. "Avrom, please kindly take your inspection documents and go back to Topan. You may threaten me all you want, but there is no way that you can perform on me a fate worse than death, for I do not exist. And for somebody that does not exist, the last thing I need is to be recorded. How do you write that 'non-people,' perhaps? If you are through, I have a child here who is very frightened and probably very hungry and tired as well."

Still clutching Mynerva's hand, she spun around and walked the child up to the building.

***

Year New 612

Mynerva walked along the beach and around the curve to the post, an outcropping of rock that narrowed and then widened again just into the water. Five minutes with a pickaxe and it would be considered an island. She jumped the narrow part and hopped a couple times to get her balance again. Not her best effort. The grasses grew tall on the post and she slid through them until she came to the rock that they used to keep lookout. It also doubled as her quiet spot and she hopped up on it, looked around, and then sat back down once she was satisfied she was alone.

So much had happened since she left The Manor, so much that she couldn't explain or process it all yet. But this spot, this was her spot to regroup, to center herself and take a few deep breaths without hearing anyone else breathing. She put her head in her hands and cried for a long time, and when she finally wiped her eyes, one of the dual red suns was already dipping at the horizon, the sky turning a darker shade of pomegranate. She stood back up on the rock and looked around, still nobody, as she expected. They didn't always patrol this area.

Mynerva pulled off her blouse, skirts and underclothing, and lay down in the grass, looking up at the stars. Total nudity, exposing *her*. Exposing her flat torso and her misshapen form. The only giveaway that she wasn't exactly as she appeared to be. Silently, she cursed Avrom for having ever checked when she was born, a product of a Topan government that strove for perfection instead of harmony. Cursed her sister, Ursule, for having screamed at their mother about it, instead of keeping quiet. She had no idea what the other planets were like, but she was certain that anywhere else she could have blended, been exactly what she wanted to be. But not here. The population was small, but certainly large enough that if she had reinvented herself, not everyone would have remembered her from before. She still had nightmares about that night. How long would it be until they were gone?

A noise in the grasses behind her caught her off guard and her breath stuck in her throat. How had somebody gotten that close to her?

"Mynerva, are you out here?"

"Emmerus. You scared me."

Her husband mumbled his apology and crossed the grasses until he saw her clothing and then her.

"I needed the privacy." The weight of everything still clung to her, and she often found she couldn't get that anywhere else. Too many people looked at her like she was in charge, even though she didn't want to be. Knew she shouldn't be.

"Should I go?" He stood still; the last thing he wanted to do was leave.

Pulling herself up on her forearms, she turned and looked at him finally. "Why do you love me?"

"Because you're beautiful."

"But why?"

"Look around. Look at what you've done. You weren't content to stand still and wait for your life to end, weren't content to be stricken from the record. You've made a difference, Mynerva."

"You loved me before that. We built our house years ago."

"Doesn't mean I didn't look at those qualities and see them then." He stripped off his clothes and crossed over to her so that he could curl up with her, pulling her back against his torso, and wrapping his arms around her.

She could feel his muscles press into her skin. She was muscular too, but not like Emmerus was, and she always felt safe and protected when she could feel him near her. He rubbed his hands across her stomach, one resting just over her belly button, and one just under it. Her breath caught in her throat and he could feel her heart pound.

In response, he kissed the nape of her neck. "I love you for what you are, not what you were. You are my *wife*, and that is all that matters to me." His hand slid down a bit further, to her first scar, and stopped there. Their breathing fell into rhythm, and they soon fell asleep.

***

Year New 605

The weather was gorgeous – a little too gorgeous, really. The rain had just given way to fog and it was already clearing out during the day. Inspector Avrom Mikkalistr drank the last of his morning glass of mint tea, kissed his wife goodbye, and grabbed his hat on the way out. As a high ranking government employee, Avrom lived on the government isle, the bridge from the mainland to the government was controlled with armed guards. This part of Topan was almost as disconnected as the Manor on the other end of the settlement, some would argue more so.

Avrom crossed the bridge on foot, his satchel thrown over his shoulders so that it hung down his back. At the end of the wooden walkway, he waved at the guards and continued on. He had been at this job long enough that he was there when the guards were born; he was the one who registered their numbers and approved their names.

He had a number of stops to make, and he decided that he would start on the far side of the island so that he could enjoy a long walk on the beach on his way to his first stop. The beach was his favorite place in Topan. No matter how cluttered and crowded Topan would ever get, the beach looked out onto the water – onto a peaceful expanse of blue-gray and away from the hustle and bustle of the city. Now, he had to say goodbye to the calm waters and hello to his first case, which was two pregnancies and a funeral.

As he turned to head up the walkway, somebody appeared at the edge of the Woods. "Inspector Avrom? We need you. Please hurry."

The man disappeared into the forest, crashing through the brush to leave an almost path for the inspector to follow. He wound his way through the thicket – and away from the path – in circles, hoping to confuse the Inspector at least a little bit. The Inspector wasn't from the mainland. His father had been government, so he was raised on the island that he still resided on. He had no idea how things really worked in Topan, because they ran differently. In contrast, having grown up next to these woods, the other man knew every tree as well as he knew every one of the sixteen people who shared his cave.

The two men finally crashed out of the trees and onto the beach at the far end. Two other figures were huddled on the beach – one lying on the ground, another crouched next to him.

Inspector Avrom stood, panting, as he picked twigs and leaves out of his hair. "What –" pant, pant "-can I do to help?"

"He's hurt, sir. I don't know what to do."

The inspector made his way across the sand to the man on the ground. Once there, he leaned over him. As soon as he did, both figures grabbed him and put a gag in his mouth. He struggled but they flipped him on this front and tied his hands together behind his back. A fourth person pulled a waiting boat into view. They rushed to get the Inspector onto it. The fog was almost gone and they had just a very small window of opportunity to get him off the mainland and across the channel. They waited as they watched the bridge sentries. As long as they were crouched, they were out of view, but if they stood up, the sentries would see them for sure. The sentry turned around and they jumped up and launched the boat. As soon as they did so, a boat was launched from the island as well. They passed in the middle at full speed, but neither looked at each other. Mynerva, Emmerus and Zain knew their mission was too important to get distracted – even by the people in it with them. On shore, they passed the boat off to a couple of others and followed a path into the trees.

"Here!" a voice called out. They turned and saw a woman waiting for them. "I have clothes for you. Yours will be obvious from the very beginning." The trio stripped immediately and changed into the clothes that were handed out to them. "I'm Katha, by the way. A good friend of Ursule's growing up. I… I'm a government employee, too, but I have the same bridge transportation pass that Avrom has."

"How did you get your credentials? What job do you have?"

"I don't want to talk about it. It's safer that way for all involved. Besides, we need to move now."

"Come," Mynerva said, leading her friends and cohorts into the woods. They made quick time behind Katha, running into the forest as fast as they could. With Avrom out of the way, they only had a day or two before the rest of the government sprang into action. By now, he was locked into the small niche on the island, in a cage custom built for him courtesy of their friend Wain's incredible carpentry skills.

It was a long walk through the entirety of the woods. "Where are we coming out, Katha? Near the top?"

"Well, not exactly." She stopped suddenly and yanked Mynerva behind a clump of trees. The guys followed their lead. They held their breath as a class of students came around the corner and down the path, the teacher at the front lecturing about the forest as they walked. The children were young and there was little doubt that most of them were completely ignoring everything that she said.

When the last footstep was a memory, the group went back on the path, careful to make as little noise as possible. Katha reached into her pocket and pulled out a handful of security badges. "Put these in your front left pocket. You have to be able to pull them out and show them at a moment's notice."

Zain flipped his open. "bu-bu-bu-bu-but there are pi-pi-pi grrrr –pictures on them. How will we grrr use them?"

"There are pictures, yes, but they are blurry. We used your real first names, but for last names, we had to invent them because, well, you don't have them. Side effect of the Manor and all, that family names – family period – doesn't matter or count. If anyone asks, just say agent and your first name and flash it quickly. Most people don't look anyway. They think the flashing is just a formality that the government has to do whenever they do anything. Like wiping your ass after you shit. If we have to give them more than a flash, I'll let them see mine, tell them that you're up for review and I'm the one in charge. Officials are up for the review all the time, you got it?"

Zain let out a low growl in response and clamped both of his hands over his mouth. "This was grrr maybe a bad idea. I should have stayed grrr on the Island and let one of them come."

"NO! We need you. You've been out the longest. We can't find your family, let alone trust them, without you, do you understand that?" Mynerva hissed. "Look, this isn't just 'shut up and nobody will know' like it was before. This is life and death and everything else that that entails. Do you get it? Do you understand?"

"Grrr. Yes." His arm twitched back and forth, shaking and twisting in the process. He caught Katha's gaze as she stared at it. Of course a government employee would have never seen anyone with the likes of him – they were all sent away immediately, after all, that was the point. "This will grrr keep me quiet for now. It takes too m-m-m-m-m-much ener grrr gy to do it for too long."

"Just go, Katha. We need to get inside somebody's dwelling as soon as we can." Emmerus started walking, hoping everyone else would take the hint and keep up with him.

Katha pushed back to the front of the group and led them further up the trail until it split. She turned away from the city and stopped near a cluster of bushes. "We have to get behind these, but be very careful that they don't look disturbed."

"Try this way, then. Even if there is a broken twig or two, it won't be as noticeable on this side," Emmerus suggested. "Here." He took great care in holding the bush back so that the other three could get behind it, and shuffled in behind them. They all crouched down and waited as Katha exposed a short gate in the fencing. "This is the gate to the outer woods – forbidden territory. The gate was put here for safety, as if that issue ever arose. I'm not sure it's been used since it was last put up. The fence was last maintained over seventy-five turns ago. It's hearty, for sure, but let's see about the gate." She pulled a key from around her neck and stuck it into the lock. It turned with surprising ease, but the gate itself proved to be another matter. She pushed a couple times and finally had to scoot over while Emmerus kicked it open. It still took him two attempts, and the gate screeched in protest. They sat for a minute, holding their breath, and hoped that nobody was close enough to hear the noise.

It felt like an eternity before Katha finally crawled through the gate and came out in the outer forest. "There are no trails here, as I'm sure you know. Find a way to remember where you are, or we'll never find you again, do you understand that?" She pulled a second key from around her neck. "This one key works all the gates to the fences.

Look for very thick clusters of bushes or other features that don't quite seem accidental when you look at them. When the fences were built, they hid the gates, short enough to not be seen, no matter what. There is a second one on this side down before you get to the water."

"Wain, it's up to you to keep track of that, okay? You have the mind for it."

He growled, shook his head and started again. "Two gates, this one and then one further grrr down before the water. I got it."

"Let's go three trees deep," Mynerva suggested. "Three rows up should be far enough to not be detected unless somebody is very close to the fence itself. But close enough to it that we should be able to have visual contact with it and know where we are. For now it's the best way."

"I agree," said Katha. "Three trees it is. Follow me, please."

They continued up the hill and then turned left at the third tree. It was true; the trees provided excellent covering, and what little visibility there was of the foursome blended in with the surroundings. Their new clothes were more in the style of the mainland than the island, but the color palate was also much less conspicuous, Ursule having chosen browns and dark greens so that they could hide in the foliage if they needed to.

They continued through the woods for quite a distance, Katha pointing out gates in the fence as they went. It was long goings getting around this city the far way, and by the time they made it to the fence next-closest to the government building, it was almost dark. Katha and Emmerus pulled the gate open, much more quietly this time, and the group tiptoed out behind the school building. After an all-clear from Katha, they walked up the trail and through the small supplemental garden that the school used before ending up on the main path.

Zain took the lead now, and led the small group down a residential row to a cave, rushing them inside after a quick peek to make sure it was clear. An older woman heard the noise and came out, screaming as soon as she saw the group. Zain rushed to her and clamped his hand over her mouth. "I need you to be quiet when grrr I move my hand, Gran. Okay?"

She nodded a couple times and waited for him to lower his arm. "I never thought I'd see you again!" She wrapped her arms around him, squeezing so hard that it felt painful to the rest of the group. "You're not dead, how were you treated? Have you eaten?" Her words came out in one big whoosh.

"Ma'am, if you could maybe calm down?" Katha said, flashing her badge as much out of habit in hopes it would help. "Look, we don't have a lot of time, and we're too exposed in the front room. Is there somewhere else we can go?"

"Oh, right. Come back here." They went down the hall to the last bedroom. "This was Zain's when he was here. His parents left him with me when it started to get bad. Hoped they could protect him."

"He's fine, ma'am," Mynerva said. "The Manor is in many ways better to us than this world is. But we need your help and we need you to trust us and listen very carefully. *Nobody* can know we're here. Not your friends, not your family, nobody. And later, if somebody asks, you've not seen Zain since they took him, or us, ever. Pretend he's nothing to you anymore if you have to."

Shakily, she sat down, almost missing the bed. "I need to know something."

"You really don't. But since we need you, I will tell you only that we are here to make things better."

"Better."

"Better," the group repeated.

"Well, if you're hoping for that, I'm going to have to get you some food first. You look weary and half starved."

***

Year New 612

The first of the suns was rising casting a pinkish glow on the grasses, and making the water look not quite as grey-blue as it usually did. The couple had shifted at some point and Emmerus was now mostly on his back, Mynerva curled into his torso.

It was she who woke up first, and she nudged him awake, kissing him gently on the cheek.

He fought sleep, rubbing it from his eyes the best he could. "Why?" He cried, one eye open.

She giggled. "Come on. It's morning. They're going to worry where we've gone to, and besides, the council is today. Or did you forget?"

"I'd like to forget." Council meetings happened just a few times a year, but they were necessary to discuss what was going on in their new city. While they needed to know that the crops were okay and be ready to add extra builders if they ran out of housing for the waves of people still coming in, it didn't make the meetings any shorter or any less boring.

He sat up and looked at Mynerva. The wound in her shoulder had scarred, as angry and jagged as the people who put it there, and although it had lightened over time, it would surely never go away.

She scratched at it subconsciously and reached for their clothes.

***

Year New 606

Zain had spent the week intermittently visiting their old friend the government and taking care of a few other tasks for the master plan. It was an odd job he had, but rather easy. His regular, low growling kept Bruice, their government puppet, on edge. For the most part, the man was ready to jump on his command. It was the easiest way, really, and he took to growling even when he wasn't doing it automatically. The government transition was going smoothly for the most part, but Bruice was still a weak link. On one occasion he had tried to tell a comrade, only to find himself staring down a weapon. It was not a good situation, and everybody knew it. If the threat made its way into the Commander's sights, their entire plan would be screwed before it had ever gotten off the ground.

Today, Zain took the last few steps to the fourth floor and opened the door. Bruice was in the hall, flagging down the commander. "Hello!" he shouted.

Zain let out a low growl and watched the color drain slowly from Bruice's face as the commander approached.

"Nice day, isn't it?" the commander asked.

Bruice mumbled agreement and disappeared from sight, shaking a bit now that he knew he'd been caught again.

That night, under cover of darkness, Zain put him on a boat and sent him off to the island with Avrom. The cage was small for the two of them, but at least Avrom had somebody to talk to.

In his absence, he left a note saying that he would be taking care of a sick relative back in the mainland of Topan. Nevermind that the letter was actually written by Zain after the fact.

Then the day of announcement came. The 100th day of the year. In Topan, it was marked with the reading of announcements from the government. Once read out loud to the masses, anything said would be considered law. This time, Mynerva had switched the scroll. Instead of announcements about farming, she had written in about the restructuring of where everyone lived and how, greatly decreasing the government's influence while expanding the free will of the people and opening The Manor as Bryor had wished.

As the appointed official started the reading, a tattered figure appeared on the beach. "STOP! I've been held prisoner and have just now escaped!" Everyone turned to look at the man, some needing more than a few minutes to realize it was Inspector Avrom who was dragging himself towards the platform. He was screaming about a breech, people hidden amongst them that were there to cause them harm.

Mynerva looked at her ragtag group of people. They quietly backed out of the crowd and then ran down the beach. A cry of "STOP THEM" rang out and several government people ran after them, a few eager townspeople jumping in to help. Mynerva knew that people like Katha and Ursule would be safe, able to return to their lives and pretend they had no part in it. But Mynerva and Emmerus and the rest of them had no hope. They wouldn't make it back to The

Manor and even if they did, they'd be killed for sure, all their work for naught.

Without a better plan, she grabbed the gun from her belt and fired two shots into the air, towards the water. The townspeople screamed again and grabbed whatever they could rip up from the ground to use as weapons. The group ran faster now, sure that they'd be dead if they stopped for even a minute.

They got to the impassible pass next to the government island and dove into the underbrush, weeds pulling at their clothes. Another shot rang out, hitting Mynerva in the shoulder. She screamed in pain and collapsed to the ground. Emmerus tried to help her but she waved him off, crawling on her good side until she was totally hidden. Another couple of shots rang out, but they managed to miss everybody. They answered back with a round of shots high above the crowd's head. They didn't want to hurt anybody, only get out safely. Their whole plan was about stopping hurt, not causing it. They got through the weeds and into the back path that the sentries used. It was deserted, exactly as they needed it to be.

One of them pulled an aide kit out of his pack and tended to Mynerva. "It didn't hit anything important, I don't think. I just need to stop the bleeding."

"Hurry up. We need to run, not sit here," Mynerva said.

He yanked the bandage tight and tied it so that her skin turned white. "I know that it might go numb, but you'll want it to."

"Then let's go." She stood up and started down the path.

"Somebody's already behind us," Wain called, running back up to them.

"Then we run. We know they way, they don't."

The group ran as fast as they could up the path. It was a long climb to get to Landing's Pass, the site of the original crash, but they made the four kilometer trip in half the time it should have taken them. They danced through the foliage until they joined the old remnants of the path and wound their way up to the wreckage site. It was fortunate that after so long part of the plane remained. They dove towards the small opening they knew was there and crawled inside the twisted metal cage, careful to cover the opening up behind them.

Once safe, they took a minute to catch their breath. Emmerus had been tending to his wife, but he addressed the group anyway. "Look, it's been a long, trying day, but everybody was far enough behind us that we should be safe. We replaced the sentries from within Topan, not from within the Manor, on purpose," he said. "I am entirely confident that we will be safe tonight. So we rest here. Once the first light creeps in, we will work on another plan."

There were murmurs of agreement and the group huddled into what was left of the sleeping bags; meant to hold one or two people at a time, these were now filled until three or four people were crammed into each one. It was going to be a long cold night.

The next day, Wain went out and scouted the area around the landing. On the main trail, there was evidence of a search party, as many of the branches of the thicker bushes had been broken or disturbed. He took great care going back into the thicket, not wanting to do any more damage than had already been done. He wandered around until he found food and water, and retrieved a member of the party to help him bring rations back to the crash site.

By lunch time, they had done little more than find water and consume it, but it was something, at least. The group was dejected. All of their hard work had ended in Anarchy. How had Avrom managed to get out of the cell? Why did he have to appear at that very moment? Another day or two and the plans would already have been underway for Great Change, committees formed to figure out different aspects of the list. But now – objections were raised before the reading of the list was finished by a high ranking official. Now that they were out of the Government and they were on the run, they had no power over anybody to do their bidding.

Mynerva said it best when she shouted "FUCK!" and kicked at the side of the ship.

Everybody turned and looked at her.

"You know what? Screw it. We tried to help everybody, but now we have to help ourselves. It's just the way that it needs to be. Today, we rest. Some of us need a chance to recuperate. Tomorrow, we head the other way on Landing's Path and see what we come across. Just because Axl came one way doesn't mean that there was nothing in the other direction."

There was agreement in the group, although some of the members started to say something. "Mynerva –"

"You're free to go back. Surrender if you need to, but don't say anything else about those who wish to stay. Remember, you're the dredges of society, so surely you can't be held accountable for your actions, although who knows. Nobody's ever been held against their will anywhere but The Manor before, and we took Avrom and kept him. The choice is up to you."

There was very little said after that. A few of the members of the group sat off to the side, deciding whether an unknown fate was better or worse than going back. If Topan had done this, they would have been set adrift – put on a boat and pushed out to sea. What of their families? They knew the risk was great, but nobody considered that their families might be targets. It was okay for Mynerva, everybody had known her as Garricke before, so they wouldn't have a clue who she was. But the rest of them… Some of them hadn't been gone that long.

"If you want to leave, I will promise you safety at the Manor. Follow along the woods until you see the beach on the island and wait until night to cross there. Bryor will give you safe lodging as long as you shall need it." Mynerva stood up and left the wreckage.

Outside the crash site, she busied herself by walking up the hill a little more. Clearly, Axl and Abelia had left the crash site and walked down hill – the history never talked much about how they arrived at the site, just that they did. But upward, the hill stretched for an entire kilometer. It would have been easier to start off downward, especially if the natural trail that was there now existed in their day.

She made her way through the foliage as carefully as she could, careful not to disturb anything too much. On the off chance that an expedition came through this way, she wanted no evidence that they were ever there. It was the safest option for sure.

As the hill crested, she faced a plateau, wide enough for two or three of her little huts and ten times as long. She walked along this and looked out. Below her, another open plain, a lot like that which was currently Topan, but many times larger. Beyond that, the water stretched as far the eye could see. Her plan *could* have worked after all. Here was the proof – equally habitable land for those who wanted to leave Topan. She wanted to search for a way down the mountain, but she knew that the deepening of the red sky above her meant that night would fall soon. She needed to get back to the wreckage site as soon as she could.

Mynerva worked back down the trail and neared the crash site. She was suddenly aware of an unnatural glow, so she stopped walking and ducked low. From where she was, the crash was unnoticeable, but the danger to her friends was unmistakable. A group from Topan, led by Avrom, had come back into the woods, torches blazing.

The dozen or so people that were with Avrom had branched out and were combing the nearby brush. Mynerva held her breath and watched as they came closer to her. Fortunately, directly in front of her was a large thicket of briars and the man searching decided not to check there.

"Nobody else has been up here for years."

Avrom stared at him. "And what makes you qualified to make this judgment?"

"None of the bushes are broken or disturbed, there are no footprints, unlike where we've been walking –"

"You morons have trampled everything. There could have been evidence, but now we won't know."

Mynerva shuddered, but breathed a quiet sigh of relief as she watched them turn and head down the hill. She stayed where she was until dark had settled. She was finally about to move again when she heard a twig snap.

"Mynerva!" the voice whispered. "Where are you?"

"Emmerus?"

"Mynerva? You okay?" He sounded hysterical.

"I'm coming! Get low and stay where you are!" She crawled back through the brush until she ran into him, sitting directly in her path.

"Thank God you're okay!" He pulled his wife towards him and gave her a big kiss.

"I heard Avrom up here, so I wanted to lay low."

"I guess so. You lay half the day, I think."

"I didn't know what else to do. What is he going to do to the people they caught? Set them adrift, martyrs for our cause? You know I didn't want that!" She started rambling, all her fears for the day coming out all at once.

"MYNERVA!" His cry stunned her into silence. "Please, get a grip, dear. Nobody is going to be a martyr for our cause. Everyone here has chosen to stay with you. Anyone caught, well, they made that choice on their own. You're offering a good way of life, and the people who have followed us are hungry for it. We've regrouped and we're strong enough to continue. In the morning, we'll figure out a new plan.

When they got back to the wreckage, everyone stared at her. "I just want everybody to know that I didn't run away. I decided that you needed space to talk over your decisions, so I went walking. I found something incredible. It's quite a hike and there's no trail, but there is a new place to settle. A second city where we'll be on our own and safe."

She scanned the crowd, but nobody took advantage of the moment to speak, so she continued. "Tomorrow morning we eat and refill the water and food and then set off. It's about a kilometer up the mountain and then we arrive at a plateau. Down from the plateau is an area of land much like Topan but twice as large at least. There's green space, trees, water, just like there is in Topan. We will have more than enough room to start a settlement of our own and grow it. "

Emmerus looked at the group and then back at his wife. "Then we wait till morning and go."

***

Year New 643

"That's it? What about the third city?" one of the little boys in the audience turned his big brown eyes towards Mynerva. Of course they knew about the third city; now that travel was unrestricted, people visited all the time.

"The third city. A very good friend of mine, Travys, was sent out to scout. He went around the island the other way and found an entire second city with a population even larger than Topan."

"But where did they come from? And how come nobody knew?"

"Under the old rules, Topan was blocked off by the fence, remember. Nobody was allowed to cross it. Turned out that the 'fate worse than death' was actually a blessing. You see, people who were given that punishment were tied into a boat, pushed into the water and held there with a tether. When it broke, the boat drifted away and was never seen again. But past The Manor and around to where we couldn't see anymore, there was another similar area. And the boats made their way there. As more and more people survived, a city started, people re-settled. Another glorious place like this."

"But why did *they* leave," another child asked.

"Some wanted to. As the government of Topan got worse, more and more people were sent off. Boat building became a full time job. So the third city – called simply Fate – grew up and became heavily populated. Too heavily, if you must know. So some people asked to come here. They liked what we had done, they were related to some of ours, whatever. There were many reasons."

A chorus of oohs drifted up from the group, and in the distance a bell rang, noting the passage of time for the city. "I think that's enough history for one day," Mynerva said. Although she hadn't told the kids most of the story, talking about any of it always brought all of the memories bubbling up to the surface. How and why she got to The Manor, who she really was, all things she kept secret. Luckily, the kids agreed, grabbing their things and running off towards home.

Mynerva stood and stretched her limbs, taking extra care with her stiff shoulder. They hadn't managed it the way they wanted to, but they'd managed nonetheless.

SEVENTH DEGREE

BY HERIKA R. RAYMER

Riley Mason was anxiously waiting in the Serp Oak Café, her food was barely touched and she turned her drink periodically as she stared blindly out the window. Around her, the general noise of chatter, clink of utensils to platters, and occasional crash of pans being banged together in the kitchen made up the mundane atmosphere of the place. Outside, solar and hydrogen cars sped by meandering pedestrians who window shopped the stores as they leisurely made their way to their next destination along meticulously kept sidewalks routinely decorated with a gated tree. Watching them did nothing to ease her tension, so to distract herself she allowed her gaze to roam the café. It did not help.

To the rear, and not entirely hidden, a carefree couple was engrossed with one another. So long as they did not start copulating in public, they would be ignored. Still, watching them kiss and fondle one another made the pit in her stomach even tighter. It reminded her of why she was here. Turning away did not help either, because at that moment she saw a transport bus carrying its usual load of toddler passengers from their school to a predetermined field trip stop. She knew where they were going; she should since she was one of the teachers as she recognized the school colors on the bus. She should be with them now, except for the fact she had taken off this week in the hopes of fulfilling a dream.

The dream of being a mother, except now that dream was shattered.

The babble of the group of girls at the next table became distracting. After all, it was not that long ago she had been a secondary education student. She remembered being fresh and having conversations similar to the one going on right now.

"Wait, wait, wait, listen to this," one of them was saying and began to read in an affected deep tone. " 'Due to the irrational treatment of people of different skin colors, sexual orientation or practice, and even gender in the centuries before The Decay, it was not uncommon for jobs to be left unfilled or even for those employed to be overlooked for promotion'." She made an exasperated sound. "Can you believe how idiotic that was?"

"Or how frustrating it must have been to live then?" another asked. "To not know if you'd be able to keep a job, or even live in a your own house?"

A third giggled suggestively. "I've even read books where it said they had separate districts where sex was sold!"

"No way!" the second one gasped and then giggled.

"Oh yeah," the third confirmed. "Can you imagine? Living in such a repressed world that you couldn't even be with whomever you want?"

"From what I understand it was a pretty bad time," the fourth one finally spoke softly.

"What do you mean?" the second one asked.

She lowered her voice conspiratorially. "They tried to regulate sex, or confine it to relationships, because people were copulating with their own siblings or children and propagating."

"Gross!" the third one exclaimed.

"I am so glad that is not a problem now," the second one said. "I mean, I cannot even imagine wanting to breed. I would hate to get that fat!"

At that point, she turned her attention away from the girls. Pushing a strand of hair behind her ear, she tried to hold back tears. '*Not everyone feels that way*', she thought.

She still could not figure out how she had been disqualified, it seemed as though her application had been met with favor. With each interview of the process passed, she had gotten closer and closer to her dream. There had been seven of them, and mostly easy in the beginning with just the filling out of paperwork. She was university-level educated, had her own place and was financially solid, she did not participate in any political arenas and abided by the Dictates, and there was no evidence of civil disobedience on her part or of anyone she associated with. All her preliminary testing had been favorable, even her request to keep the child rather than have it raised by the CP, or Civil Prepotence, had been granted due to her background in the public instruction of young minds. She was well versed in the what-to-do's and the why-for's, and had even been complimented on her devotion to the proper tutelage of a developing mind. Yet when she got past the fifth interview, the one pertaining to her knowledge about her own medical history, things had gotten strange.

If only they had told her why, maybe she would not have taken such desperate measures…

The sounding of the bell interrupted her musing. She looked towards the door to see a couple enter, the woman was wearing a particularly unusual rose in her hair. It had a yellow bloom with lovely orange stripes.

These must be the ones she was waiting for.

She raised her hand in greeting, forcing a smile even though her face muscles hurt at the attempt. Everything had to seem normal, that was what the instructions had said. She had to behave as though she were expecting these people.

The woman raised an answering hand and said something to her companion, who turned and walked towards the music selection area. There was already a tune playing, despite the cacophony of conversation, but he stood there while she approached Riley's table. Before she could stand to greet her formally, the woman smoothly sat into the seat as if they were old friends.

"It was so wonderful to hear you still lived here!" she began breathlessly, as if the two of them had not seen each other in a long time. "I'm so sorry we can't stay long, but you know him," she went on with a dismissive gesture to her escort. "He's always on the move, getting product sold and moved. Still, it gives us a chance to see the Demenses."

Initially overwhelmed at her friendly tone, and then finally realizing she was establishing a rapport for anyone who might be watching via The Eye, Riley allowed her smile to widen into a grin. "How many have you seen?"

"Oh let's see," she purred as she tapped a finger to her lips, her eyes giving warning for a moment. "There was Achter Cull, nice city with a wonderful virtual reality screening."

"Pardon?" what was this woman doing? They were here for a reason!

"Oh," she made another dismissive gesture, though her eyes seemed troubled. "The CP there uses virtual reality to screen their citizen applicants. Nice place to visit, but I would not want to live there."

"Uh..."

"But Beulah!" she went on with a delighted clap of her hands. "The view of the ocean there is just divine!"

"Don't forget Lyster," the young man added as he sat down. He tapped the table three times with his thumb.

The woman watched his hand and nodded. "Yes Lyster, just follow the river from Beulah and you get to quaint Lyster."

"Excuse me..." Riley began, wanting to get control of the conversation and steer it to what she contacted them for.

"Miss?" the stranger called to the servi, ignoring her.

A young woman dressed in the café's uniform sauntered over and smiled at him invitingly. "Anything I can get you?"

He grinned and gave her a complimentary eye roving. "For now, could I have two drinks?"

"Anything specific?"

"Tea will suffice."

She gave him a wink and sauntered away, looking over her should just once to be sure he was enjoying the show. He was, as were several other customers. Normally this would not bother Riley, but today was crucial. What was going on?

The music changed, the low beat of it thrumming through the floor like a heartbeat.

"Now we can talk," the woman said as the man turned back towards the table, his arm draped over the back of her chair as he began to nuzzle her neck.

Riley eyed him curiously.

"He is keeping an eye and ear on the café while partially obstructing The Eye's view of us," the woman explained. "We have as long as this song."

"For what?" she asked, trying desperately to keep up.

Her visitor was patient. "To get you what you need."

Her heart leaped and she was sure her face blushed. Hope surged through her again as she realized she had not been wrong, these were the people she was waiting for and they had known all along what she was there for. "You can do that?"

"Partially," she reached over to take the other's hand in seeming comfort when she saw the downcast expression. "This will get you started."

When she felt the small card-shaped package box being slipped to her, she almost broke down into tears. "What is it?" she asked softly, barely controlling her emotions.

"False identification," her savior replied. "Only it will not work at a Hospital, you have to go to a Dash Clinic."

She grimaced. "Why?"

The music was peaking, so the woman spoke fast. "You know why, the DP monitors and controls all breeding. Hospital security is thorough. If you were to go in there with this, especially after receiving the Seventh Degree Fail, you would immediately be recognized and

flagged. At best, you would be arrested. At worst, you would be immediately executed. The DP does not tolerate disobedience of any of their Dictates."

She swallowed and nodded as she gripped the woman's hand, realizing the gravity of the situation and how much everyone at the table was risking. The couple was risking their lives getting her this Pass, and she was risking her own by even thinking of going against the Dictates of the DP, or Demense Prepotence. Yet she was willing to give up everything to have a child.

She looked around her, at the people of her region. How could she be so unhappy in the midst of such perfection?

Everywhere she looked there was plenty of food and drink, people were employed and had individual homes, and there was a general feeling of camaraderie. Health was no longer an issue due to select breeding, the children were taught by the CP (such as herself) unless someone wanted the time-consuming responsibility of doing it themselves, everyone had a job and a place to live, and there was not a want for anything really. The DP had gone to great lengths to ensure that all needs and wants were provided for, and the citizens, for the most part, were happy. All the shackles of the past had been left behind. There was no preferential treatment on the basis of skin color, Demense of birth, or even gender. From what she understood there was even a time when one or all of these determined what job a person could get, and this was no longer the case. If someone was suited for the job, they were hired. Why, even the worry of disease or pregnancy was addressed by the DP Dictates, hence the Hospitals and Clinics. They mainly ensured that the populous engaged in clean copulation and guaranteed that all citizens were sterile and disease free.

The DP Dictate of mandatory sterilization was its answer to the after-effects of The Decay. The general health and intelligence of the populous had degenerated due to generations of inbreeding caused by either intent or ignorance, mostly in the later 21st and 22nd centuries in attempts to garner public assistance. In addition to the economic strain, the result was that everyone was related within seven generations of one another, and the accompanying damage to the genetic code had been almost catastrophic. In a massive effort to salvage humanity, every citizen was rendered sterile at the onset of puberty, the men via the gel injection RISUG and women via contraceptive injections. This method allowed the bodies to develop naturally while not interfering with hormones or bio-chemistry or neurology, and it was reversible so anyone who wanted to breed could apply and, if approved, get the injection to allow them to have children. Techniques involving the retardation of growth were banned, unless it was a physiological condition; transgender operations were less invasive now though still screened, people were encouraged to accept the gender they were born with; abortion was banned, due to physical and psychological damages never truly addressed; and pregnancy was by permit only, granted only to applicants who passed a series of screenings. The history books claimed there had been an outcry in the beginning, mostly based on opinions of identities being tied to sexuality. However, after so much time these arguments proved baseless since gender identity no longer really mattered. Due to the blending attitudes of the forefathers, a laizze-faire attitude was practiced towards the genders and especially towards sex. There were a few restrictions, but otherwise citizens were allowed to be with whomever they chose. There was no guilt, no commitment unless mutually agreed, and no repercussions. It was a new world, a better world, one that the citizens could be proud to live in. The air was cleaner due to responsible fuel usage, the lands were less tainted thanks to the use of cremation and recycling, and the water was more pure due to proper filtration and less dumping of waste in the waterways. Everything was obviously better than they had been in centuries past, according to the historic tomes.

So why was she so full of discontent?

It was those last interviews, they had seemed so odd. With health problems of old addressed by the stipulations of the breeding process, there should be little to no genetic damage remaining. So why was breeding still being controlled?

The music was reaching its end.

"We've done our part," the woman was saying. "Though as a final warning, don't go to the Hospitals for the Scheduled Check-ups."

"Then where can I go?"

"All you need to know is in there," she answered. The music stopped and an upbeat modern song took its place. "Oh sweetie, I'm so sorry to hear that," she went on smoothly, patting Riley's hand. "Well, I'm sure things will work out."

She just nodded, not sure how to respond.

The man whispered in his companion's ear, to which she giggled. This time she could see the acting. They were putting on a show for The Eye, so no one would think their meeting odd. The woman turned toward her companion and began kissing him deeply and passionately. After a few moments, she turned with a grin. "I guess you don't want to join us?"

She turned them down with a shake of her head.

The woman shrugged. "Well, I can't just leave you with nothing."

She reached up and took the peculiar rose from her hair and handed it over. "Wear it wherever you go, I'm sure it will bring you luck."

With that, the couple stood and left.

She stayed a few moments before settling the bill and leaving, eager to open the packet.

* * *

The Dash Clinic did not look like a regular Clinic; it was more like a bed and breakfast. She could see people eating through the front windows, and knew that the rear and the upstairs were entertaining different business. Breeders entered and were superficially identified, which is what made it safer to go to than a Hospital. After all, this was not where someone went for an exam. This was where some of the more 'archaic' breeders went to meet their donors face-to-face. This Dash Clinic catered to such interaction. It operated much like the old time Date & Dash, where potential matches sat and talked for five minutes and, if they cliqued, were given a room for as long as they needed. Thankfully the Clinic provided pregnancy indicators which informed the woman just hours after conception. In the meantime, meals and comfort would be provided until the business was complete. From what she understood, impregnation should happen within 24 hours if both had waited seven days after receiving the injection to reverse each party's contraception.

She hoped what she heard about Dash Clinics being able to supply the Reversal were true, otherwise all of this would be for nothing. There were two types of impregnation: insemination and direct copulation. Riley could not have insemination done due to her faux identification; the Hospital would spot it immediately. This was a bit more risky than she had in mind, but she did not mind. In fact, before her interviews she had already decided that she wanted to do have direct copulation. She was no stranger to sex, this was true. However, this would be her one chance to choose who the father of her child would be. For whatever reason, she felt compelled to at least know something about him before she accepted his seed.

She needed to get going before she lost her nerve.

Reaching into her jacket pocket, she pulled out the ID card sized felt box and opened it to reveal its contents. Snugly fit into the container was a Breeder Permit, a needle with a strange liquid in it, and another small disk that looked like it fit in her phone. Taking it out, she placed the disk in one of the side slots and placed the earpiece in her ear while she waited for it to load.

"After this recording, destroy the disk," intoned the computerized audio. "Included in your packet are your permit and the Reversal injection so that the Dash Clinic's reserves do not read any lost inventory. It is not unusual for a Breeder to bring their own supply, so do not worry about drawing attention. In fact, they prefer it because it tells them that you are Approved since Reversals are only available through Hospitals, so be sure to have it in view when you are put through security. Budget is set for fourteen days, so do not overstay. After you are finished, it is strongly recommended you have your Scheduled Check-Ups at a Clinic where the Hot Tea Rose is in the window. This location will change, so always wear your rose when you visit the Clinic to help the nurses know who you are. Good Luck."

Riley's stomach clenched, and she quickly pulled out the disk, exited the car, dropped it, and ground it into the pavement with her heel as she shut the vehicle door. All this sly maneuvering was slightly exciting, but also scary. Was she sure she wanted to do this?

A couple walked by pushing a stroller, with a small baby looking around seated inside. The women looked so proud, and the baby so lovely. She felt the all too familiar longing surge through her.

Squaring her shoulders, she crossed the street to the Dash Clinic and ascended the steps.

She was not sure what she expected when she entered, but the mere normality of the inside was a little startling. Looking around, she took a few moments to take in the friendly atmosphere. The couples sitting at the tables were laughing as they ate, seeming like friends rather than one-time lovers. It was encouraging. Seeing the clerk at the far counter, she made her way across the dining area. When she got there, she smiled. The clerk smiled in return.

"Identification?"

She nodded and pulled out the felt box. Opening it, she handed over the faux permit, making sure to have the small injection in full view as she handed over the ID card. The clerk noticed it, and she could almost see the man's shoulders relax. It helped ease her nerves.

"First time?"

She nodded again, her throat too tight to answer.

He smiled reassuringly at her as he spoke again. "Place your forefinger in the reader."

"Okay," she breathed as she did so. She was familiar with this; it was the lie detector which was standard for all interviews.

"State your name."

"Riley Mason."

"Age?"

"25," this was important since all Breeders had to be above the age of 21. Something about the body's chemistry changing every seven years, so it was selected as the best age beyond puberty to begin allowing pregnancies.

"Previous pregnancies?"

"No," her voice was a bit confused, had he not asked her if this was her first time.

He smiled as he heard her annoyance. "Standard questions, miss."

"Oh," she grinned sheepishly, "sorry."

He nodded to her and typed in some information.

She remembered then that Breeders were only allowed a certain number of children, and that was dependent on their health. Any Breeder who tried to go beyond that was, at best, severely reprimanded and punished. She hated to think of the worst case scenario. Now that she thought about it, disobeying a Dictate was almost a guaranteed death sentence. Was she sure she really wanted to do this? Looking around, she reminded herself that this had always been a dream of hers. Right now she was sure she was being tested, how far was she willing to go? Apparently, all the way – she was willing to risk death.

His voice interrupted her thoughts. "Are you sexually involved with an immediate family member?"

She shuddered. "No," she answered firmly. Aside from the Dictate against it, it was unthinkable to her. Not to mention it was rather difficult to accomplish given that Breeders were usually selected from separate Demenses as their progeny.

He continued to type. "Are you sexually involved with a minor or student?"

She was proud to say, "No," to that one. Though she had begun having sex at fourteen, like many others, it was strongly discouraged to have sex with someone beyond your age group. Apparently before The Decay, adults used to take advantages of minors' need for acceptance and abuse was common, so it was no longer tolerated. In addition, any adult in a position of instruction over young minds was strictly forbidden to copulate with students. Both offenses were punishable by termination, on multiple levels. Besides, she took her position as an instructor very seriously, and would never abuse her position of trust.

"Last question," he seemed to tense, "do you practice bestiality or necrophilia?"

She could not suppress the shudder of revulsion. "Absolutely not."

He relaxed. "Apologies. Standard questions."

"I understand. But really… ick."

He made a face in agreement. Once again, aside from the fact that doing such a thing would mean death, the mere thought of it was repulsive. What kind of a place was The Decayed World that these questions had to be asked?!

"Remove your finger," he finished typing as she complied. "You do know that optimum time before insemination is seven days after Reversal?"

"Yes."

"You plan to stay here the entire time, or go back to your home?"

She thought about it. "Stay."

He took the Breeder Permit and ran the card through a reader before handing it to her. "Room number is on the key. Credits will be deducted after you leave. Don't forget to check out."

She placed the card back in its cushioned slot and looked at the clerk. "Am I allowed to participate in the Dash before my time?"

"Of course," he assured her. "Some Breeders like to use the time they are waiting to carefully select their partner. Enjoy."

She grinned and moved past him, her heart racing as she walked down the hall and up the stairs to where her room awaited.

The next few days were a bit of a blur. The shot itself was not very painful, though she was a bit sleepy the first day. On the second, she made a point of watching the Dash, to get an idea of how it worked. Fairly straightforward: participants sat across from one another and tried to impress each other within five minutes. If it did not work, a bell chimed and the men shifted position – she liked how the women were the only ones sitting still. By the third day she was sitting in the Dash, and the thrill of it rushed through her as she received numerous pitches.

Too needy.

Handsome, but too self-absorbed.

Too chatty.

Too quiet.

Too self-centered.

It was amazing to her how many different personality types she could meet in one day of these Dash encounters. All the while, she was waiting for that reaction that would tell her that, at the very least, she would not mind bedding the man. On the sixth day she met him, or rather heard him. His voice was like a beastly purr that tickled along her skin. She barely was able to concentrate on the man in front of her, and waited eagerly for the bell to chime. When he sat before her, she was a bit surprised to see that his face and physique did not match his voice. She had half-expected to see a rugged appearance and a burly frame, but the man was slender and his features were average. However, his voice was heavenly, he was intelligent, and had wit. Apparently she impressed him as well because when the bell chimed they stood and left the Dash arena for the dining hall, where they spent her final day talking and enjoying each other's company before sealing the deal.

His name was Carlton, and to be honest he was perfect for her even beyond what they were here for. She had no complaint, especially since the sex was fabulous. He was attentive and giving, not to mention patient. After all, there was no real rush, and they were determined to enjoy one another. She made sure she was as thorough with him, drawing sounds from him that made her skin tingle with delight. It was not long before she was pregnant, and they both shared a laugh and a hug. She was getting what she wanted: a child by a man who wanted to breed and, as a bonus, it was a man she desired. In fact, she would not mind keeping his contact information and staying in touch with him afterward. A sentiment he apparently shared since he gave her his card.

Day ten saw her checking out, satisfied on a multiple levels.

* * *

Riley wondered for the 'n'th time if she had made a mistake.

Sitting in the Hospital exam room, she felt a chill that had nothing to do with the temperature control. She had not wanted to come here, but she had not thought she had a choice. After visiting the Hot Tea Rose Clinics suggested by her 'contacts', she realized she was not going to be able to keep it up. She could not claim it on her insurance without flagging her illegal condition so the cost involved was coming out of her account, especially since it could not be funded by the government. She had not known how much the regular check-ups would cost, but she knew now that she could not keep it up. Initially it had not been so bad, a check up once a month she could handle. Yet now she was beyond the three month mark and had been told that the check-ups would have to be more frequent, especially approaching the time of birth. She was an instructor; she could not afford this without help.

She dared not ask Carlton, even though they had been seeing a lot of each other since the Dash Clinic. He had been more than happy to accompany her on the scheduled check-ups, though he did express initial confusion at her not going to a Hospital. She was only partially honest when she told him she now preferred Clinics since it reminded her of how they met, and was delighted when he accepted that explanation. She wished she had asked him to come with her here, but as close as they were getting she still had been too afraid to tell him that she had gotten his child illegally. She was afraid of what his reaction would be. Would he turn her in? Would he be sympathetic? Would he even be as curious as she was why she had been denied? If only she could puzzle that out.

That, and the odd pain that she was experiencing. The Clinic doctors could find no reason for it, and it was not constant. So she just reasoned it had to do with the pregnancy. Still, at times it was so intense that she could not move and was using up her paid time off at work. This could not keep up without someone getting suspicious. Especially now that she was starting to show, well a little.

In a moment of weakness, she had gone into the Hospital to get a thorough exam with better technology.

Yet it was taking too long. They had drawn blood and taken her ID card, surely it did not take that long to find out if anything was wrong with her or her child. But what if something was wrong? What if her child was malformed?

The door opening interrupted her thoughts.

A nurse quickly crossed the room and gathered her clothes. "Get dressed."

"What?" she repeated blankly, automatically taking off the hospital gown and donning on her clothes.

"You were told **not** to go to a Hospital!" the woman hissed as she peeked out the door. "The doctor is calling you in as we speak. Your ID has been flagged and no Hospital or Clinic will give you sanctuary now, not to mention the Enforcers will be hunting you. We have to get you out of here… now!"

"Wait…" she hesitated as the woman led her down the hall. "They won't hurt me… will they?"

The nurse gave her a scathing look. "You disobeyed a Dictate, used falsified information to steal a child, and were dumb enough to go to a Hospital."

She paled with each word, remembering why she was going to the Hot Tea Rose Clinics to start with.

"You'll be lucky if they wait to terminate you."

"Terminate?" she squeaked.

"Yes, terminate," was the rejoiner. "Not aborted, as that is stopping something before it happens. Not erased, as what has been done cannot be undone. Terminated. You and your child will both be killed."

"B-but…"

The other woman shushed her and dragged her down the service elevators down to the parking lot. When the doors opened, she hesitated. The nurse looked at her expectantly.

"What about my baby?"

With impossible patience, the woman answered, "I am taking you to the Coterie. They will help you."

"The Rebel Underground?" she practically squeaked.

The woman narrowed her eyes. "Who do you think gave you the number to call when you were denied?"

She thought back to that day, sitting listlessly in the after-interview room and wondering how it went wrong. Someone had walked by and dropped a card in her lap. It had a number on it, and when she called she was asked just how badly she wanted to have a child.

The other snorted a strange and unladylike sound. "If you'd just waited until after the birth, everything would have been fine. Do you realize what kind of stress you're going to endure now? You are on the run."

A fugitive?!

"The facilities are not as advanced," the nurse was continuing, "but we will not hurt you or your child. We will provide shelter and security as best we can. You can be certain of one thing; they will certainly kill you if they get the chance."

"You can't know that."

There was a haunted expression to answer that. "I've seen it happen."

The thought gave her pause. She did not want to die, but going to the Coterie was a definite act of treason. Even if she was exaggerating about the punishment for disobeying a Dictate, doing this would seal her fate. Still, she could not risk her child's life on the assumption all would be forgiven if she turned herself in. "What if something goes wrong?"

The woman's face softened then, and stepped forward enough to place a hand on her shoulder. "Pregnancy is never a sure thing, something can always go wrong. You will not be alone." Her face hardened. "Then again, this can still be stopped. Do you wish to terminate the pregnancy?"

"No!" Her stomach plummeted at the suggestion as she grabbed her midsection protectively. She went through too much to get her child!

The nurse softened again. "What if the baby dies?" she asked pointedly. "What if you die? Not even a Hospital can prevent that."

She thought about it, and then felt the distinct fluttering inside her that announced the life inside her. It was a risk, a terrible one, but one she was willing to take. Besides, if the DP found her now they would surely terminate her. She wanted a fighting chance!

"Lead on," she said with more steadiness than she felt.

With no further discussion, the woman led her out into the parking lot. They took pains to keep along the walls or between the vehicles. She was not sure why until she remembered that The Eye was undoubtedly hooked into the security here. When her rescuer gestured to Riley to get in a car, she did not hesitate to obey. Her rescuer then shoved the car in reverse and sped out of the parking lot. "So much for that job," She muttered.

"I'm sorry."

She hugged herself in the passenger seat as the landscape around her faded to a blur.

What was going to happen to her and her baby?

* * *

Riley was tired and ready to have her child.

Six months on the run had been more than she bargained for. The nurse had been right; being a fugitive was incredibly frightening. Her former life was left behind: her job as a CP, her home, her friends, and Carlton. The new life she led with the Coterie, the group who had supplied her with her Breeder Pass, was filled with anxiety despite her new friends' attempts to ease the tension. She always had to worry if someone recognized her when she went anywhere, had to pay for things with prepaid credits provided by the Underground – which meant always being on a tight budget, and endured the care of the Hot Tea Rose Clinics while hoping that the information they gathered did not get back to the DP. She never recalled a time when she had so many concerns. It was unnerving to always be looking over her shoulder, being aware of where The Eye was so that she walked just right or made sure someone was in front of her to lessen the chances of being identified. Granted she was always with someone, but it only helped to lessen her fear not alleviate it.

Her fear would never go away, when she and her daughter were found they would kill them. Even after the birth, because she had been foolish enough to go to a Hospital. The Coterie was offering to transport her to another Demense, but they dare not do it until after the baby was born. It seemed it was farther reaching than she initially thought, having contacts, hubs, and operations within all of the nine main regions and the waystations in between. That was how they knew about her. The contact she had made to simply get a child directed her to them, and in turn they used their Underground operations to provide her the material and advice she needed. It would have ended there, had she just listened to them.

It was impressive, how prepared these people were. They were not the disorganized teams talked about by the media and DPs. Everyone cared for each other and shared what they could, but work was required. Everyone had a skill, no matter what their age. The only ones given any leeway were the children, who were allowed to play but were also trained for when they reached adulthood. However, just like anywhere else, the people here practiced sterilization, but not necessarily for the same reason as above. Aside from other reasons, it gave them the pass they needed to infiltrate Hospitals to get Reversals. Other than always moving with the awareness of The Eye watching, there were many aspects about the people which were similar to those she used to know. What she could not get accustomed to was the atmosphere.

There was a kind of hyper-vigilance that kept her jumpy, and she was finally able to identify what it was about the Clinics that bothered her. She looked around as she thought about that, as she was now sitting in one of the sympathetic outfits. On the surface, they looked the same as a Hospital; it was the patients and clerks who bothered her. The patients either had an attitude of aggression, desperation, or borderline defeat about them; and the clerks were often annoyed, exhausted, or close to apathetic. It was not overtly obvious, of course. She was sure it was due to her condition and her being oversensitive to things lately that brought these things to light.

"RM3802?" the speaker called out.

Her escort stood and helped her to her feet. As usual, a sharp pain accompanied to the movement. The doctors still had not been able to tell her why that kept happening.

She felt warmth spread down her leg.

Looking down, she was alarmed to see her slacks darkening.

"Medic!" her companion cried out as he took a firm hold of her arm and encouraged her to sit back down.

Nurses came running out and immediately began tending to her. They asked her a succession of questions: was she light-headed, when was her due date, had she been experiencing any pain, blah blah blah. Everything they already knew if they had her file, which was supposed to be carried by collaborators between clinics. She tried to answer as best she could, but she was feeling strange.

"She is bleeding heavily," one of the nurses was saying. "We have to get her to a Hospital."

At the word, she reached out and gripped her guard's arm firmly. Was he going to risk it?

He looked at her, his eyes full of concern, and then touched her hand sympathetically. He moved away as the nurses did their best to make her comfortable. She could see him using his transmitter, and began to feel hope. It was not long before the paramedics arrived. As they were placing her on the gurney, he approached again.

"You the partner?" one of the men asked as they strapped her to the wheeled bed.

"Yes," he lied, sounding breathless.

"Where to?"

"Sece."

They paused to look at him oddly. "That is not the closest Hospital."

"It's the one covered by her insurance," he replied, looking a bit dazed.

Accepting that, they resumed their task and rolled her out of the Clinic. Since he had said he was her partner, he was allowed to ride with her. He held her hand, maintaining the act of being scared.

"It'll be alright," he assured her. "I called ahead and they know to expect us."

That did a lot to relieve her fright. If the Coterie knew what was happening, and they had people in the Hospital they were going to, there was a chance she and the child would leave alive. Hope kept her conscious. As she felt the vehicle navigate traffic, her mind focused on her child again.

Why would the Demense Prepotence kill her and her child? Sure she had disobeyed a Dictate by obtaining the child illegally, but the child hadn't done anything wrong. Maybe she had been foolhardy to think that once she was pregnant they would not hurt the child. If they had just allowed her to be inseminated in the beginning, she would not have taken such drastic steps. Thinking about that brought to mind her interview again. Once again, she puzzled over why her application had been denied. She had the proper training to keep a child instead of turning it over to the CP's, and everything else was optimal. It had been when the screening reached the personal medical that the interviews got strange.

The fifth interview established her sexual health. Like anyone else, she had no serious partner (at the time, it might have been different had she been allowed to keep in touch with the baby's seed father), and she was sure to report to a Clinic once a month. She was clean and thus passed.

The sixth interview examined her genetic background, which apparently had been acceptable because she had been moved forward. Only that took longer than the previous test, and she had not been told the results. Why not? Not to mention she always had the impression that she barely passed it.

It was the seventh interview that she failed, the one that took a closer look at her medical history. The Hospital had taken current physical, blood, and genetic information. She had stayed there for ten days, waiting for them to tell her something – anything. Finally, she was told that she was unfit to be a Breeder. Which made no sense, after centuries of selective breeding one would think that most if not all genetic damage had been addressed.

Wait… a thought occurred to her as the ambulance arrived at the Hospital.

What if the problem was not that her child would be damaged in some way? What if the problem was her? What if there was something wrong with her?

A lance of pain and more warmth between her legs gave credence to that thought.

'*Oh no*,' her heart raced as panic took the place of fear. '*Please no, let me have my baby. Let me hold her… if just once!*'

They rolled her inside the Emergency Entrance and to the preparatory rooms. As she was raced along, she was encouraged to see the Hot Tea Rose pins on several of the nurses' uniforms. She reached out blindly, the pain getting worse and her focus blurring –

though whether from blood loss or her tears she could not say. A hand grabbed hers.

"Save my baby," she cried.

"You'll be fine," someone answered.

"No!" she was insistent. "In my ID pack, there is a card… The seed-father… Carlton… If I do not make it, please contact him."

There was a pause and then, "Ok."

"Promise me!"

A new blurry figure came up and took her other hand. It was her guard. "I promise."

Somewhat assured, she surrendered to fate. There was no guarantee he would want anything to do with the child, but she could think of no one else. She did not even know who her own seed-parents were, and now she regretted never finding out.

In the birthing room, there was a mixture of collaborators among the others. She had been granted time, as since this was an emergency there would be little background check until after. Not to mention that the nurses who had been forewarned were able to provide the necessary medical information the Hospital would need for this procedure. Thankfully the main doctor was also sympathetic, and coached her through the process. It was excruciating, even after they gave her anesthetic. She could not be given too much, in case it affected the child. However, determined to at least see her child she endured. With every push, she felt herself getting weaker, despite the fluids being fed into her.

Finally, the wail of a child awarded her effort.

With a sigh/groan of relief, Riley fell back onto the bed. She had never felt so weak. She could see the blur that was her child, being held up for her. She reached out as much as she could.

"Please... let me... hold..."

Without hesitation the doctor handed over the baby. "A girl." The nurse said.

Holding the small body in her arms, she could hardly believe her dream was finally here.

"Have you selected a name?"

She nodded. "Tessa," and leaned down to kiss the warm forehead. "I love you," she whispered.

The tiny eyes opening to look at her were the last things she saw as she blacked out.

* * *

The baby was held by Riley Mason's guard held while they tried to revive her. He backed away to give the nurses a chance to help. They worked on her, but she never regained consciousness. As if on cue, the baby began to cry.

A nurse came forward to claim her and take her to be examined and fed. He complied, see it was an ally and knowing the child would be cared for in private. Right now he had to be sure the body was removed before an official examination could be done. The less evidence of Tessa's beginnings that there were the better chance she had of living outside the Coterie. No one was forced into that life, it was mainly a last resort to those who thought they had no other choice but who did not want to die.

His business done, he went to the private nursery to check on the newborn. One of his cohorts was there, feeding her.

"The mother should never have gotten herself pregnant," she was saying. "She'd be alive now."

"The DP never explains its decisions, you know that." he reminded her firmly.

"Still, if she'd known she might not have gotten pregnant."

Looking at the small form, he answered, "Don't be so sure. She was told of the risks, and that this could've happened - she chose the child. Anyway, she should have the freedom to choose."

The woman's lips thinned, but she nodded. The DP did not even allow that.

The Hospital would be told the baby was a SIDS case, with autopsy reports to support the claim. Then the baby would be taken to the Coterie nursery where she would be cared for until it was certain she was strong enough to survive. After which, the seed-father would be contacted. It was important that the mother's wishes be honored. It was the least that could be done.

After all, she had risked death to achieve her dream of having a child.

THE JOB HUNTER

BY SHAUN AVERY

The guy outside the Job Place is playing Russian Roulette with a rusty old gun, running it in and out of his mouth and grinning gap-toothed grins with every squeeze of the trigger.

From the look of him, it's the only thing that's passed his lips for a while.

I look down on him.

Though not the way I once did.

The bulge at the ankle of his trousers tells me all I need to know.

He notices my gaze and looks up at me and says, 'three months today?'

I nod.

Then head inside the place that I've come to loathe so much.

***

They log me in at reception and I make the same old fruitless search on the Job Machines they keep near the front.

I'll apply for every vacancy I see, and I suppose there's nothing new about that. But there'll be a little more urgency involved by the time I leave here today. That's only natural, when it's your life that's on the line.

My Personal Employment Advisor, a guy called Brian, seems to recognise this fact, and is more sensitive than usual as he ushers me into the usual seat facing him. This surprises me; I hadn't considered him capable of emotion, much less empathy.

'Big day today,' he says. 'But nothing to worry about. I'm sure we'll have you up and working within weeks.'

He said that years ago.

When I first came here.

As he speaks, the security guys come towards me.

The ones with the specialist training.

The rest of the Job Place goes quiet, watching, as they strap the tag to my ankle. As they set the timer running, as they hook up the needle, as they fill the vial connected to the tag with a painless but fatal poison, one that will be released into my bloodstream at the end of a three-month period if I am not employed by then.

The clock is ticking on my existence.

Time to get out there and find work.

***

Funny thing is . . .

I supported the scheme when they first brought it out.

'They' being the newly elected Government Earth, fresh into power and keen to make their mark on things. Which they did first of all by attempting to tackle the country's crippling unemployment problem.

Well, *they* called it a problem . . . but to most of the people claiming Job Hunt Allowance, their work-free status was anything *but* a problem. I saw them, hanging out on the street and getting drunk without a care in the world, and like the rest of the luckily employed I resented the taxes that I was paying to keep them in booze.

But life moves on.

Things change.

People become unemployed.

And I was one of them.

So yeah, it's pretty easy to support a scheme that will kill people when you're exempt from the death list.

Not so easy when there's a poison injection strapped to *your* leg.

Funny, that.

***

The guy with the gun is gone when I emerge from the Job Place. But I don't need to see him to know I will *never* turn out like him. I won't give up.

But my housemate, Terry, is less optimistic.

'You know the percentage of long-term unemployed that go on to find work?' he asks me. Then brings up the data he's referring to on the computer before him.

I stare into my box of personal belongings as he speaks.

Stare at the wedding ring I once wore.

Thinking, a job's not *all* you lose, when you lose a job.

'Tell me,' I say. 'Cheer me up.'

'It's a low one.'

'I thought it might be, Terry.'

'Twenty five per cent.'

'That's a quarter.' I shrug. 'That's not so bad.'

What *is* bad is our living together in the first place. But that wasn't through choice, believe me. After Rhonda left, after all the arguments which culminated in her throwing her ring into my face, I tried to hang onto the house in which we'd lived together. But that was about as pointless as trying to hang onto the memories we'd shared. So I'd gone looking for a place to rent, thinking I'd go it alone, but new government legislation said that I *had* to share with another Job Hunter, the thinking behind that being you would motivate each other into work.

'Can I see it?'

I look up at him. 'See what?'

He points at me.

More specifically, at the tag around my ankle.

I already want to be rid of the damn thing. But, of course, it's all monitored via a Job Place computer system. The moment it stops detecting skin next to it, an alarm goes off. Worst of all, I'll miss out on that week's benefit. And how am I going to find a job with no money to go looking?

'How does it feel?' Terry asks.

This is such a ridiculous question that for a few seconds I'm tempted to take on a new, self-given role: that of murderer. But it's hard to stay mad at Terry. I'm too busy being mad at myself for ending up in this situation.

'You'll find out for yourself soon enough,' I say, and leave him to stew on that one.

***

Next time I see Brian, he has a black eye.

Not all Job Hunters are as placid as I am.

'Trouble, Brian?' I ask.

'Never mind that,' he says, and his irritated tone makes me smile. 'How's the Job Hunt going?'

'Fine,' I tell him, and for once I'm not lying.

See, I have an interview tomorrow.

It's a job in Customer Services, and I know I have the experience for it. But I also know, because Terry told me, that according to government statistics an average of fifty people show up for a single vacancy nowadays.

Still, I pass this news on to Brian. And then I decide to push my luck by asking for a clothing allowance.

Remarkably, he agrees.

I must have caught him on a good day. Either that, or the punch that provided his black eye has done something to his mind.

He comes back with a voucher – they stopped handing out money to people when they realised just how much of it ended up being sprayed against alley walls – and tells me all the clothing stores in which I can use it. Then, just to prove that the punch didn't do *too* much damage, he adds, 'and don't forget to bring back the receipts!'

I probably *will* forget, just to get him in trouble.

Such is the complicated relationship between advisor and claimant.

***

I hit the clothing stores, and it's been so long since I've had extra cash, even in the form of a paper voucher, that I'm momentarily overwhelmed by choice. Of course, I *don't* have a choice, not really; this voucher is to get nice clothes for an interview, not to splash out on one of those nice Hawaiian shirts they have in the window. Still, it's nice to look.

After much perusal, I eventually pick out a nice suit.

Making sure, of course, that the trouser leg fits around the ticking time bomb on my ankle.

They considered using actual bombs, by the way, instead of poison. But they thought there might be too much collateral damage – i.e. bad publicity – if a particularly vindictive Job Hunter with only seconds remaining decided to go boom-boom in public.

Maybe they were right.

Would *I* choose to go out that way?

But I don't want to think about that. So instead I pay for my suit, and I flirt with the woman behind the counter, and it's going pretty well until I have to hand over the voucher. That's when she sees the Job Place stamp, and she's suddenly all business again.

One more reason to get a job, I think. I can't wait to be the one doing the sneering, not the one being sneered at.

So I go home without the girl's number but at least I have a nice suit. Though that's little comfort when I realise that Terry is planning on killing himself.

***

And he's not alone.

Which surprises me.

I didn't realise he had friends.

But here they are, in our house, a bunch of sad-eyed losers, and you don't need the worthless degree I've got to suss out that they're the long-term unemployed. Although, I realise as they look to my tag and gasp in awe, they're not quite long-term *enough*.

Their reaction to my imminent death gives this whole scene a borderline surrealism. But it doesn't quite veer off into *actual* madness until Terry walks into the room with a balaclava over his head.

'What's going on?' I ask. Not, I'm sure you agree, an unreasonable question.

'Jack!' he says. 'Good to see you. Guess what?'

These two words are normally a precursor to a torrent of government data. Today, though, I sense something even worse coming down the chute.

I'm right.

'We're planning,' he says, 'on robbing the Job Place.'

I hope I've misheard him. 'What?'

Turns out, he goes on to tell me, that he's been in contact with this group for a while. 'This group,' of course, being the people currently standing with us in this house. He's been talking to them online, because that's how he talks to *everyone* other than me, and they've all decided that they can't take the Job Hunt anymore, and they also can't wait the time it takes to get their tags. So they're going to break into the Job Place and take the poison for themselves.

I listen to all of this patiently.

Rationally.

And then, and only then, do I drag Terry into the next room.

A room that, before I'd left the house earlier, you would have called 'the kitchen.' Now, though, I'm not sure *what* you'd call it. See, Terry has been busy with his statistics again, and it seems he has hooked the printer up to the machine, too. Because there are print-outs of Government Earth statistics covering every inch of each wall.

Looking up at them, seeming to take strength from them, he says, 'you know the odds against us ever working again?'

'A little bit more than *you* do, sunshine,' I reply, and bump my tag against his leg.

He spreads his arms wide. 'So what's the point, Jack?' Then his tone turns petulant as he adds, 'I mean, it's okay for you – you already *have* your tag.'

'What,' I snarl, 'you think I want this? You think I want this thing on me?'

He looks down at the tag and there's so much lust in his eyes, lust coupled with a complete lack of hope, that I know he *would* swap places with me.

In a heartbeat.

And, God help me, I'd let him.

But I can't.

So he's doing the next best thing.

'They must keep a supply of the poison on-site,' he says. 'We're going to take it. And then *take* it.'

I make one last attempt, saying, 'think they'll just keep it out, where anyone can get it?'

'No,' he says. 'It'll be locked away in a safe. But I've found a guy that's good with safes.'

Then he does something he's never done before.

He holds out his hand to me.

Requesting a farewell shake.

And I wish I had the words to make him hold on, to make him believe that brighter days, *working* days, are just around the corner. The words that Rhonda had once said, then shouted, to me. But his ears would be as deaf now as mine were then.

So all I can do is take his hand.

And watch him walk out of my life.

***

With an interview tomorrow I probably shouldn't do it but what the hell.

I get drunk.

Terry will either be stupid enough to kill himself on the Job Place premises or wise enough to do it someplace else, but his disappearance will eventually be noticed. Maybe not until he misses his appointment with his advisor, but it will be noticed all the same.

What'll that mean for me?

And will it stop me getting a job?

Funny, how quickly that question becomes the only thing that matters. It was for me, even *before* the tag. I guess Rhonda sensed that. She always knew she wasn't as important to me as getting a payslip for a hard day's work. No wonder she left me.

And here we go with the self-loathing, right?

Better take another drink.

I remember the Head of Government Earth, the day they'd brought in the Unemployment Death Act. We'd all cheered at that, Bill, Chester, Arnold and me. My friends. The guys I'd worked with. Drinking then, too, down the pub, and laughing at the lousy jobless bum counting out his Job Hunt Allowance pennies to pay for the cheapest drink on the menu at the bar. We'd laughed and I'd said, 'he'd be better off dead,' and you know something?

I'd believed it.

That was how much work meant to me back then.

It still does.

It means everything.

And Bill, Chester and Arnold?

Well, they're not my friends anymore.

Why?

Answer's easy.

They didn't lose their jobs when I did.

Now I'm 'friends' with people like Terry. Terry who should be poisoning himself right about now. Terry who gave up . . .

I won't be like him. Won't be like the guy playing with the gun outside the Job Place. Won't be a quitter.

Ever.

But I'm fighting off a hangover as I head for the interview.

***

For once, Terry's stupid statistics were right.

'Fifty applicants for a single vacancy,' he'd said.

Looks about right.

But I'm not the last to arrive, thankfully, and I take a seat in a huge room with the rest of the would-be workers to await the start of proceedings.

We all sit in silence, all sizing each other up. Most of us trying to suss out who the competition is, but I'm doing something a bit more personal.

I'm looking for the ones that are tagged.

There are a few of us, and the rest of the applicants try to keep a distance from us, as if what we have is contagious.

Maybe it is.

I lock eyes with another of the tagged.

He nods slightly towards me.

Then the interviewers come out.

***

There's a bunch of them, three guys and a woman, but there's a clear pecking order between them, and it's the oldest of the guys that says, 'welcome to the interview. My name is Donald.'

You can tell from his demeanour that no one ever shortens it to 'Don.'

'This is a role working with the public,' the woman chips in, 'so anyone that we feel is unsuitable for that role, we will tap on the shoulder and they will have to leave the interview.'

Jesus. Something else to fear. The dreaded tap.

But I'm determined to get this job and as they stand us all in a semi-circle and then bring out a large beach ball I try to calm myself.

'I'm going to throw this ball to one of you,' Donald announces, 'and when you catch it I want you to tell everyone your name, plus one interesting fact about yourself. Then throw it to someone else in the circle and they do the same. And so on, until we're all introduced.'

This is more panic-inducing than it sounds. I'm not sure I can remember one interesting fact about myself. How can you be interesting when you haven't got a job?

Luckily, though, it's not me that gets the ball first.

It's the tagged guy.

The one that nodded at me before.

'My name is James,' he says. 'And if I don't get this job, someone might die.'

The room goes silent.

No one knows quite what to say.

'And that someone is . . .'

Again, he pauses.

Then grins.

And shows his tag.

'Me.'

Everyone laughs then, but the sound has nothing to do with humour. It's more the laughter you get when a tense moment has passed.

But I'm still irritated.

Jimmy-Boy just stole from me the one interesting fact I have to give.

***

'No,' I say, standing behind the counter. 'We don't serve giraffes here.'

Before you assume I've lost the plot, let me explain.

We're doing a 'roleplay' here where you have to show both good and bad customer service to the rest of the group, and there are five words you have to use as part of it. One of them is 'giraffe.' Hence me barring a giraffe, played by another applicant called Janet, from my shop.

We put our roleplay together in four separate groups, each one watched by a different interviewer. We got Donald, the big man himself, so I went out of my way to show how vocal I was, how passionate. With the whole giraffe thing, I think I did pretty good.

But one of the other words you had to use was 'helicopter,' and James, the tagged guy, pretends to *be* a helicopter, spinning across the room, making whirring noises, actually being, I hate to admit it, pretty damn entertaining. And I laugh along with everyone else, but inside I'm praying for his tag to malfunction and poison him now.

Because he's the competition.

I see that now.

Soon they whittle us down to just ten and we await the final outcome. But since there are only five roles to fill, they tell us they'll need another day or two to decide.

They'll be in touch.

James and I are the only tagged left, and I watch him warily as he comes towards me.

'How much longer you got left?' he asks.

'More than "another day or two" – so don't get your hopes up.'

He laughs at that.

And for some reason, I'm sure I can still hear him laughing

behind me as I head on home.

Where I find the police waiting for me.

***

Seems that Terry pulled it off – him and the rest of his hopeless brigade.

I'm scared to see the law at my house, but they're immediately at pains to stress they don't suspect me of anything – I mean, why would they? No, this is all just routine stuff. 'What was the state of his mind, did he leave a note,' that kind of thing.

Plus they take his computer.

I'm glad to see the damn thing go.

But I'm also wondering what will happen to me.

If I get to keep this place, if they'll move someone else. If I'll get that damn job, or if James or someone else will beat me to it.

The police finally leave, and I step out of my suit and then try to relax with a shower – keeping, of course, my tag out of the water at all times. But the interview I've just attended runs through my head, and I find myself constantly picking apart everything I did, wondering if I've done enough to make me shine above everyone else.

I'll find out soon enough, I guess.

I step out of the shower and into a gown and the first sign that something is wrong comes when I feel the draft against the bare skin of my legs.

A draft that is coming in through the open door.

The open door that I just closed, when the last of the police had left.

I look around myself nervously.

'Terry?' I say.

That's a stupid thing to say, of course. But it's the first thing that springs to mind.

Then:

'Rhonda?'

That's probably even stupider.

I cross to the door and look outside.

No one.

Nothing.

I close the door gently.

Head back into the kitchen.

And hear the soft footsteps of someone behind me.

Then I turn and see James.

And the knife in his hands.

***

'Followed you home,' he says. 'Had to wait for the police to leave.'

The entertaining guy, the guy that made us all laugh back at the interview, seems nowhere in sight. Instead, his voice is dulled, robotic, and his eyes are dark yet blank.

'James,' I say. 'What are you doing?'

'Making sure,' he says, 'that it's *me* they pick.'

'You're crazy, man,' I tell him. 'It's just a job.'

'Not when you're tagged,' he replies. 'Then it's your life.'

I could run.

But I don't want to turn my back on him.

Or that knife.

So I begin to circle the kitchen counter.

Walking backwards.

He follows.

'So, what?' I say. 'You're going to take mine?'

He cocks his head, looks at me strangely. 'No,' he replies. 'I'm just going to take care of the competition.'

He comes closer.

I move backwards again.

'There were eight others, James.' We're still circling the table, and the door is within reach, but I can't chance it yet, I still have to keep moving. 'You going to kill them all, too?'

'It'll be you or me,' he says. 'We have the most to lose.'

A sudden grin splits across his face.

'And when they can't get hold of you . . . when you're lying in a pool of blood and it's *whoops* sorry you can't get to the phone . . .'

He looks at me.

'It'll just be me.'

That's when he lunges.

And my first instinct is to turn and run, but I realise that this move is suicidal, is just as much about giving up as Terry's attack on the Job Place was. So I face James head on, and one hand seizes the wrist that bears the knife and the other forms into a fist and drives itself into his gut, and there are years of anger and frustration in that punch and it feels *good*.

His eyes still look dead, but some small spark of life must be driving him on, because he's still striking down with that knife, trying to lay me open.

'James,' I try again. 'Stop this. It's just a job, man!'

But the words seem to mean even less than they did before.

To both of us.

And I know there's only one way this can end.

I drive a knee into his groin.

Watch him sink to his knees.

Then take the knife from his hand.

I'm breathing fast.

But not just from exertion.

He looks up at me from the floor.

'It's . . . just a job?' he offers questioningly. Hopefully.

I smile at him.

Then I reach down and take care of the competition.

***

There's a knock at my door the next morning.

I haven't taken care of James yet, but you can't see him from the doorway so it's fine.

I open up.

And see standing there . . .

Brian.

Both eyes blackened now, and one arm in a cast.

Though he still looks better than James does at the moment.

'I miss an appointment?' I ask. 'You come to stop my money?'

He doesn't say anything.

That's when I know.

They've got me.

Somehow the tag let the Job Place know that James is dead, and someone saw him coming here and . . .

But then Brian amazes me by doing something.

He laughs.

And I think, *Brian can* laugh?

Wonders will never cease.

'No, no,' he says. 'Just come to see how the interview went.'

'Pretty good,' I say. Then, improvising, add, 'but it dragged on until the wee hours.' There's an understatement and a half. 'Can I tell you about it next time I'm in?'

Brian looks up at the rays of a new day dawning and says, 'Jack, I truly believe I won't be seeing you again. I think this job interview's the last one you'll ever have to go to.'

I glance back at the dead body in my kitchen.

And reflect that my advisor might be right.

THE ULTIMATE SALE

BY DEEDEE DAVIES

I'm an Offliner, and I'm damn proud of it.

Okay, so I don't get the perks; the life of ease and effortless fulfilment, the great prize of 'self-actualisation' bestowed on those who chose to live the dream. I have to get by with the burdens of miserable weather, hard graft, and whatever food I choose to incinerate on my 2-ring Calor-gas stove. But the key word is 'choice'. I made mine a good thirty years ago, and rheumatism and cataracts notwithstanding, I wouldn't change it for the world.

I never watched much TV - I never saw the need to delve into the endless repeats, the cheap low-brow laughs they churned out in a stream of gaudy absurdity that pandered to people's vanity and self-obsession. The 'Net, though, that was a different matter. In times of boredom, I'd spend most of my spare time idly surfing sites that interested me - and plenty that didn't. I even had a whole circle of friends that I communicated with solely through that electronic interface. If I were more of an existentialist (or paranoid), I'd wonder if any of them really existed, or whether they were purposely-generated pieces of software, tailored to the words I typed into search engines.

One night, about thirty years back, I surrendered to the lure of mindless entertainment: those few cheap laughs were looking like my idea of heaven after the day I'd had. I managed to sit through two hours of programming, most of which was so shredded by the adverts that I began to wonder whether I was following the story of a dysfunctional bunch of animated 'toons, or the ongoing saga of Ludo Pizza. I turned off the TV and tried to remember why I'd subscribed in the first place.

Advertising.

In some small, indirect way, it was controlling my choices. I panicked, picked up the phone (an all-too-rare occasion, even then) and cancelled my subscription. At least, I tried: the sales rep on the other end of the 'phone was so persuasive that I kept the damn thing. From then on, I kept the set unplugged as much as possible, but when my resolve failed, and I fell to watching a few minutes of broken storyline from behind my trusty cushion, my paranoia grew. Where was the control, the censorship of these adverts? Why was no-one stopping these insidious little invasions into the private life of every individual with access to cable TV or the Internet? By and by, a horrible realisation dawned. I saw the true reason for it, and now that my mind was attuned, I saw the evidence for it too.

We were being reduced to a nation of sedentary slugs.

Everything in the media was aimed at ensuring we had to leave the house as little as possible. Provided you lived in the right areas, you could get food delivered to your doorstep, videos hand-delivered or downloaded online, and catalogue shopping for clothes and home goods was already a long-standing tradition. You didn't even need to go to the bank to get money out to pay!

In the interest of 'Equal Opportunity', businesspeople were allowed to work from home, their meetings now conducted via an entirely virtual network. Of course, from there, things just got progressively worse. The reality game show mingled with the new 'stay-at-home' lifestyle with disastrous results: why would you want to go abroad when you could watch the beautiful people do it on TV?

People were snared, fished in, hook, line and sinker. There was no escape: the advertising companies had created a false dependency on the Internet, then inundated people with advertisements in a flickering kaleidoscope of 'must-haves' and 'can't-do-withouts'. Slowly but surely, the insidious lethargy wormed its way into the lifestyles of the shiftless and the indolent, bringing a relaxed and euphoric calm that had not been seen since the psychedelic sixties. Some people no longer needed to go outside. The Ad magnates preyed on the impressionable, the bone idle, the greedy; people who would buy anything if it was on sale - even agoraphobia.

Of course, not everyone was susceptible. There were those of us too stubborn, too scared to be seduced by them. We are now by default the workers, and we spend our lives grafting to enhance and maintain the luxury of the Onliners.

There were a lot of stories when it was all new, a multitude of theories - each more improbable than the last - as to who or what had brought about this split in society. I can say now with definite certainty that it was the Adbots: virtual entities who existed in cyberspace, created inadvertently by a dotcom who needed roving, evolution-capable robots to boost their sales. They took their programming to heart, extrapolated it to the nth degree and reached self-awareness - in no small part due to a joke motto about a captive audience that had ended up in their core code: “The less they move, the more they buy.”

Whoever coined the phrase had no idea what he or she had unleashed. By 2025, all those who could afford it (any many who could not) had their own BOI (Bionic Online Interface), which was wired to the ‘Net. By 2040, everyone had bought Virtual Reality stimulator kits that enabled them to experience an infinite variety of physical sensations without actually leaving their plumbed-in chair-beds. By 2050 the market for physical objects - like clothing, musical instruments and cars - had folded. Heavy manufacturing was replaced by the production of newer and more efficient ‘Net interface equipment, protein supplements in a million unlikely flavours, and heavy duty blinds. The sun burned their skin through the windows, you see.

And work? Oh, work still exists. It’s part of the human psyche, much as we’d like to deny it. We need work to give us purpose, and so, with the advent of the Cerebral Interface came the Thought Exchange. Before long, people were once again working together, using their acquired talents to create new music and films in virtu-space alone, using a collaboration of minds that was unprecedented. Meanwhile, virtual businesses flourished, selling products that never existed to people who would never physically hold them. Holidays were taken in cyberspace on Saturn’s beaches, or at Hogwart’s, or Hobbiton, where tourists could spend their time soaking up the atmosphere, or challenging nightmare enemies through terrifying - if safe - landscapes.

But if there is one adage that holds true, whether in cyberspace or the real world, it is that things change. Finally, after a good run of thirty golden years for the advertising industry, they ran out of new things to sell. I saw the physical advert for it, on one of the few billboards they still maintain in the vain hopes that some more of us Offliners will one day be drawn in by their promises.

Not likely!

What they're selling now is the ultimate experience, something that has been lost or ignored by the Onliners for many years. It is a rather unusual product, as apparently it comes with such high risk that only those in their prime, with suitable liability insurance, will be able to obtain it. To my old eyes, it's the ultimate irony, the proof that the world really does turn full circle.

"Sign up now for the ultimate experience - Offline roving adventure!

Try out our NEW free-form Exterior Holidaying Packages. Savour the scent of Fresh Air; walk in the City streets; buy a solid, softcover magazine from an authentic newsstand.

Unique Opportunity - £20,000.00 per 24-hour adventure.

Please note: This is a challenging product, and is not recommended for anyone who has been online for more than 10 consecutive years.

Health Warning - requires disconnection from the 'Net."

THE BIRD BELOW GROUND

BY S.C. LANGGLE

Subland, Year 220 P.E. (Post Explosionum)

Liam knew he should have given the photograph to his mother the moment he found it. Photos were rare in Subland, and his mother could sell it to the Preservation Room for a good price, or the black market for a better one. They needed the money—Liam couldn't deny that when he heard his baby sister Tessa wailing, even though she'd been given the largest portion of the *tipiog* porridge, or when he felt the twinge of empty space in his own belly. And his mother had barely taken a single bite for herself all day. How long had it been since they'd had one of Subland's delicacies, the rare *narancia* fruits or *karoton* roots, which danced on your tongue and filled your stomach with warmth the way *tipiog* never could? The money from this photo could buy an entire bushel of *karotons*, and some new clothes and blankets besides. They didn't *need* the extra food—a few bites of *tipiog*, along with one of the huge vitamin pills distributed for free by the Leaders, would fulfill all their nutritional requirements for the day.

But it was hard to trick a stomach that longed for grains and proteins to digest, a tongue that craved new flavors and textures. Sometimes, Liam had decided, you could have everything you *needed*—and still want more.

Like the photograph. Liam didn't need it—not the way Tessa would need an entire new wardrobe in a few months, if she kept growing the way she was—but in the few days he'd kept it hidden in his pocket, it had seemed to become a part of him, and now he couldn't imagine going on without it. Whenever he was alone, he would slip it out and look at it: the picture of a yellow canary, wings outstretched, flying against a blindingly blue sky. The colors alone, so different from the dull grays and browns of Subland, were enough to entrance him for days. And the wings... Liam had seen pictures of birds before in school, had learned how they once flew through that blue, blue sky in Aboveland, somewhere far past the dark rocky ceiling of Subland. But despite the photographs, despite the written records of long-dead Abovelanders, the existence of birds had always seemed more myth than reality, too miraculous and impossible to believe—as impossible as the sky itself.

Now, though, since he'd spied that sparkle of yellow and blue hiding between two rocks in the corner of the schoolyard—since he'd picked up the paper, so thin and fragile it threatened to dissolve into dust, and unfolded it to discover the strange creature within—it seemed more real. Not just a dream, but a possibility. Almost like he could reach into the paper, into that blue blue sky, and stroke the outstretched feathers. Would they feel smooth and cold, he wondered, like the rocks that littered so much of Subland's surface? Would they be warm and fleshy, like Tessa's tiny fingers when they clutched his hand? Or would the wings be made of an entirely new material, something Liam couldn't even imagine? The possibilities kept him occupied for hours.

For once, too, Liam was actually glad he didn't fit in with the other middle school students, the crowd of boys and girls who spoke so loudly and quickly their words sounded to Liam like a foreign language. If Liam had spent his school break playing kickball with the boys, or watching the girls jump rope, he never would have found the photo. If anyone had come to talk to him in his deserted corner, had even dared to approach him, he might have been forced to share his discovery. So what if the girls said Liam had a weird look on his face, like he was staring at something that wasn't there? So what if the boys said he asked too many questions in class, and odd ones besides? Liam had a secret, a miraculous secret, and none of them could touch it.

There was writing below the photograph, too, and while some of it was illegible, marred by a water stain, Liam could make out enough to guess the page had come from a textbook or an informational guide of some kind. "Canary, or *Serinus canaria*," it read, "a small passerine bird of the genus *Serinus* in the finch family." Imagine that—there had once been whole families, even genuses (whatever that was) of birds in the world Aboveland. Were they all so colorful, so bold and so bright? Liam could barely believe it, yet he couldn't stop trying to picture it—a place and time where color existed in excess, in motion, spinning and whirling in an endless expanse of space above his head.

At the bottom of the page, a larger piece of writing had escaped the stain, but Liam wanted to wait till he had a good chunk of time to himself to read it. Between school, homework, and helping his mother cook the *tipiog,* feed Tessa and clean her and play with her and sing her to sleep, his chance didn't come for nearly a week. Even when his opportunity came, he had to fight the sleep bearing down on his eyelids—the night before, Tessa had fussed till the early hours of morning again, and their house was too small to escape her cries—as he huddled under his covers with his flashlight. Tessa and his mother had fallen asleep together in the rocking chair a half hour ago, and Liam had covered them with the thickest blanket and turned out the weak overhead light. Now he aimed the even weaker beam of the flashlight on the photograph, illuminating the canary. That thin, anemic electric light was the only thing you could possibly call "yellow" in Subland, but it certainly didn't compare to the canary. People told stories about the sun that had hung in the blue sky in Aboveland, a brilliant ball of orange and yellow fire that must have outshone even the canary's feathers, that had illuminated and warmed the entire world. *Fire*—that was another thing that might be yellow. But like birds, Liam had seen fire only in ancient photographs. He didn't know how it was created or what it was made of; he knew only that it was very dangerous, and thus it was forbidden in Subland. Better to be a bit cold than to risk more destruction.

Now, moving the electric beam from the canary to the words below, Liam read:

Canaries were famously used by miners as a sort of life insurance policy…

Liam had only a vague idea of what a "miner" was, from some Aboveland history book he'd read: they were Abovelanders who'd dug tunnels into the ground, long before Subland existed. Why, Liam couldn't remember. For now, he read on:

Carried below ground in cages, the birds' highly sensitive metabolism detected methane and carbon monoxide gas traces that signaled potential explosions, poisoned air or both. As long as the air remained high in oxygen, the canaries would chirp and sing in their cages—

Sing? The birds sang too? Liam didn't remember learning about that in school. They'd learned about other animals that made noise—dogs, which had once been human companions and made a rough sound called "barking," and wolves, who had let out a high wailing like the sirens that sometimes rang through Subland, signaling an emergency. But *singing*—Liam had thought that talent belonged to humans alone. To possess such bright colors, and the ability to make music as well… It seemed almost too much. The words continued:

But if carbon monoxide levels grew too high, the canaries would have trouble breathing. Once the canaries were no longer singing, miners would know the gas levels were rising, and they needed to return to the surface. As the gas levels increased, the canaries would display noticeable signs of distress, swaying on their perches and falling, and many would even die.

At the last word, Liam felt something knot up in his throat, like a lump of undercooked *tipiog. Die?* They would take the canaries underground to *die*? If there were just one canary in Subland, one bright yellow, winged, singing creature, Liam imagined the entire community would band together to protect it. But those Abovelanders…they had something so extraordinary before them, in their very hands, and what did they do? They led the creature to its death.

Liam tried in vain to read on, but it was useless—all the other words on the page were stained beyond recognition. Finally he gave up, clicked off the flashlight, and fell into darkness, still holding the photograph in one hand.

Liam was trapped. Ahead and to both sides of him were craggy rock walls, so close he couldn't extend his arms. When he turned around, tried to move back the way he'd come, he saw a cloud of swirling dark smoke moving toward him. He tried to breathe in, and gritty particles flew into his mouth, choking and burning him. Far away, he heard a low, keening cry, like the sound he imagined a bird might make in distress…

Liam sat up in bed, covered in sweat despite the cold air. Tessa was wailing, but when he peeked into the next room, his mother had woken and was rocking her. Already her cries were growing softer. Liam gulped in huge breaths of air; at least it was fresh and clear, if very cold. His mother finally noticed him, and she smiled. A tired smile. "The morning bell hasn't rung yet," she whispered. "You should try to get some more sleep."

Liam nodded and crept back to his room, which now felt smaller and more closed-in than ever. It wasn't until he was back under the covers, on the edge of sleep once more, that the real significance of his dream occurred to him:

It wasn't just the canaries who died. The miners died too.

***

All through the next day at school, while they studied new techniques for plant growth underground in Science class and new methods of preparing *tipiog*—the only plant growth that had proved successful for the Sublanders so far—in Life Skills, Liam thought about the miners. He already knew that the Abovelanders had been careless with life, human and otherwise. In Abovelander history class, they'd learned about the wars in which Abovelanders slaughtered each other, the diseases they spread while denying medical care to those who couldn't afford it. Even the disaster that had destroyed Aboveland entirely, replacing the air with poison gas and killing all living things other than the original Sublanders, who'd escaped underground in time, had been caused by dangerous human experiments.

But somehow, what had happened to the miners and the canaries seemed even worse to Liam. He didn't remember much about the miners—he was going to the Preservation Room as soon as possible to try to learn more—but he did know mining was a job, something certain Abovelanders did almost every day for most of their adult lives. And that was what Liam found so hard to understand: why would anyone who lived in a world of warmth and light, of blue sky and colorful winged creatures, choose to leave that all behind, to risk his life in the darkness beneath the earth?

***

In Subland, nothing was more important than preserving human life. They heard it every day at school in the Subland motto, *vita carissima*—life is precious—repeated at the beginning and end of morning announcements. They read the same words inscribed over the threshold of every official building in the community, from the school to the Preservation Room to the Leaders' Meetinghouse. But really, the message began much earlier, before the new citizens of Subland had learned to read or even to speak. All newborns were kept in incubators for at least the first six weeks of life, where they were monitored every second of the day until the doctors had determined they were healthy enough to go home. Children under the age of six visited the doctors every week; from the age of six on, the mandatory doctors' appointments were biweekly until adulthood, when they decreased to once per month. The doctors had shots for everything, for diseases with names so odd, they sounded to Liam like a child's nursery rhyme—*mumps, measles, malaria*—and sometimes Liam felt his left arm was no more than a human pincushion.

There were no weapons in Subland—none of the strange guns, or bombs, or toxic chemicals Liam had learned about in Aboveland history class—and fighting was unheard of. Even harmless physical activities, like the kickball games and jump rope most of Liam's classmates loved, were strictly monitored: they were to take place only under adult supervision, in the center of the schoolyard with its soft foam floor. In fact, injuries were so rare in Subland that Liam had seen blood only once, when he was seven and he'd tripped over his own two feet and landed on a pebble. He was so stunned by the vivid red color—almost as vibrant as the yellow of the canary—that the pain didn't even register. His knee was barely scratched, but his mother rushed him to the hospital anyway, where they cleaned the wound with stinging antiseptics and covered it with layers of bandages, forbidding him to remove them himself. When the doctor finally took the bandages off a week later, Liam's disappointment at finding the last traces of blood had faded to a dull, muddy brown hurt far more than any cut or scrape ever could.

***

Nearly a week passed before Liam found time to visit the Preservation Room. The photograph was growing wrinkled and more fragile than ever in his pocket, but he couldn't bear to leave it at home all day. He'd gotten in the habit of rubbing the paper between his fingers every time another student glowered at him, then turned and whispered to a group of giggling friends, or simply came right out and called Liam "freak" or "mutant." The photo had become a bit of a good-luck charm, and he'd examined it so thoroughly that all he had to do now was close his eyes, and the canary would appear in his vision, wings stretched in flight.

Despite its name, the Preservation Room was much more than a single room. It descended far below the rest of Subland—kids in Liam's class placed bets on how many floors there were—and held the thousands of books and artifacts the Sublanders had managed to gather before the final disaster. But most of those treasures were strictly off-limits, far too delicate and precious for the Sublanders to touch or examine. So for the average person, the Preservation Room consisted of the small lending library—copies of the most important Abovelander books, as well as the textbooks and other guides written by Sublanders—and the computers with their huge database of information.

The Preservation staff member on duty, Jeremy, recognized Liam and waved him in, telling him to just ask for help if he needed it. That was convenient; Liam didn't even have to explain what he was looking for or why. He went right over to one of the many empty computers—the Preservation Room wasn't exactly the most popular place in Subland—logged on, and began searching.

A half hour later, Liam had determined that miners had indeed died while doing their job—and far too often. More than 100,000 killed in the United States alone; that was more than 100 times the population of Subland. It made Liam dizzy just thinking about it.

Next, Liam wondered what could possibly make this coal so valuable, that it was worth so much more than human lives. He found coal could generate electricity—but there were other ways to do that. They used the underground river here. The Abovelanders had also used coal to heat buildings. And…to power *steam engines*. Liam had heard of trains that crossed the vast Aboveland, great mechanical beasts that carried humans from one end of the country to the other, past the varied landscapes he could only imagine: forests full of towering plants called trees, mountains where the earth rose in immense humps, cities of human-made buildings standing tall against the blue sky. Yes, the trains did seem wonderful—but not nearly as wonderful as being alive in Aboveland, able to walk through all of (or just one of) those many strange landscapes. Not as wonderful as a gleaming, singing yellow bird, soaring through the sky.

***

The days passed, blurring one into the next just as the grays and browns of Subland all smudged together into one dull shade. Liam choked down more *tipiog* and tried to ignore the hole in his stomach. He listened to his teachers drone on and tried to tune out the whispers aimed in his direction. He lay in bed at night and tried to pretend Tessa's cries were actually a beautiful song. And as the days passed, Liam thought. According to the several articles he'd read, the miners' canaries died because they didn't have enough oxygen to breathe. Liam knew about oxygen—they'd learned in Health class that all humans took in oxygen from the air, that every cell inside their bodies needed it to survive. But it had never occurred to him that oxygen could *run out*. Liam understood that some aspects of the mining process had been especially dangerous, had caused explosions and buildup of dangerous gases. But, still… Miners died because of lack of oxygen. Oxygen came from the fresh air above ground. Subland existed far below the earth's surface, without any opening that Liam knew of. So why, in over two hundred years, had their oxygen never run out?

No one knew how far below the earth's surface Subland was located. Well, the Leaders and some of the scientists must know, Liam supposed, but it certainly wasn't common knowledge. And it wasn't the type of thing you could research in the Preservation Room, either—the databases there held information only on Aboveland society. Liam, like most of the other kids, had always imagined Subland located miles and miles beneath the surface. There were even rhymes about it, written to match the rhythm of the jump rope:

Down and down and down they ran
to escape the poisoned men.
Down and down and down we'll stay.

Miles below, we're always safe.

But now, Liam thought maybe the rhymes and stories were wrong. There had to be an opening somewhere, a way for fresh, oxygen-filled air to travel down to them. And if there was an opening, maybe they weren't so far below the earth that the surface was little more than a dream, a fantasy. Maybe…maybe there was a way out of Subland. Maybe there was still a world above, a world of sky and sun and birds that flew.

There was no point waiting for Liam's science teacher to bring up Aboveland or oxygen or how many miles Subland extended beneath the earth. It wasn't going to happen. So one day in school, when Mr. Abithen followed yet another lecture on subterranean soil with the words, "Any questions?", Liam decided to take him literally. He might have chosen a more tactful method, might have approached Mr. Abithen alone after class, but Liam was beyond that now. His curiosity had grown so strong, it seemed to have developed wings of its own, and now it was soaring beyond Liam's control.

"Mr. Abithen," Liam began when the teacher called on him, "we all breathe oxygen, right?" He could already hear the titters from either side of him.

Mr. Abithen cleared his throat. "Yes, Liam, but I don't see what—"

"And the oxygen has to come from somewhere, right?" he went on before he could lose his courage.

"Well, yes, but let's get back on—"

"The oxygen must come from the surface." Liam let the words out in one long rush. "There must be an opening to the surface somewhere in Subland, or else we'd all be—"

Mr. Abithen's face turned hard, then, as hard as the stone ceiling that hovered high above Subland. "There is *no* opening. The air in Aboveland is poisoned, and if any of it was seeping down here, we'd all be dead."

"But the disaster was more than two hundred years ago," Liam protested. Unconsciously his hand went to the photo in his pocket, gripping it for support. "Things might have changed since—"

"*Nothing* has changed. Aboveland is destroyed, and we can never go back. Indulging in silly daydreams is not only pointless, it's dangerous. We need to focus on our life down here."

Around Liam, the other students' whispers and giggles had faded in the wake of Mr. Abithen's booming voice. None of them had ever seen the teacher so angry.

"Do you understand, Liam?"

For a moment, Liam couldn't speak. His mouth didn't seem to work.

"Liam?"

"Yes, sir. I understand."

***

That evening, Liam took the photograph from his pocket and examined it one more time. He memorized every detail of the picture: the spot where the bird's yellow surface shone even brighter, he supposed because the sun was hitting it; the little wisps at the edge of each wing, tugged at by an invisible breeze; the piercing black eyes that stared straight ahead, into the endless blue. Then he gave the photo to his mother, as he should have done all those weeks ago. He didn't need it anymore. The bird was inside him now.

All evening long, as they ate *tipiog* and Liam did his homework and his mother played with Tessa, talking all the while about the new clothes and luxuries they'd buy, Liam thought about the opening hidden somewhere in Subland, leading to the surface. Despite what Mr. Abithen had said, Liam was as sure as ever that it existed. And maybe in Aboveland, there *was* life again. Maybe there were towering trees and rolling mountains, dogs that barked and wolves that howled. Maybe right this very moment, far above Liam's head, a bird the color of the sun was flying on outstretched wings.

And maybe one day, Liam would find his way to the surface and see for himself.

That night, when his mother was ready to put Tessa to bed, Liam said, "Let me." He laid Tessa in her crib and watched as she reached her chubby arms up, up, grasping instinctively for something just beyond her reach. Finally he extended his own arm, just far enough for her to grab one of his fingers and clasp it tight. Her grip was warm and surprisingly strong; she let out a gurgling sound of pure pleasure and gave a big, toothless smile.

And Liam smiled back.

THE CHOOSING

BY MICHAEL O'CONNOR

Ninah sat in the hollow she had scooped out for herself and stared unblinkingly ahead at the expanse of lilac sand. The Copses were close behind her, and the tight-knit collection of thirty variously sized residence-domes and other buildings known as Gamma Town was a little to her left. But despite this proximity, she knew that as long as she kept her eyes fixed in one direction she would eventually be able to convince herself that she was alone and safe from the obstructiveness of other people.

She had been brought to Graal as an infant, fourteen years earlier. "We fled the noxious ball of pollution which the over-industrialised Earth had become to seek the riches buried within a brave new world," her father had once told her in an uncharacteristic moment of verbosity. Though it was hot and dry and the Copses sighed poison at night, Ninah loved the tiny planet which was the only home she knew.

The yellow sun had already dipped below the horizon and the more distant red one would soon follow. Automatically, she put out her hand and let it fall onto her night-hood. Once it became dark, all the plants on Graal would start to draw in the breathable air and exhale a noisome gas which humans could not tolerate without transmutation. The gas was rendered harmless at red sun rise. Night-hoods contained the necessary filters and chemical devices that make it possible to breathe outside after dark, but they were expensive to buy and to maintain, and Ninah would get into serious trouble if she lost hers. Satisfied that the hood was safe, she ran her fingers through her short, carrot-red hair. She had asked her mother to cut it that way because the long ringlets she used to have were taking up too much room in the child's night-hood she used, and her parents would not buy her a new one until after her Choosing. Just in case they did not need to.

She picked up the night-hood and stared at her reflection in the black visor, angling it up and down to take in her whole body. Her slight build and spiky hair had not worried her before. She had never really cared what she looked like. But that was before Trum came, trekking across the desert by day and night on a sand-scooter from Kappa Town which lay in one of the further segments of Graal. His parents had died in a mining accident and he had an uncle in Gamma Town who had invited the youth to share his home. Trum was tall and bony with dark brown hair which was always falling into his green eyes, and he had a way of smiling slowly as he spoke to her which made Ninah think he could read her mind. She had grown up with all the other boys in her Town and viewed them like brothers. Trum, three years older than her and with a slight drawl in his voice, seemed almost mythic. It frightened her how quickly and how powerfully she had fallen in love with him.

"You cannot select a partner before your Choosing," her mother had told her. "However long you have to wait for it. It may not be ... appropriate, afterwards."

"Trum is male so does not get a Choosing," Ninah retorted, her voice trembling with emotion. "Why cannot he select me?"

Ninah's father sighed heavily, and glanced at his wife. "No female can select or be selected until after their Choosings," he said patiently. "It is the law. You know how things are here. You are not a little child any more."

"Then why does everyone treat me like one!" screamed Ninah, wiping tears of frustration from her eyes and running to her room. She threw herself onto her bunk and sobbed until sleep overcame her. Even the faint hum of the dome's filters coming on did not wake her. They started to pump out a slight aroma to indicate that they were operating properly, and, in the next room, Ninah's parents slid under the warm sheets of their own bunk. Slowly the residence-dome became imbued with the reassuringly sweet scent of violets.

The following morning, Ninah had eaten her breakfast in sulky silence, then returned to her room and switched on her Tutor. "Today's lessons will begin with history..." crackled the artificial voice of the computer, shaped like a smiling head with a view screen representing its shoulders. Ninah sat there and worked, without stopping to eat and ignoring her parent's occasional calls from the communal area, until late afternoon. Then she suddenly stabbed at the over-ride button. "Individual research," she muttered loud enough for the machine's sensors to pick up her command.

"Subject?" queried the Tutor.

"The Choosing," Ninah replied, after a moment's hesitation. There were severe punishments for failing to keep up with the tuition programme, and she had already fallen several days behind. She knew she could catch up on two or three day's work without too much trouble, but the present backlog was starting to worry her, which was why she had dedicated so much of the day to her studies. But now she was bored, and wanted to investigate what really mattered to her.

There was a pause before the Tutor responded. "Note that this is the recommended lesson for persons of your standard. If you require a higher level response, please ask an adult to join you and enter his or her code." Biting her nails impatiently, Ninah sat and waited. Satisfied that nothing else was going to happen, the Tutor continued. "Graal has never produced enough males for its needs. Consequently, young females on Graal are given the opportunity to choose which gender they wish to be for the rest of their lives. There are generous awards given to those who elect to become males. That is all." The Tutor emitted a low tone to signal that the response was complete.

Ninah punched a button to switch it off. It was the same curt message she had heard for the past five years. When would she be old enough to hear a more detailed account? She wanted to find a loophole that would enable her to partner Trum straight away. She could not bear the thought of having to wait until the Central Administrator's office contacted her parents to say it was time for her Choosing. Though it seemed to be long overdue already, nevertheless it could still be days or months or maybe even years away. She could not endure for so long. Pulling a green tunic over her brown one-piece, and automatically snatching up her night-hood in case she decided to stay out late, she crept out of her room and was through the main door of the dome before her parents had time to look up from their workstations. She knew they would not pursue her. It was too important that they meet their work unit quota each day, and they scarcely had time for meals and sleep as it was. As long as she was not in obvious danger and was not breaking any important rules, they would let her alone.

The dry heat hit her as soon as she was outside, but the air was fresh and clean and she gulped at it hungrily as she ran past the hydroponic farm and the Supply Depot out onto the warm, shifting sand which surrounded Gamma Town like an ocean around an island. Very few of the settlers came out onto the sand unless they had to, regarding it as one more unpleasant feature of a generally inhospitable planet, but Ninah loved it. She loved its warmth and its mutability, and the way in which its soft lilac tones lightened and darkened according to the time of day and the positions of the suns. She had scooped out a hollow and seated herself facing away from the Town, and from the Copses where the towering Ghuign trees shared space with a mixture of smaller but equally sturdy plants and shrubs and maintained the breathability of the daylight air.

She sat there, feeling the heat seep through her linen clothes and embrace her slight body, and desperately tried to think of a way in which she and Trum could be together without having to wait until the Administrators saw fit to summon her to her Choosing. "Widow Sarich," she suddenly said aloud. "She is the oldest person in the world. She will know all there is to know about the Choosing. She will know if I have to wait for it before I can be partnered."

Scrabbling her way upright, and frightening several inquisitive Nards, mauve-skinned sand lizards whose camouflage made them very difficult to hunt, it took Ninah only moments to reach Widow Sarich's tiny one-person dome on the outskirts of Gamma Town. She placed her hand on the sensor by the door and waited for the old woman to identify her. After a few minutes' silence, Ninah grew impatient and banged on the white plastic wall, shouting her name. The door slid open and the girl entered.

A faint humming and the distinct scent of lavender alerted her to the fact that Widow Sarich had somehow gained permission to leave her filter on all day. The old woman never left her dome and seemed to distrust even the daylight air, though Ninah could not understand why she did not simply accept that everyone else could breathe it perfectly well so there could not be anything wrong with it. Widow Sarich's husband had died many years earlier, long before Ninah was born, when his night-hood had broken down during an exploratory expedition which had got lost and been forced to stay out all night. The old woman had grown increasingly reclusive over recent years and some of the younger children mocked her for her eccentricities. But Ninah had a fondness for her which she could not explain.

When her eyes grew accustomed to the dim light inside the old woman's dome, Ninah realised with a shock that Widow Sarich was wearing nothing but a flimsy underdress, stained brown and yellow and concealing little of her sagging plump body. She was sitting by one of the filter's outlet grilles, staring sightlessly towards the open door. She had been born on Graal in the early days of its settlement, before many of the birth defects which were common then had been eradicated, and she had come into the world with moist white eyes which had no pupils. As she came closer, Ninah saw that the wide eyes now contained a number of dark blood spots, which floated idly across them like tiny red boats on a lake of milk.

"How are you, Widow Sarich," Ninah said politely, touching the old woman's wrinkled hand with her own. "I have come to visit you."

"You are the only one who ever does, Ninah Tressard," Widow Sarich said, with affection in her voice, though she snatched her hand away as if she had been stung. "But I suppose there are no other little girls left to do so, are there?"

Ninah did not reply for a moment, because she had to bite back her anger at being called a little girl. But she knew how irrational the old woman could be sometimes and did not want to upset her. "Well," she said at last. "There are the two toddlers that belong to family Eflond and the five girls who share my tutor group, but they're all quite a bit younger than me. They are what could be called little girls, I suppose," she concluded pointedly.

"And you sometimes wonder what became of those who were older than you?" asked Widow Sarich, rocking her head so that the shaft of sunlight from the open door seemed to slap her face back and forth. "You weren't always the eldest girl in Gamma, were you?"

Ninah found a stool and sat down on it, staring intently at the blind woman, wondering if she had some magical way of discerning what it was she had come about. "The big girls all took the award for choosing to become male," she answered. "Their parents were all poor, I think, farmers and builders and suchlike, so I suppose they needed the money. Mine work with their brains so I don't have to worry about it."

"Indeed brainwork is always better rewarded than muscle work," Widow Sarich said, as though the thought had never struck her before. "The Tressards administrate the farm, don't they?"

"Something like that," Ninah agreed. "They have to plan when crops go in and come out and that sort of thing. I don't really take much notice."

"No, I don't think you do. And neither does anyone else. No-one on Graal ever takes much notice of what goes on except an old blind woman who knows better than to go out and remind people she's still here. Did any of the older girls tell you before they went that they were going to choose to let the Alpha Town Nanotechs and Bio-engineers make them into males?"

Ninah shrugged her thin shoulders, then remembered that this gesture would be lost on her companion. "We never talked about it much. It's a bit ... embarrassing, when you're young. I think Greya was considering it because her father had gone missing and her mother couldn't manage very well on just the one wage. But some of the others were planning to take partners. Phaedra was desperately in love with one of the farmers, I recall, though he was much too old for her. Even so, I remember thinking it strange that she didn't come back after her Choosing."

"So they still alter the changelings' memories and send them to different towns afterwards?" Widow Sarich asked softly.

"Yes. They say it's easier to start a new life somewhere that you're not known and when you can't remember who you used to be. Besides, it's at the mining towns that the males are needed because the digging machines don't work very well on Graal and they need men's muscles to get the minerals out. You don't need many males in a farming town, so there wouldn't be much point in them coming back here if they'd chosen to change."

"No point at all," the old woman agreed. "No point at all. I am glad you learn your lessons so well. You don't want to be thinking wicked thoughts such as men are cheaper than machines, do you. Or that they are more resistant to underground vapours than even physically augmented females. But I am tired now, Child Ninah, so just run along home would you. Shouldn't you be doing your schoolwork?"

"I wanted to ask you about the Choosing," Ninah protested. "If there is a way I can ..." She stopped, suddenly shy. "If anyone can select a partner before their Choosing."

The deafening noise of a descending Transport Ship rocked the dome. The old woman covered her ears and flung herself back and forth as if in a fit. "Get out and shut my door -- don't let them come for me!" she screeched in terror.

Ninah ran outside and closed the door behind her. The sleek saucer-shaped ship had settled on the landing bay beside the Supply Depot, and most of the townspeople had come out to look at it. An unscheduled visit was of considerable note in the small place.

"Ninah Tressard," crackled a loudspeaker from somewhere on the surface of the gleaming vehicle. "It is time for your Choosing. Collect your belongings and enter."

Ninah stared in astonishment, her heart racing, her mind in tumult. Part of her was frightened, worried because she had not received the usual week's notice allowing her parents time to organise the traditional party. But a more jubilant part of her realised that her loneliness and suffering was at last close to ending. In a few days, she and Trum would be able to be partnered for life.

She scampered over the cobblestone grounding of the town to her dome, where her parents, efficient as ever, were already packing a travelbag for her. "It's a bit sudden, isn't it?" her mother snapped at her as she entered. "What have you been up to?"

Ninah shrugged her shoulders. "Maybe they've just remembered me," she said. "Phaedra Collan was months younger than me when it was her time, and she was the oldest ever. I was starting to think they'd forgotten me and I'd end up alone like Widow Sarich."

Ninah's father nodded his balding head slowly. "The administrators have certainly been busy lately," he muttered, his deep voice contrasting with his wiry frame. "They have a hard job keeping the mineworkers nourished on such an arid planet as this. Our predecessors were stupid to destroy so many plants before they realised that they drew water up to the surface. Graal could have had thirty or forty more hydroponic farms if they hadn't wiped out so many Copses."

Mother Tressard cleared her throat uncomfortably. "It doesn't do to speak ill of the administrators," she murmured. "People can only survive here by sticking strictly to the rules. You wouldn't want to be shipped out ... or worse."

Father Tressard looked uneasy. "I wasn't speaking ill of them," he said, his voice unnaturally loud. "Just commenting on what the first settlers did. It wasn't anyone's fault ..."

"Well, here's your bag, Ninah," said her mother, clearly changing the subject. "I'm sorry you haven't had a party. Maybe we'll have a late one for you, if you get back."

"When I get back, you mean," said Ninah truculently. "I have no intention of being turned into some hairy giant of a man, whatever award they offer me. I don't expect it'll be more than a couple of days before I'm home again. And then you'll have something really important to celebrate!"

She took the bag from her mother's shaking hand and glanced around the dome. Sparsely furnished, and with much of its communal space given over to her parents' workstations, it was hardly cosy. But it was the only home she had ever known, and her eyes tingled as she looked around it.

Her father suddenly strode across the room and shook her roughly by the hand. "I hope it goes well, Ninah," he said unsteadily. "You'll have to excuse me. I am getting behind with my work." He walked back to his vidscreen and pressed a few buttons on the fascia beneath it. Then he just sat back and stared at his reflection.

Mother Tressard put her soft hands on Ninah's shoulders, as though she were about to give her a hug. But she just nodded and cleared her throat. "Whatever happens will be for the best," she said, enunciating each word slowly and distinctly. "Have a safe journey."

Ninah smiled. "I'll see you in no time," she said cheerily. "No need to get all silly about it."

She ran out of the dome and towards the landing bay, without seeing her mother's eyes fill with tears and her mother's lips mouth the words "Goodbye, my child."

The ship's door slid open as Ninah approached. She paused and turned to take another look at Gamma Town. Many of her friends and neighbours stood by the doors of their domes, waving and smiling encouragingly. Mother Eflond held both her small daughters, one in each arm, while her plump little husband stood beside her staring expressionlessly at the ship. Father and Mother

Collan had walked over from the farm, but stood too far away for Ninah to hear what they were saying to each other. Several other farmers stood beside the Collans, waving cheerily, and the doorways of the supply depot were crammed with workers jostling to get a good view. Ninah knew that Trum would be among them, but would be too gentle to force his way to the front.

It was a great rarity for so many people to be outside at the same time, and for a moment there was an air of festivity. But it was only a moment. "Enter at once, Ninah Tressard," crackled the loudspeaker impatiently, and Ninah did as she was told.

The door slid shut behind her before she could look to see if Widow Sarich had come out to see her off, so she took a couple of steps forward and sat on the hard green plastic bench which ran in a semi-circle along half the diameter of the ship. The pilot's area was closed off and the rest of the cabin was featureless, so Ninah pursed her lips and made herself as comfortable as she could.

She was scarcely aware of the craft rising into the air, but felt distinctly queasy when it shot off towards Alpha Town. She looked in her bag for some sweets to suck, but her parents had never been in favour of anything so unhealthy and all she found was a small packet of travel-sickness pills. Not for the first time, Ninah thought of the effective way her mother and father always took care of her, even if they seemed to do so without much tenderness. She took a couple of the travel pills with a can of processed rhubarb juice, and devoted her time to imagining what she would wear to her partnering with Trum. Somehow, it never occurred to her to wonder what he would wear. When she pictured him in her mind, it was always in the sand-stained blue jerkin and breeches he had worn when he first scooted into Gamma.

Eschewing the narrow bench for the comparative comfort of the floor, Ninah eventually lay down and dozed, the barely perceptible throbbing of the craft's engines making her feel strangely at ease. It was quite a shock when she awoke to the sound of the door sliding open and an irritable voice calling her name.

She got up and, remembering just in time to pick up her bag, walked out of the ship to find herself in a covered landing bay. A dozen slender blue pillars supported its slightly domed roof, and the floor was grimy and pitted with holes and scratches. The place smelled like the noisy machines that trundled around her parents' farm.

A tall man with white hair and a long beard, dressed from head to toe in a dark grey robe, was standing outside, tapping on the metallic ground with a stick made of glistening black wood. "Follow me," he barked, when Ninah appeared.

He led her into an adjacent building, the largest the young girl had ever seen. It would have been big enough for the whole of Gamma Town to fit inside it three or four times over. Inside, though as sparsely furnished as most places Ninah had been, it was cool and bright, and there were even a few windows spaced along the exterior walls. Through them, Ninah could see several large Copses and a corresponding number of hydroponic farms. There were also a few other large buildings, though none rivalled the staggering dimensions of the one she was in. A cluster of residence-domes filled the cobbled space between the larger buildings; Ninah noticed that most of them were one-person domes, and that they all had their doors open as though their inhabitants had no sense of privacy.

She scuttled along the winding corridors behind the tall man, barely keeping up with his long strides and too out of breath to ask him any questions, wondering whether the tap-tap of his stick would be loud enough for her to follow if she fell too far behind. Occasionally a man or woman would pass her, walking swiftly in the opposite direction, or hastening up one of the sets of staircases which punctuated the inner wall of the corridor. Ninah smiled at the first three or four strangers she saw, but every one of them stared straight ahead as though they did not see her, so she quickly gave up.

Almost before she had time to stop, the tall man swung round and walked up a flight of stairs. He moved much more slowly, and leaned heavily on his stick, so Ninah was able to catch up with him. "Where are we going?" she asked. "...Sir," she added after an interval, thinking it might be wise to show some respect.

The old man turned his humourless face towards her. "To your Choosing, of course," he snapped. "You should have been taught about it by your Tutor. I'll have to make a complaint ..."

"No," Ninah interrupted. "I do know about it. I just meant where are we going this very minute?"

The man scowled. "Never interrupt me," he said. "You farmer children have no idea how to behave properly. The sooner you are processed the better." He paused at the top of the stairs and caught his breath. "We are going to the medical examination area," he told her.

In silence, Ninah stumbled along as he led her into a very bright room crammed full of gleaming white machinery, covered in dials and switches and flashing lights. In the middle of the room stood an old wooden desk, half buried beneath piles of papers and books. It seemed out of place amongst all the technical equipment. There was a tall blonde woman sitting at the desk, slightly older than Ninah's mother and wearing a green smock. She looked up when the pair entered and her thin lips formed a smile but her cold grey eyes did not change. "Ninah Tressard from Gamma Town?" she asked.

The tall man nodded before Ninah could answer.

"Welcome to your choosing, Child Tressard," the woman said,

standing up and approaching the young girl. "I am Doctor Chadwick. Please take your clothes off and stand on that pad." She pointed towards a glass cubicle in the corner where the open door revealed a thin grey mat on the floor.

Ninah coughed nervously and looked at the tall man, who had taken a seat beside the desk. The Doctor's eyes followed her gaze. "That is Administrator Lucas," she said curtly. "He is responsible for your Choosing. He has to remain."

Ninah clenched her fists involuntarily, wishing there were someone with her that she knew, who could advise her what to do.

"Be quick, Child," snapped Lucas. "I have much work and cannot afford to devote all day to one farmer's brat."

Her heart racing, Ninah stepped over to the cubicle and, seeking some element of privacy from the head-high computers which abutted it, slowly stripped off her garments. The Doctor took her by the arm and walked her up onto the pad, roughly forcing her to turn towards the Administrator. Though she closed her eyes, Ninah could feel the old man's dispassionate gaze slide over her naked body, appraising the slender torso, the small breasts, the narrow bony hips, the fuzz of red hair between her skinny legs. Ninah felt as though she were suffocating, and her skin had turned almost as red as her hair. "Not very womanly," muttered the Administrator to the Doctor. "But she's older than most of them." He stared straight at Ninah. "Are you a virgin, Child?"

Ninah cringed, trying to cover herself with her hands. She nodded rapidly, unable to speak, fighting back tears of humiliation. She had never imagined her Choosing would be like this.

"It makes no difference to the procedure whether she is or not," the Doctor muttered. "Let me carry out the physical examination." Forcing Ninah to rest her arms against her sides, the Doctor attached a number of tiny sensors to the girl's shivering body. Ninah jerked her head back and bit her lip when the blonde woman's cold hand pushed her legs apart and slid something metallic inside her. A spot of blood dripped onto the girl's chin. "Stand very still now," the Doctor ordered her. She stepped back and closed the cubicle door. Ninah felt her whole body tingle and could make out a faint humming which seemed different from that of the dome filters; it reminded her of the moaning sound the Nards made when their throats were cut prior to them being gutted and cooked. She had no idea of how long she stood there, but was close to collapse when the tingling and the humming sound stopped simultaneously and the Doctor opened the door and disconnected the sensors. "You can get dressed now, and the Administrator will take you to your room for the night."

With her back to the staring man, Ninah hurriedly put her clothes back on. A little of her confidence returned when she had done so. Though she could look neither of the adults in the face, she asked the question that was paramount in her mind. "When do I make my Choosing?"

"What are you talking about?" Lucas asked her crossly. He stood up and began walking towards the door.

"Who do I tell that I Choose to stay a female?" Ninah asked plaintively. "I am not interested in any award."

The Doctor had reseated herself behind her antique desk. "We don't do that any more," she said curtly. "Not enough girls were volunteering, and we are desperately short of males. It is we who do the Choosing now, depending on the suitability of the subject. You will find out in due course what our decision is, after I have processed your tests. You probably already know that your Town is unusually productive, and has given us a hundred per cent acceptability rate in recent years. Please go with Administrator Lucas now."

It seemed to Ninah that the room had suddenly started to spin, and that she was about to be flung against one of the walls. She reached out her hand to steady herself, and the tall man grabbed her by the elbow. He dragged her outside and further along the featureless corridor. Before she had regained her self-control, she found herself lying on a narrow bunk in a tiny bedchamber listening to the only door click locked behind her. Satisfied that she was at last alone, she made no further effort to hold back her tears. Sobbing uncontrollably, she lay alone and ignored until unconsciousness overcame her.

She was wakened by the click of the door being unlocked before it slid open. Doctor Chadwick stood there, holding a large glass of milk. "Drink this," she ordered.

"What is going to happen to me?" Ninah asked, her voice tense. "When will I be told?"

The Doctor thrust the glass into Ninah's unsteady hand. "A decision has been made. You will learn it when the Administrators give their formal consent. Now drink!" She stared unblinkingly at the frightened child. Though the surface of the milk seemed to be sprinkled with tiny black dots which were moving back and forth like boats on a lake, Ninah was too frightened to disobey. She gulped at the warm nutmeg-flavoured liquid, finding it surprisingly refreshing, then meekly handed the empty glass back to the Doctor.

Without another word, the blonde woman turned and walked out, locking the door behind her. Ninah stared at the blank wall for a moment, then began to feel extremely drowsy. As she lay back down, her body started to itch from the inside as though it were full of spiders. But she was too tired to care.

***

A loud siren woke Ninah with a jolt. Both Administrator Lucas and Doctor Chadwick stood in the doorway to the tiny room staring at the dazed figure. "When you have eaten, the Transport Ship will take you to Kappa Town where your new life will commence," the grey-robed man announced, in what was for him almost a gentle tone. "I'm afraid it will take several hours for your memory to adjust. We cannot avoid that. Do not be too long getting ready."

Ninah looked down, as if from a great distance, at the body that had been resculptured and completely reformed during the night by the nanites still working within it.

He screamed.

TOMORROW'S CHILDREN

BY DELPHINE BOSWELL

It is now thirteen years since the 9.5 magnitude quake occurred on March 3, 2078, the largest quake to hit North America, destroying most of the state of California with the exception of the Monterey Peninsula. Although the quake only lasted fourteen to sixteen seconds, it managed to kill almost all of the 36,000,000 people who resided there. Life would never be the same. The joyful noises I had known turned to a deadening silence. My home of light and love had turned into a sanctuary of ash. Broken pieces, broken lives.

My name is Adhara Canis Major, named after stars in the galaxy; I am a reporter for the "Domicile Daily "and one of the ones lucky enough to have survived the ordeal without a scratch. What did remain of the peninsula floated out into the Pacific, soon to become known as the Island of Domicile, a damp, foggy, and windy mass of land outlined by a rocky seacoast. Add to this, there is a terrible undertow right off shore and a swarming group of Great Whites. There is no use for our pocket optic-audios here or our supersonic speed messaging as the towers were destroyed during the quake; hence, there is no use in trying to make contact with the rest of the world. Truly, Domicile is an isolated swell of land in the middle of nowhere.

After the initial shock of the quake wore off, people on Domicile grappled about in a state of confusion and uncertainty. Many expressions appeared glazed and almost mesmerized, not knowing what to do, not knowing how to cope. There were many who had lost family and friends. I recalled seeing two women huddled together, crying. Strangers reached out to strangers. As if by some God-like quirk, the Community Hospital of Monterey, a Trader Joe's, a couple of Seven-Elevens, and one elementary school remained standing, totally intact, suggesting that the quake might have been a mere mirage. Several soldiers guarded the doors to the quick-food places as people waited in lines for supplies. Despite the limited quantities, there was no pushing or shoving as I remembered how people were before the quake. I heard people saying, "Thank you," and "God bless you." Someone raised an American flag. Out of tragedy arose altruism as the survivors spoke to one another about how grateful they were to be alive.

Over the next few weeks, however, much of the camaraderie and good will was exhausted. I saw a group of men pilfering; their arms filled with Hostess cupcakes, loaves of bread, and cans of soup.

"What in the hell gives you the right to think you can just up and steal what little is left?" one older man said to the thief. One of the robbers struck the elderly man with the end of a broken tree branch; blood dripped from an open head wound.

Like dogs playing tug-o-war, I saw two, young women arguing over the contents of a bag. "You, little bitch. It's mine," said one; the other scratched the woman across her face, leaving bloody gauges.

Eventually, after months of seeing the Domicilians responding more to their emotions than to rational thought or logic, when things seemed to get as bad as they could, a group of military men, from what was the former Naval Postgraduate School, as well as some soldiers from what was the Presidio of Monterey, came forth stating the importance of forming a government that could run and control the outbursts of the people.

On a negative note, the new government, known as a Napocracy, run by the Napos, or National Association of Patrolling Officers, resulted in anarchy. Some believe the Napocracy provides them with freedom—freedom from having to make choices, to bear responsibilities. To me, I view the government as oppressive. And, perhaps, the worse example of this came the day the Napocracy enforced the Anti-Conception Law to prevent the population of Domicile from growing and established the Cryopreservation Center, demanding that children be frozen until a time when the government deemed it necessary to reestablish the society.

It was then that Gemma my supervisor at the "Domicile Daily" asked me to write a story on the influx of children to the Cryopreservation Center. People were lining the asphalt walks leading up to the doors, and parents who were both angry and saddened to be offering up their children to be frozen, were getting into verbal altercations. I was asked to go down to the Center to speak with those who were waiting, to get their stories, and to write up a column. It's paradoxical, really, in that Gemma wants public-interest pieces, but yet she doesn't want anything published that goes against what the government dictates. "We agree for the betterment of all," she keeps saying to me.

When I arrived at the Center, I found myself surrounded by

crying infants; restless, whining children; and parents who obviously were beginning to lose their tempers. A heavy rain fell and large black clouds hung low, adding to the dismal picture I stared over. The people were drenched. I chose not to bring an umbrella as I wanted them to see me as one with them. "Hello," I said. "My name is Adhara Canis Major; I'm a reporter for the 'Domicile Daily,' and I'm writing a column. Could I speak to you for a moment?"

The woman I addressed frowned. Her face was wet, her hair dripping onto her collar. Her black dress and white apron were soaked, and her black oxfords stood in a huge puddle. "What is it that you want to know?" She held the hands of two toddlers who appeared to be around three- and four-years of age. Both of the children were crying and trying to find shelter in the folds of the woman's dress. Periodically, they would peek out and stare at me with their big, round eyes.

"How long have you been standing here, waiting to get into the Center?" I asked.

"Six hours, maybe more. My children are hungry. . . thirsty. . .cold."

"Understandable. This is a terrible day to be outside. Have you been offered any umbrellas or cover-ups?"

"Really? Did you expect that the Napos would be that considerate?"

"What's the reason for the hold-up? Have you been told?" I assumed some explanation had been given to the women.

"It's a process, a Napo told us. First come, first serve. They say that with so many freezers beginning to start up at the same time that it has caused some power outages."

That explained the grinding coming from the building, like an engine trying to start when the batteries had almost but given out. The noise would stop momentarily, and then start up again.

"Must you wait? Can't you return when the issue is resolved?"

"To start all over again? To wait in this line, to lose my place?"

I continued to jot down what the woman was telling me. It was clear that there was no system in place regarding the processing of children and, worse yet, the Center could not handle the amount of voltage that was required to run so many freezer units. I wondered why someone hadn't considered this before now, but, then again, the Anti-Conception Law and the Cryopreservation Center were issues that had come up quite abruptly once the government decided that something had to be done immediately to stall population growth.

I looked at the woman's two children. I could see the fright in their eyes. I couldn't imagine what it must be like inside the Center when the children were to be pulled from their parents arms, screaming and hollering in hysteria. I thanked the woman for her time and offered her my compassion.

Then, I stopped another woman who looked to be much less stressed. She placed her weight on one foot and fingered the rope around her waist, using it to wipe the rain off her face. Her child, probably eleven or twelve, played with some type of game that involved black tiles with red dots. He arranged them and rearranged them on the pavement. He attempted to wipe them dry with his wet uniform shirt and placed them back in position.

I introduced myself to the child's mother and asked her what her feelings were about having her only child frozen.

"Maybe, this sounds heartless to you, Ma'am. It's obvious from the tattoo on your forehead that your position on Domicile pays well and that you are one of the intellectuals here. It's not like that for me." She brushed her soaking hair off of her forehead and revealed a tattoo in the shape of a large "A," which stood for "mentally incapable." I assumed that meant that she worked for the Napos in a servant-type capacity, not thought to have the intelligence to handle anything more challenging.

"I know what your insignia means, but I'm not sure I understand how your position makes it any easier for you to turn your child over to the government," I said.

She moved closer to me, within inches of my face, looked me directly in the eyes and said, "I need the money, lady."

"Money?"

At the sound of the word, two women ahead in line began to push each other; one woman pulled the other's hair that was pinned behind her ears. Their children looked on like gawking birds.

I excused myself from the woman I had been speaking to and rushed to the side of the site. "Please, please, stop. "What's wrong?"

"This bitch here called me a fuckin' whore."

Two of the children covered their ears with the palms of their hands.

"She's full of shit. I never said such a thing."

I tried to push myself between them and held up my arms. I explained who I was and told them that I would appreciate hearing their stories—both sides.

The second woman spoke. "You see this kid at her side? It's the sixth kid she has brought to the center."

I couldn't quite understand why that would matter or of what concern it would be to the woman. I must have had a confused look on my face.

"Don't you get it?"

I shook my head.

"The more children, the more money. Why this idiot could care less what's happening to these kids."

At this point, the first woman put her hands in fists and started pounding on the woman's shoulders.

Before I could stop the fighting, a Napo carrying a large black umbrella, who had apparently been working his way through the line, stopped, grabbed the angry woman by her arm, and threw her to the ground. "You see the end of the line? Get your ass over there."

Her children followed her like sheep.

I saluted the Napo, the required form of respect for authority, and explained who I was. I thought he might be a better person to ask as to what was occurring here.

By this time the woman causing the grief had done what the officer demanded.

The other woman kept repeating, "It's not fair. Something should be done."

"What does she mean?" I asked the Napo.

He adjusted his grey cap with his free hand and cocked his head in an arrogant poise, complete to his right eyebrow raising. "It's quite simple. The woman with the six children stands to make herself quite a bundle."

"I hope I'm misunderstanding you."

"No. You're getting it just fine. Six children equal $150,000."

"This can't be. The woman is selling her children to the

government for $25,000 a child?" I could hear my voice rise.

"Quick math skills, you have, Miss Adhara."

I felt myself lightheaded and suddenly queasy. I grabbed for one of the handrails along the walk.

"I told you. Six kids by six different men. She could care less about the kids. And, to make matters worse, she's making money off of them," the second woman said.

I glanced at the Napo. "But, isn't this exploitation? How can the government buy children only to freeze them?" I couldn't believe what I had said; it was so out-of-character for me to risk asserting myself in this way.

"Why not?" the Napo said, in a sarcastic voice. "Do you think this broad really cared about her kids to begin with?"

"That's not the question," I said.

"She's nothing more than a fucking whore," the Napo said. "My guess is probably fifty percent of these women in line are no different."

The second woman nodded her head. "That's what I tried to tell the journalist here."

"I'm still confused. Even if she didn't care for her children, why would the government be interested in buying them?"

"It's all part of the plan."

"Huh?" was all I could say.

"Someday there will be those who will pay good money to have a child of their own, and when they do, the government and the children will be ready," the Napo said. "You see, it really is a win-win situation."

I could not believe what I was hearing. Not only was the government demanding that children be taken from their parents and frozen until who knew when, but the Napos would, in the long run, actually be making money in the transaction. I could not help but ask myself what life had come to, when children were viewed as nothing more than a commodity and, worse yet, as a means to an unthinkable end.

I excused myself. I had more than enough information to write my article. But. . .there was no way that I could. In my heart, I knew what was being asked of these suffering women. It was cruel and unforgivable. I knew that the buying and selling of children for whatever purpose was appalling and hideous. Yet to expound on either of these issues would mean that I would be immediately sent to solitary confinement if not the Assisted Suicide Center. I wanted nothing more than to speak out, to make sure my voice was heard. I went back to my office, but the helplessness I felt prevented me from beginning my article. I could only think about the women and their children, waiting in snake-like lines as the rain poured down on them; perhaps, for some of them, washing their guilt down the drain, and for others washing away their sadness

YOUR COMFORT IS IMPORTANT TO US

BY TANITH KORRAVAI

Please accept our appreciation that your sponsors have chosen us to service your medical needs. This is a once in a lifetime experience, and we have provisions for every possible contingency to ensure you minimal discomfort in the days leading up to the blessed event.

By now you should have received your supply of medications. Please follow along as I explain each item to make sure your packet includes them all and that you understand when to use each.

First, you should see a brown bottle of liquid. This is a skin softening oil made from the fat of your young, er, compatible young animals, enhanced with many optimizing nutrients. Use this twice daily on the affected area. This will allow the skin to adapt with minimal discomfort.

The bag labelled '794' contains twelve bright blue tablets with the word 'GREX' on them in white letters. These are for the first three days of your confinement. You may take up to 4 per day as needed to reduce feelings of strangeness and disorientation.

Side effects from the blue pill may include headaches and cramping of the tongue. Rinsing the oral cavity with the bright green liquid in the vial marked 'PLERK' will alleviate the discomfort. Extensive tests have been performed to ensure its efficacy. The unfortunate taste in your mouth will be temporary.

After three days you will need something stronger. These are the light pink pills in the pale yellow baggie. These may appear orange as a consequence of color theory, but you can easily distinguish them from the actual orange pills by the number 38461 printed on them in large friendly letters.

Take one of these pills each day upon waking for days four through eight, assuming you are still able to sleep. If not, take them each morning. If nausea occurs, which is likely, take with food, if you can still stomach food. Otherwise, take them in conjunction with the optional dark purple caplets to relieve minor digestive distress.

If you take the actual orange pill by mistake instead of the light pink pill in the pale yellow baggie, your host can provide a dark green pill to counteract the effect, but be advised that this will greatly decrease the effectiveness of the greenish-yellow pill.

By day six, you will start to experience some discomfort and swelling in the area around the injection you have just received. This is normal and nothing to be concerned about. Since your comfort during this process is important to us, we have provided several palliative options.

If your sponsor has purchased the Silver Plan, you are entitled to a visit from a massage therapist every other day for the remainder of your confinement. Your therapist has had special training in pain management, pressure relief, and techniques of disassociation. We think you will be surprised at how effective these will be.

If your sponsor has purchased the Gold Plan, you may have a live-in therapist for the duration. The live-in therapist has other techniques available, some of which are not so much directed at your comfort as at enhancing the growth of the offspring. These techniques have been proven to result in healthier and more intelligent offspring, and you are requested to cooperate fully with the therapist's efforts, even if they result in some distress.

For those at the Bronze Level, we offer this booklet of stress management techniques and a lovely squeeze ball in the shape of a cockroach.

By Day Twelve you may be unconscious; in that case, feel free to ignore the rest of these instructions.

If you are one of the 37% who will still be conscious and capable of feeling pain, please take note of the six red sublingual tablets. These will dissolve instantly under your tongue and be absorbed into your bloodstream. We suggest that you reserve them for the final hours of your confinement on Day Seventeen.

On or about the fifteenth day you may experience shortness of breath, accelerated heart rate, and an increase in blood pressure. While this is understandably worrying, it is not serious, and you may take it as a sign that your confinement is proceeding normally and has only a few more days to run.

On Day Sixteen it may seem that the pain cannot possibly get worse, but in fact it can, and will. Know that your pain serves the highest needs of our society. Children who emerge from those who remain conscious up until the end have much higher levels of social integration.

You will achieve maximum benefit from the red tablets if you wait until the first nymph pokes its claw through your skin and begins to feed.

At this point, take them all.

You will spend the remaining few hours of your service in bliss, knowing you have given the greatest gift in your power to allow your sponsors the privilege of reproduction without being devoured by their own offspring. This process has enabled our civilization to evolve and flourish for over 1000 years, as parents are now able to pass on the wisdom of their experience to the next generation.

You are a vital part of our progress, and we thank you for your participation in our evolution, whether voluntary or conscripted. Rest assured, regardless of your origin, your name will be entered into the rolls of honor and your host brood will offer a sacrifice in your name at their ascension.

The anesthetic you received prior to your injection may be wearing off now. As you return to your sponsor families, feel free to ask for anything that might make you more comfortable - an extra pillow, a favorite food, even an extra hour of television watching - educational programs only, of course.

Your sponsors are very grateful and will accommodate any reasonable request you are able to communicate. We have provided an environmentally friendly wipe board with a nontoxic marker, as your voice box has been removed so that your screaming will not traumatize our children when they

USELESS

BY ELLEN BROCK

"You're small for twelve," one says, leaning forward, a finger pointed at my hollow stomach.

They watch me with dark eyes, pencils slapping their clipboards. A table separates them from the rest of the long gymnasium packed full of equipment for sports, the military, weight lifting. There's even a row of guns of all shapes and sizes, and I wonder if anyone's ever used them on the judges.

"Can you lift weights?" they ask. "Can you dance?"

I shake my head. My mother prepped me for this, told me to speak loud and firm, to stand tall with my head up. But my shoulders are tucked down like a school dunce and I can't find my voice.

The one on the end shuffles through my file, stopping on a bright orange paper. His eyes raise from the clipboard and scan my body. He's searching for the scars, traces of my accident. I turn my bad foot out straight like my mother told me. I grit my teeth against the pain.

He leans over and whispers across the table, too quiet for me to hear. I am not new to this judging. This is the final stop, the end of the line, where you go when no one else wants you. I've already been through the math judges, the reading/writing judges, the music/theater judges. There were dozens of them and they all turned me away, sending me on to the next room to be somebody else's problem.

For most of the jobs, I'm too stupid. Some of my brain cells were left behind at the scene of the accident, smeared across the black cement. For other jobs, I'm too ugly, deformed, my body broken and battered. The other stupid kids are given jobs where you don't have to think too hard, like packing boxes, stocking shelves, even prostitution. But I am not good enough for any of those things because of my foot and my scars. They say I am broken both in mind and in body. I am problematic.

The men lift their heads once more. They don't smile, don't try to make me feel comfortable. There is even a hint of anger on their faces, perhaps annoyed that I've made their job less than easy.

"We have nothing for you," they say.

My chest burns and so do my cheeks. I squeeze my hands together, twisting my fingers, not sure if I should stay or leave.

The one in the middle rolls his eyes, leans forward, and yells towards the door, "Next."

I swallow hard and back away. A tall boy with strong shoulders and muscled arms passes me at the door. This is not a last resort for him. He is here because he wants to be, a smile beaming on his face. He will make a good boxer or football player. I will probably see him on TV someday, making our great nation proud.

* * *

The air is chilly as I walk home, and I pull my jacket tighter. It is size extra small, just like me. I clutch my file against my chest, inside it says I will only grow to five feet. I am sure this is part of what makes me so useless to the judges. Mostly I don't blame them.

I turn at the big building with the red shutters, just like Mother told me. Since my accident I have not been able to understand signs. My vision is perfect, crystal clear, but I cannot read. I can't write. I can't work numbers. The doctors say it is some kind of acquired visual processing disorder. Three years ago, when I was nine, everyone said I would be a great scientist. I won contests. My teachers were proud. But now my brain is scrambled and I am useless, assigned no job at all, not even a bad one. I have never heard of this happening. I don't think it ever has.

I turn left at the park and I'm almost home. I don't know how I'm going to tell my parents the truth, so I drag my feet. I will take as long as I possibly can.

When I was seven my neighbors had a baby girl. She was deaf in both ears and had crossed eyes. They let me hold her, carry her around the neighborhood, pretending she was mine, but when she was two months old, they took her away. Her parents did not cry, and I didn't either. She was a useless thing that would never do anyone any good. She was bad for our great nation.

If I were a baby, I'd be gone too, taken away, thrown in the undertaker's furnace. But I am almost grown up so I think killing me is against the law, even if I'm useless, even if I am just a burden on our great nation.

Mother is on the porch. Even from the end of the road I can see her arms waving, her big smile. Father stands behind her, arms crossed against his chest. He doesn't believe in me like she does. When I was nine we were best friends. He spent hours setting up experiments, challenging me to grow my brain, but now he stands away from me, watches from a distance. At night sometimes I hear him cry.

I wish they had not seen me so I could keep dragging my feet, delay the truth for just a little bit longer. I walk as slow as I can while still seeming normal.

"How was it?" my mother asks, nearly flying from the porch in excitement.

"Come on," my father says, waving us inside, propping open the door with his foot. There aren't any neighbors around, but I understand how he feels. I understand his embarrassment.

We pass through the entryway and into the living room. I sit in the big chair and my parents drop down on the couch. Mother's eyes are wide, eager, but Father's are dark, focused low on the ground.

"How was it?" Mother asks again.

I bite my lip. I don't know how to tell them, don't know how to choose my words so I just shake my head.

"What is it, sweet pea? Not what you expected? Whatever it is, it's okay."

I shake my head again, eyes burning.

"What happened, sweetheart?" She leans forward, so far her behind is barely in contact with the couch.

My father jerks up suddenly, eyebrows scowling. "Out with it, already," he shouts, and I jump.

I suck in a breath, my heart banging in my chest. "They assigned me nothing," I say, voice a quiet squeak.

My mother's face falls, lips quiver. "What do you mean, sweet pea?" She tries to smile, but it's sad, quivering, and it's all my fault.

"Damn you, Ishka," my father says, his face red. He used to call me Princess, but not anymore, not since the accident.

I hang my head. I really am sorry. I never wanted to be an embarrassment to my father or my nation.

"If you had just listened," he shouts, standing up, pointing a finger in my face. "If you were just an obedient child." Mother grabs his arm and pulls him back down on the couch, shushing him. He shakes her off. "Don't shush me." His eyes pin on me. "What am I supposed to do with you now?"

I shift my eyes to the floor in respect. He is so much better than I am, especially now. I'm not worthy to be his daughter.

"Well?"

I swallow, head bowed. "I don't know."

"We cannot try for another child with you at home," he says, then he looks at mother, scanning her up and down. "There's still time."

Tears run down her cheeks as she shakes her head, grabs hold of his arm. "No," she says, but it is weak, not the strong voice I grew up loving.

They both turn to me, watching, waiting, and I don't know what to say. My parents are not rich. Mother was a dancer, retired since I was eight, and Father screws bolts in a factory. They only earn enough for one child, for me, their only hope. And now I am useless.

"I could stay home, keep the house clean, cook the meals." It's stupid, but I have to say something, have to at least try to give them a reason to keep me around.

Father jumps up again, thrusts his hands on his hips. "That's your mother's role. Should I throw her out instead?"

I shake my head. My heart breaks thinking of Mother on the streets, begging for food, eating from garbage bins.

"I'll go," I say, but it comes out as only a whisper.

Mother drops to her knees, shakes her head, grabs my hands in hers. "No," she says, but Father grabs her, pulls her away, and points to the door.

I slip into my bedroom and gather some things I might need: extra clothes, some matches, a picture of my mother. I shove them all deep into my backpack and walk straight to the front door. Their eyes bore into me, but I don't turn my head. My mother is sniffing, but my father is silent, like a rock.

I pull open the door and close it behind me. The cool air bites at my skin. The sun is just starting to set.

As I walk away from my house and my parents, my feelings are not hurt. I understand their decision. I respect their choice. They will need someone to take care of them in their old age, someone who can provide more than just love. And that position is not mine. It can't be. It belongs to anothergirl or boy, one who is yet to be born.

* * *

The streets are dark. The moon is high and full and yellow. My jacket is little help against the whipping chill of the wind.

There is no one around. I'm all alone in my walking, a single small person under an endless sky. Lights are on in the houses. They are warm and loving. The one on the left belongs to my old friend Bennet. We were in the judging house together earlier today, but he left after the second set of judges, assigned to be the city accountant. Inside, his parents have undoubtedly baked him a big cake. They will sing and dance and present him with his new uniform, the one reserved for those in job training. I guess I will have my child's uniform forever with its soft gray pants and gray jacket. As far as I know, there is no uniform for the useless.

There's a big house at the end of the road and I turn right. There are no houses now, just businesses lining both sides of the street. They're closed now, shut up tight. There is a buzzing sound coming from between the eye doctor and grain store. I slip into the dark space, a small alley with a dumpster on one side and a gray box on the other. The box is what's making the humming. It's a heating unit, probably left on by mistake.

I sit down beside it and warmth washes over me. I smile with relief. With my eyes closed, I can pretend that I am back home, sitting on the couch, watching a science program on the TV. My parents sit next to each other holding hands. When I look back at them, they smile at me.

"Hey."

My eyes snap open. There is a man in front of me wearing a black suit and tie. He is bent down, reaching a hand towards my arm. I jump up and back away, shaking my head. This is the undertaker, the man with the furnace. Did they send him to come look for me? Do they throw older people in the furnace just like the babies, burn them to ash?

"It's okay," he hisses. "I won't hurt you."

I stumble backwards, twisting my bad foot. I fall hard and smack the ground. He reaches down and grabs me by the arm, pulling me up. I have my footing again, but he's still holding on tight, fingers like talons.

"Come with me. Everything will be fine."

He pulls me down the back of the alley. I am not sure if I should fight to get away or just go willingly. I don't want to be burnt up in a furnace, but I don't want to be a burden either. I don't want to bring down my great nation, and I don't want to spend the rest of my life on the streets.

We come out on another commercial road and he pulls me along it. The big gray building at the end is the undertaker's. No one ever goes inside it except for him. He brings the bodies to the ceremonies on his mechanical cart. He doesn't get help from anyone.

He drags me to the side door and sweeps his head left and right, as if looking for spies, then he pulls the door open and pushes me inside.

It's dark and I stumble forward. The door closes and the lights flick on. He checks the drapes on the windows, pulling them back and forth, straightening them, blocking out all the light. Then he turns to me, his face serious, and he jerks his head towards a closed door.

I am sure that this is where the furnace is kept. He'll open the door, push me in, and turn it on. In a moment it'll all be over. Maybe that won't be so bad. My parents can have a new child, a perfect one, and they will never see me huddling in the street to keep warm. They will never feel sad or ashamed.

He twists a key in the lock and shoves the door open. I squeeze my eyes shut and take a deep breath.

"Watch the stairs," he whispers, grabbing my shoulders like he wants to help me, protect me. It reminds me of my father before the accident and a shiver runs down my back. I guess if you're going to put someone in a furnace, you will at least be nice to them first.

He reaches back and closes the door, locks it, then keeps moving forward. There's a turn in the stairs and I see light, lanterns hung around the walls. There are people sitting at a table and chairs. A man with a hunchback, a woman with a thick body and twisted face, and an old man with white eyes. There are beds along the walls and a little girl sits on one, blanket wrapped around her body, face turned away.

"Guys," the undertaker whispers, "There's another one."

They turn to see me, and I look down at the floor in respect. Perhaps these are the people who run the furnace, but why would there be a little girl?

"Head up," the undertaker says, tapping my chin with two fingers. "We are all equals here."

I do as he says and the people in the room are smiling. The girl has turned now and I see her crossed eyes. She is my neighbors baby, I'm sure of it, the one that was taken to the furnace. She tilts her ear towards me, and there is a strange plastic thing around and inside of it. It must help her hear because she seems to understand what's been said.

"What about the furnace?" I whisper.

He chuckles and grabs my shoulder, squeezing me into him. "That old thing hasn't worked in years. Not that I ever used it in the first place." He puts a hand on my back and pushes me forward towards a bed against the back wall. "This is where you'll sleep from now on."

I climb up onto it and wrap the blanket around my shoulders. This place is chilly, smells wet, and there are no windows, but I am grateful to the undertaker, grateful that there is no furnace.

"I can't promise you much," the undertaker says, "but I will feed you and keep you safe for as long as I can." He heads back towards the stairs. "But for now I have to go. Don't want to look suspicious. See you in the morning."

He disappears up the stairs and all eyes turn to me. The man with the hunchback grins wide and nods. "I'm Tip," he says. "I'm thirty-three but my brain is seven."

I don't know exactly what he means, but I smile and nod. "I'm Ishka. I'm twelve."

"I'm Igson," the old man barks, much louder than necessary. "I'm blind as a goddamn bat."

I open my mouth, not sure if I should apologize or laugh, but I'm cut off by a high-pitched cackling. The woman with the deformed face smacks her fists against the table.

"Bat," she says and laughs. "Bat. Bat. Bat."

"Hush, you," Igson says, eyebrows pushed together. He turns his white eyes towards me. "She's a goddamn loon. They're all goddamn loons."

The girl on the bed, the one I carried around as a baby, looks over at me with wide, crossed eyes.

"What's your name?" I ask.

Her mouth is a straight line. "Bay," she says. "And I'm not a loon."

* * *

There are footsteps on the stairs and I open my eyes. It's the undertaker. He grabs the nearest lantern and turns up the flame, then moves on to the next one.

"Good morning," he says, but there is no indication it's morning. It is just as dark as it was when I climbed into bed.

"Morning. Morning. Morning," the deformed woman says. She sits up and claps her hands.

Igson grunts, throwing back his covers. "It's too goddamn early."

Me and Bay just sit quietly, shivering under our blankets.

"My trainee is coming this morning," he says. "I don't want to keep the kid waiting nor do I want him poking his nose down here before I know if I can trust him."

I wonder which of my classmates is his trainee. While not luxurious, undertaking is a respectable career. His parents are surely very proud. I am just a tiny bit jealous that it isn't me.

He drops a basket on the table. "Two buns each. No fighting." He eyes Igson, then winks at me.

***

Two Months Later

It is not so bad living in this basement. It is quiet and there is not much to do, but it's better than being burnt to ashes. At night I still imagine my parents and what they're doing without me. Sometimes I pretend that I am sitting with them, that we are together and happy, that my accident never happened.

There is a sound from above, steps on the staircase. The undertaker shakes as he makes his way down, basket in hand. He sits it on the table and smiles, but he looks weak, defeated. He coughs.

"I'm not feeling well today," he says to me and Bay. We are drawing pictures with the crayons he brought us yesterday.

In his eyes, there is a haggard look. There are lines on his face. It never occurred to me before this moment that the undertaker is an old man.

"There's enough food for tomorrow as well, in case I can't make it back."

I don't know what to say. I don't know what to do. I just smile at him and say, "I hope you feel better."

* * *

My stomach growls. My guts are burning. Beside me, Bay's body is limp. She breathes softly. There is a dryness to her skin, a tightness.

The undertaker has not visited in a long time. Without windows there are no days or nights, but I know it has been much too long. We've gone to sleep and woken up four times, but without the undertaker to tell us goodnight and good morning, we don't know if we slept at night or day.

"I'm so goddamn hungry," Igson grunts.

The woman with the deformed face is crying in the corner, her wails filling up the small room.

"My belly hurts," Tip says, rubbing his stomach.

If the undertaker is gone for good, then surely the trainee has taken his place. People do not stop dying just because the undertaker is sick. Or gone.

I stand up and walk to the stairs. I can feel their eyes on my back, but I don't turn around. I don't want to lose my confidence. At the top of the stairs I stop and grab the doorknob. It's locked so I jiggle it, but it won't budge.

"Help," I scream. "Somebody, anybody. Please."

I scream and scream and scream. And there is a noise, a shuffling sound, like footsteps. My heart races. A key is inserted into the lock and the door opens.

A boy stands on the other side, eyes wide. He looks me up and down. His mouth opens, then closes, then opens again. I recognize him from school, but I do not know him well.

"I'm Ishka," I say, shifting my eyes to the floor. I hope this sign of respect is enough to soften the hard look on his face. "The undertaker takes care of us down here. We are useless to our great nation, but we need some food and water."

"Useless," he says, and the word is disgusting on his lips. "If you are useless, then why should I waste the resources of our great nation on you?"

It's a good question and I have no answer. I don't know what to say.

There is a loud cackling from downstairs. It's the deformed woman. If I do not deserve resources, I'm certain he will think worse of her.

"Please," I say. "We are ashamed of our uselessness, but one of us is very small, a tiny girl. She needs some water."

The boy huffs. One shoe taps the ground. "I will give you

nothing. The undertaker is dead. I am in charge now. You useless must leave. Now."

He steps aside, as if to let me pass, but I do not step forward. I shrink back down the stairs to get Bay, to get the others.

Igson, Tip, and the deformed lady stand at the bottom of the stairs, eyes on me.

"Go on up," I say, pushing past them. I pick Bay up off the bed and she moves just enough to wrap her arms around my neck. She is more than half my size, but I have to manage. I follow the others up the stairs.

The new undertaker stands at the door with his arms crossed. We pass him and head towards the front of the building. Bright afternoon light streams through the window and it is a wonderful thing to see. If we find nowhere to go, I am glad to see the sun one last time.

I reach past the others to push open the door and step outside. Tip guides Igson by holding his hand. I wonder how long it's been since they've seen the outside, since they've smelled fresh air.

People are going about their business, visiting shops, walking kids home from school. It is the busiest time of day and all eyes turn and land on us. I look down in respect, and I hope the other useless are doing the same. We do not want to look any bolder than we already are.

There is no noise, not a single word spoken, not even a loud breath. Their eyes burn my skin, piercing like needles. I shift Bay's weight in my arms.

"Ishka?"

My heart stops. I look up, tears already flowing from my eyes. Mother is beautiful in her yellow housewife uniform. She drops her shopping bags in the street and runs to me, then wraps her arms around me and Bay, squeezing tight.

"Oh, Ishka," she says, pulling away to look me in the eyes. She runs a hand along the side of my face. There is so much guilt in her eyes and I'm sure it is because of how bony and pale I've grown in the dark basement.

"I am so sorry, Ishka," she says. "I will never forgive myself."

I shush her and shake my head. "Don't feel bad, Mother. I was useless to you and to our great nation. There is nothing wrong with what you did."

"No, Ishka," she says, shaking my shoulders. "It is the wrongest thing I have ever done. Someday, when you grow up, you will understand."

"I do not think I can grow up," I say. "I have no place in our nation."

She bites her lip. She knows it is true.

"I just want to get some water for Bay," I say. If we must die, at least I can ease her pain.

But my mother is cut off before she can answer. An old woman shrieks. She stumbles forward, grabs Igson by the shoulders.

"Oh, my Love," she says, tears running down her cheeks. "My sweet, sweet, Love."

"My goddamn wife," Igson says, then smiles wide.

She wraps her arm around his back and stumbles away. I wonder if she is allowed to do that. Perhaps they will both be punished when they're caught.

"What's going on here?" A deep voice says.

It's the mayor. His eyes dart between me, Mother, Bay, Tip, and the deformed woman. I cast my eyes to the ground and my mother does the same as she stands straight.

"Who are you people?" the mayor asks.

"We are the useless," I say. "The undertaker cared for us, but now he has died and we have come out for food and water."

"The useless?" He pauses and I can feel his confusion radiating over my body. "What about the furnace?"

"It's broken, sir."

"There is no place for useless people in our great nation," he says.

"Yes, sir," I say, and I feel my fate imprinted on my bones, branded on my skin. He wants us killed.

"We will arrange transportation to the next town," he says. "They certainly have a working furnace there."

He turns and begins to walk away, and tension builds in my chest, like a fist around my lungs. If he leaves now, if he walks away, we will all be burnt, even little Bay. I can't let that happen. I must try something. There is nothing for me to lose.

"Wait," I say, and the crowd gasps. He turns around and I do not bother to divert my eyes. There is no point now in showing respect. "I...I..."

He stares at me, his eyes narrowed. I swallow hard.

"I don't think I'm useless," I lie, then take a deep breath.

"You don't?"

"No."

"So what are you good for?" His voice is challenging, but I will not back down, even though I am desperately searching my mind for an answer.

"I can take care of the useless."

He laughs. "The useless will be turned over to the furnace within hours. Ashes don't need cared for."

I shake my head. I have never been good at crafting stories, but I must do my best to save us, to save Bay. "The furnace is big and expensive to run and transporting us to the next town will be expensive too." I am surprised about the words coming from my mouth, but I don't stop. "If I could have just a small place, an unneeded place, I could care for the useless. We don't need much. Just a bit of food and water."

My eyes dart to the ground automatically, but I lift them up again. I am trying to save my friends' lives. I do not need to feel so small.

Chattering runs through the crowd. They are whispering, leaning towards each other, and I wish I could hear what they are saying, but it all blends together.

"What would be the point for the nation?" the mayor asks. His arms drop from his hips to his sides.

I take a deep breath. "Well," I say, thinking carefully about how to be the most convincing, "family members could come see them, come visit. That way they wouldn't lose them completely. They wouldn't be as sad. Mourning costs the nation money too."

The mayor's eyebrows crease together and I think he is really considering my lie. Even if he says no, I am proud that I tried.

Everything is silent now, even the crowd. Their eyes are wide and flick between me and the mayor. I want to look back at Mother to see what she thinks, but I am afraid to move a muscle and disrupt his thoughts.

"Okay," he says, his face softening. "We can work something

out."

I try to smile, but I am overwhelmed. This is the biggest thing I've ever done. I turn to my mother at last and she grabs me into her arms, hugs me tight.

"I am so proud of you," she says.

This is the first time I've ever been praised for a lie.

Two Months Later

The grocer hands me two bags of food with a smile. It is the food that expired today, the food he cannot sell tomorrow. I wave goodbye as he turns and climbs down from the porch.

This is my place now, for me and the others. Mother told me the sign on the door reads "Home of the Useless." I think about that name a lot, about how I tricked the mayor into believing the house was useful even though its inhabitants are still useless. It is strange, and I am surprised everyday that he doesn't catch on to the lie.

There are eight more of us now. It turns out that there were other useless ones hidden away. Some were born at home and hidden by their mothers, others were found on the streets and squirreled away, protected. They are no one's burden now. Their families come to see them when they want to and stay away when they're busy. Of course, they would not be a burden if they were dead either.

Once a month the doctor comes by and draws our blood. He takes it back to the hospital to be used on the useful people, those that contribute to our great nation. The mayor says that this is an added bonus. I am happy for my small contribution.

Inside, the deformed woman is screaming again. I named her

Silv so she wouldn't feel so left out.

"Hush. It's okay, Silv," Bay says. She is strong now and healthy. I am glad that I saved her, that I saved all of us, even if it was with a lie.

The sun is starting to set over our great nation and I am proud to be a part of it. People are saying that the next town has created their own home for the useless and it's all because of me. I hope it keeps spreading farther and farther until all the furnaces are shut down for good.

Perhaps it is bad of me to hope for such a burden on our great nation.

AUTHOR BIOS

Leslie Anderson

Leslie J. Anderson grew up falling off horses, which would probably explain a lot if she thought about it. She now works in marketing and publishes poetry, fiction, and comics. Her work has appeared in Asimov's, Strange Horizons, and Andromeda Spaceways Inflight Magazine, among others. Find her online at www.lesliejanderson.com.

Shaun Avery

Shaun Avery is a crime and horror fiction fan with numerous publications on the UK small press comic scene, as well as competition wins for his fiction and a recent shortlisting in a screenwriting contest. He spent some time out of work, and has exaggerated a few real-life events in this story. But not by much. More of his work can be found here http://descenttheatre.co.uk/category/playella/ and here http://erewashwriterscompetition.weebly.com/winners-2012.html

H. David Blalock

H. David Blalock has been a writer for print and the internet in speculative fiction for more than 35 years. Inspired by the science fiction and horror writers of the early and middle 20th century, he continues to try to bring that sense of wonder and awe he felt at that reading to his audience through his stories and novels. For more information about David and his work, check out his website at ThranKeep.com

Delphine Boswell

I have numerous short stories accepted for publication in online magazines, print anthologies, and a literary journal, as well as a chapter excerpt from a mystery novel currently under agent consideration. I hold an M.A in English (Rhetoric & Composition) from the University of Nevada, Reno and recently earned my M.F.A. in Creative Writing from the Northwest Institute of Literary Arts. I have been teaching college writing for the past twelve years.

Ellen Brock

Ellen has loved books since the day she learned to read. She also loves animals (especially dogs and rats), hot sauce, paper crafts, and geocaching. She owns an editing company called Keytop, Inc. (www.keytopservices.com), where she edits manuscripts for established and aspiring authors. Ellen enjoys sharing writing and editing advice on her blog (https://thewriteditor.wordpress.com) and is currently finishing a novel.

Cathy Bryant

Cathy Bryant won the 2012 Bulwer-Lytton Fiction Prize and is a former blogger for the Huffington Post. Her stories and poems have been published all over the world in such publications as the Andromeda Spaceways Inflight Magazine, Night to Dawn and Midnight Times. In 2012 Cathy was runner-up in the SFPA Poetry Contest, as well as winning the Bulwer-Lytton, The Sampad 'Inspired by Tagore' Contest, the Malahat Review Monostich Contest and the Swanezine Poetry Contest. Her collection, 'Contains Strong Language and Scenes of a Sexual Nature' was published recently. To contact her, email cathy@cathybryant.co.uk

Jason Campagna

Jason Campagna is a native of Western Pennsylvania where he made his living in government until he decided to go back to school.

His degree is in Communications from Pikeville College in Eastern Kentucky. He is currently studying for a Masters at Murray State University.

Carolyn M. Chang

Carolyn writes SF&F stories to escape into a world where she can control absolutely everything – kill anyone she feels like, make someone ugly or beautiful, invent any technology she wants, you get the picture. She has had two other short stories published: one in collaboration with Leslie Lee in Novus Creatura: An Anthology of Never-Before Seen Monstrosities and a second in The Temporal Element: Time-Travel Adventures, past, present, & future. Carolyn is also the proud author of two yet unpublished manuscripts, the first a multi-cultural YA/SF and #2 a dark fantasy with SF elements. She lives in Amsterdam, Netherlands with her husband and two children where she's involved in two writing groups.

Deedee Davies

Deedee is a writer interested mainly in the fantasy, horror and science-fiction genres. Inspired by turn of the century fantasy and science-fiction, she wrote a great deal as a youngster, returning to it in 2012, when she finished her first draft novel. Deedee is also a cover artist, with around 20 published book covers under her belt. She lives in Plymouth, UK with her partner, 3 spiders, 3 snakes and a scorpion.

H.S. Donnelly

H.S. Donnelly lives in Toronto with his supportive wife Anne and two affectionate, though rather demanding, cats. First Head was his first attempt at writing short stories. Along with First Head, he has had several short SF stories published or soon-to-be published in Onspec Magazine #86 (Oh Most Cursed Addition Engine) and Kaleidotrope Magazine (2014) (Stowaway to Mars).

Many thanks to the Burlington Writer's group (Sylvia, Jim, Rory, Janice, Chelsea, Gesila, Estelle, Cathy, Lynda, Rachael, Elaine) who endured a lot of re-writes to this story and to Sue Williams, in particular, who encouraged me not to give up on the story.

For more information, visit my Facebook page at: www.facebook.com/peeringintothefuture

Jay Faulkner

Jay Faulkner resides in Northern Ireland with his wife, Carole, and their two boys, Mackenzie and Nathaniel. He says that while he is a writer, martial artist, sketcher, and dreamer he's mostly just a husband and father.

His work has been published widely, both online and in print anthologies, and was short-listed in the 2010 Penguin Ireland Short Story Competition. He is currently working on his first novel.

Jay founded, and edits, 'With Painted Words' - www.

withpaintedwords.com - a creative writing site with inspiration from monthly image prompts, and ‹The WiFiles' - www.thewifiles.com - an online speculative fiction magazine, published weekly. He can also be found as a regular co-host on the Following The Nerd radio show–www.followingthenerd.com

For more information visit–www.jayfaulkner.com

Tanith Korravai

Tanith Korravai spends much of her time looking for utopia in all the wrong places. She occasionally puts in an appearance at the group blog smalltriumphs.com.

S.C. Langgle

S.C. Langgle is a lifelong lover of words and stories who has never outgrown her preference for children's and young adult literature. A graduate of the Master of Professional Writing program at the University of Southern California, S.C. is originally from Baltimore, Maryland. She currently lives in Hollywood, California, only a block from Marilyn Monroe's handprints at Grauman's Chinese Theater, though she spends more time at home with her computer than mingling with celebrities. Luckily, she has her two adorable dogs—a Chihuahua, Chin-Mae, and a maltipoo, Sasha—to keep her company, and she'd choose them over a gaggle of Hollywood stars any day. Visit S.C. at http://www.sclanggle.blogspot.com.

Mandi M. Lynch

Mandi M. Lynch started writing stories at the tender age of six, pecking out the words on her mother's manual typewriter. Although the crayon drawings have improved marginally, the spelling has not. Now, she lives in Nashville, TN, with three cats - none of which write due to lack of thumbs - and spends as much of her time in the industry as she possibly can. You can find her or her small press (Ink Monkey Mag) on facebook.

Michael O'Connor

Michael O'Connor is a writer and freelance editor who lives in Kent in the UK. His short fiction has appeared in numerous UK/ North American print and online magazines as well as in one single-author and several multi-author anthologies. He wrote the non-fiction From Chaucer to Childish: Writers and Artists in the Medway Towns in 2006 and the e-novella Cages in 2010.In addition, he has written essays and book reviews for The Baum Bugle (Journal of the International Wizard of Oz Club), and is a long-standing member of The Lewis Carroll Society (LCS), for which he edits their quarterly newsletter as well as being on the editorial board of their academic journal The Carrollian; his most recent work is All in the Golden Afternoon: the Origins of 'Alice's Adventures in Wonderland' which is available from the LCS website http://lewiscarrollsociety.org.uk/. His own website is at www.mpoconnor.co.uk

Herika R. Raymer

Herika R. Raymer grew up consuming books - first by eating them, later by reading them. Her mother taught her the value of focus and hard work while her father encouraged her love literature and art; so she has been writing and doodling off and on for over 30 years. After much encouragement, Mrs. Raymer finally published a few short stories and has developed a taste for it. She continues to send submissions, sometimes with success, and currently has a collection of stories in the works. She is the Short Story Editor for a horror magazine. A participant of the voluntary writer/artist/musician cooperative known as Imagicopter, Herika R. Raymer is married with two children and a dog in West Tennessee, USA. Her website is at: herikarraymer.webs.com

Frank Roger

Frank Roger was born in 1957 in Ghent, Belgium.

His first story appeared in 1975. Since then his stories appear in an increasing number of languages in all sorts of magazines and anthologies, and since 2000, story collections are published, also in various languages. Apart from fiction, he also produces collages and graphic work in a surrealist and satirical tradition. They have appeared in various magazines and books.

By now he has a few hundred short stories to his credit, published in more than 35 languages. In 2012 a story collection in English ("The Burning Woman and Other Stories") was published by Evertype (www.evertype.com). Find out more at www.frankroger.be .

ABOUT THE EDITOR

Robin Blankenship

Robin Blankenship, a freelance editor and book reviewer has a background in teaching and social work. When not working or reading or editing she can be found at home in Kentucky with her husband, Andrew and two children, Christian and Beatrix.

www.ingramcontent.com/pod-product-compliance
Lightning Source LLC
LaVergne TN
LVHW010052110826
845155LV00028B/301